THE DENOUNCED

BOOK 1

A GREY SUN

BY SJ SHERWOOD

Published by Blue Ned Ltd.
135-137 Station Road, London, E4 6AG.

First published in the United Kingdom in 2017.
Copyright © SJ Sherwood, 2017.

SJ Sherwood has asserted his right under the Copyright, Designs and
Patents Act 1988 to be identified as the author of this work.

A CIP catalogue record for this book is available from the British Library.

ISBN 978-1-9997929-1-6

For those who gave me their time.

1

In less than an hour my life will end.

Some of the other *Denounced* said I would mess my pants when my time came. They said worse words, of course, but I wasn't listening because I'm determined to die with dignity. It was the same when I ate my last meal of burger-and-chips followed by chocolate pudding. The dessert was served with fresh whipped cream, something I've never eaten before. I ate it slowly with a smile on my face while a guard watched over me. Jack told me it was okay to feel scared. It's normal, he said. All the boys, even the tough ones, can lose it; the girls too, when your time comes.

But I'm not going lose it, I tell myself, as three men step into my cell.

One of them I know.

Two of them I don't.

Jack is my guard and the person responsible for my day-to-day welfare. He's taken me from my cell each morning to the Court House and has looked after me as best he can in the seven weeks I've spent in the Holding Centre. He's wearing a freshly pressed, dark-beige guard's uniform and his face is more red and sweaty than usual. He struggles with his weight and he's terrified the Holding Service Corporation will find out about his heart condition, then he'll lose his job to a younger man. I told him his secret is safe with me. I'm good at keeping my mouth shut. All orphans are because you need to if you want to survive the System.

After a petulant pause, I stand. Jack throws me one of his half smiles. It's a sad smile, really. You know the type where the mouth moves but the eyes don't shine. I bet it was Jack who organised the chocolate pudding and fresh cream. It was an act of kindness that is rare in our Secular World and I'm sure Jack and I would have been friends if we'd met in different circumstances.

The man standing next to him is tall, with shiny black hair and unblemished skin. He's wearing a blue suit, a pink shirt, and a dark-blue tie. His shirt has those cufflinks that hold the sleeves together and it is his duty to make sure everything is carried out to the letter of the law. Like I give a dog's stink about that stuff any more, because the law isn't much good or that honest. Corruption is the word they use around here. It was a word I'd never thought about much until I was arrested, but I think about it now – all the time.

The third man is bald and muscle-bound with a goatee beard that is tinged with grey. His eyes look too small for his head and it makes me want to laugh. He has a permanent scowl, and he's wearing a white collarless shirt buttoned to the neck. The shirt is too tight and pinches at the front of his throat, but if I had eyes that small I probably wouldn't be able to pick a shirt that fitted me either.

He's my Executioner.

'Are you Ned 5-7-9-0-1-2-3?' the Court Official asks.

His back is arrow-straight and his head is held high in that way all Court Officials stand. He flips open his electronic notepad and taps the screen with an officious flourish. I remember my Judge tapped his notepad in the same way, but not as quickly as this man. He's younger than my Judge and more interested in wanting to impress, so maybe that's why he types quicker.

I nod that I am.

'Please answer Yes or No.'

I don't answer. Why should I? It's a game all the *Denounced* play. I'm sure he's going to ask me the question again, but he doesn't fall for it. I smile back. All I have is my dignity and that's the one thing they can never take from me.

EVER.

'You have been found guilty by a court of your peers and convicted of being a *Denounced*. You will be hanged by the neck until you are pronounced dead. Do you understand the implications of what is being said to you?'

How stupid is the guy? Of course I understand the implications – I'm going to die. I count to twenty in my head, still smiling, before I nod, knowing I'm supposed to answer *yes*, but I'm not going to unless he asks me again and even then, he'll have to wait.

'Do you have anything else you want to say? Anything you would like to add to your records that we may have missed?'

I think for a second.

'I'm not guilty.'

'You said that in Court. This is not new information. I'm only interested in new information. Do you have anything *new* to add?'

I stare him out because I'm never speaking to this man again.

'Then let us proceed,' he says finally.

Jack steps forward and handcuffs my wrists with a plastic zip-tie. They say you get buried in them. It must be true because they are the same deep-purple colour as my Holding Centre Jumpsuit. Purple is the colour of the *Denounced* and I was made to wear it over a white t-shirt with white sneakers in Court before I was convicted. I thought that was unfair because you are innocent until proven guilty, and I said so to my lawyer. She said if I complained it would only look bad, so I didn't, because you're supposed to listen to lawyers even if they are corrupt. She was young and pretty and blonde, and always in a hurry. I heard an older boy say she looked hot and he'd like to do things to her, especially to her mouth. I thought she looked cold, despite being pretty, and I didn't want to do anything to her but have her leave me alone. She said she hoped my trial would finish on the Friday, because she had a holiday booked on the Saturday and she didn't want to cancel it. In the end, it was okay for her, because I got convicted on the Wednesday. She looked pleased and she told me she had done her best before she hurried off again. I found out later that once you've been accused of being a *Denounced* it's almost impossible not to be found guilty. They call it the conveyor belt of death. The lucky few who have been cleared have gone on to become celebrities, making millions of digital credits. Someone gave me a book to read about a Survivor, but from what I could see the boy had a twin and the police had accused the wrong sibling, so he wasn't cleared in the true sense. I was convicted on hearsay. I never saw the person and they never came to court. The prosecution read out a statement that said I denounced our State and wanted to live in the Non-Secular World. It meant the Law saw me as having anti-Secular beliefs and that I secretly hoped for a return of the Terrorist Wars. None of it was true. I never said the things they said and I don't know why somebody made up those lies.

But they did and here I am, about to die.

The Court Official asks me to show him my right wrist. I twist my arm so he can see my luminous number. Everyone in the Secular World has a number embedded into their skin in the same spot. If the police find you without a number they can shoot you on sight. Mine is easy to remember. Add two to five and two to seven and you get the first three numbers. The last four are sequential from zero up.

5-7-9-0-1-2-3.

In the Secular World, you are known by your first name and number, and your number becomes the most important thing about you. You get digital credits added to it so you can buy the things you need. Your education and where you live and what you've done are all logged to it as well. You simply scan your number into Readers and you can travel or take a cab, buy a home, whatever. It all comes down to the number, but I'm never going to do any of those things.

'Height?' the Court Official asks.

I yawn then say, 'One metre eighty-eight. I'm tall for my age,' I add.

I'm not sure why I said that and I'm annoyed for giving something away about myself.

'Weight?'

I shrug. I can see he has my weight marked as eighty-two kilos. I'm closer to ninety, but I'm not fat, I'm stocky. I always have been. The other *Denounced* say it's a good thing I'm heavy. It means I'll fall harder and my neck will break quickly, like they know what they are talking about because they've had a dry run.

There are some idiots here for sure and I'm looking at another one as the Court Official taps away on his notepad. I spot he has my hair colour listed wrong. He has 'light brown', but it's what you'd call dirty blond. Does that mean they've made a mistake? My heart races as he stares at me, but then he changes the description and updates my eye colour from light blue to grey. He adds a few more comments that I can't see before he finishes with another officious flourish, closing the cover with a snap.

I hate all Court Officials, especially this one, and if I wasn't zip-tied, I'd punch him, just for a laugh.

'There are four scheduled endings this morning. You are number two. It's time to go. We don't want anyone missing their weekend because of a *Denounced*, do we!'

2

Jack leads the way with my Executioner behind me and the Court Official behind him, I suppose, but I don't turn around to check. We walk along a steel gantry that is sloping toward a security door. The pass-through points are all the same. Cubes that you enter with a choice of four exits if you include the one you've stepped through. Only one door ever opens at a time so you have no chance of escape. Not that there's much chance of that anyway. I wait for one door to fully close as I think of my family name – Hunter.

Ned Hunter.

I always thought it sounded kinda cool and it's better than Ned 5-7-9-0-1-2-3. The Secular World lets you use your family name until you go to Second School at the age of ten. It's there that you're issued your Number, which is how you're known from that point on, but like most things in my life I've been different. I was seven when I got my Number. My parents had died in a ferry accident, which my sister, Liz, survived. She is six years older than me so we're not close. I was put into an orphanage, or a Community Home, as they call it, which is why I was issued my Number early. I've lived in six Community Homes before coming here. Liz could have become my prime-carer when she turned eighteen. I would have been twelve and the Secular World would have given us a home and digital credits for us to live and eat. She would have had her education paid for, along with loads of other benefits. But she refused and I don't know why. I was told at the time she didn't want the responsibility – something about being too immature despite her age. Liz was always mature for her years, so that was a lie, but as I've gotten older, I understand. It's easier to survive when you only have to think about yourself. Liz didn't come to my trial but she did send an email saying that if I was found guilty, then I deserved my punishment. I know why she wrote those words, because life can be tough, even for family members, if they are seen to be supporting a *Denounced*. They get labelled *Doubters* and end up living in allocated camps where the police watch them all the time.

We exit another cube and enter a long metal tube. I know where we are going and I block it by picturing what Liz looks like. I can't remember her much any more. I think she had the same colour hair as me and was tall. My mother had the same colour hair too, but hers was wavy and Liz's is straight. We both get our height from our dad. The Community Home's Committee take all your family pictures from you when you enter the System. They say it helps you to come to terms with being on your own. If you want, you can have them back when you become an adult at eighteen. I asked if I could see them before my end. It was Jack who delivered the bad news that I couldn't and it made me angry for a week. I wanted to hurt someone in revenge, but I didn't, because I'm not that kind of person. I've learned that sometimes circumstances and what other people do to you, can make you something you're not.

The tunnel starts to bend to the right and I see a set of steps at the end, which will lead into another holding area. I can hear the low hum of voices, I'm guessing this is going to be my final destination. My heart starts to pump like I've been on a sprint. My legs go weak and I tell myself: I'm Ned Hunter, I'm innocent of being a *Denounced* and I still have my dignity.

I say it again and again in my mind.

At the bottom of the stairs and to my left is a steel wall with an electronic sliding door in the centre. On the far wall is a long wooden bench with three teenagers sat down. I've seen the boy to the far left in Court a few times, he is small and thin with rounded shoulders and brown spiky hair. He's cried so much he looks like he's been stung by a swarm of bees. Next to him is a tall boy – not as tall as me, but not far off. He's mixed-race with green eyes and a long, twisted-afro. He looks strong, like he's lifted weights. He's a good-looking fella and he's staring at the floor in that nonchalant way we all do to show 'em we don't care. It's another stupid game, because we do care really. Next to him is a girl with long blonde hair and light blue watery eyes, like I've never seen on anyone. She has sharp cheekbones and a pert nose all set on a muscular frame. She is beyond beautiful and it makes me forgot where I am. The next thing I know, I'm stumbling, trying to find my footing and it's Jack who catches me by the shoulders and stops me falling on my face.

My Court Official laughs.

'I'm not scared,' I snap at Jack.

'I know you're not,' Jack says with a reassuring nod and one of his smiles. 'You're one of the bravest boys I've ever met.'

I don't reply because I don't want to appear weak. I'm expecting Jack to walk me to the wooden bench to sit me next to the girl, but he doesn't. Instead, he guides me toward the electronic door and I wait outside. Another guard pulls the boy with the swollen face by the forearm to his feet and marches him in front of me. Jack tells me to take a step back. I do, glancing behind me to see the mixed-race boy next, and the girl last. My Court Official tells me to look forward. I give it a ten count before I do as I'm told. I mean, what is he going to do to me if I don't. Kill me! The mixed-race boy smirks. He knows the unwritten rules – I bet he's an orphan, too. He has that look about him. I stare forward and the boy in front of me starts to wet his pants. I can see why we are stood on a grate with a drain beneath. It allows them to wash away the smell with ease.

A guard puts a mask on the boy's face in a rough, hurried manner. Jack does the same to me, but he uses a gentle hand. This is it. My time in the Secular World is all but over. All that will be left of me is my record, which is kept in the Court Digital Files for two years. My Number will then be recycled to someone else at the age of ten, or younger, if they happen to be an orphan. I hope whoever gets 5-7-9-0-1-2-3 has more luck with it than I did. They say some Numbers are doomed and I never thought that about mine, but maybe it's true after all?

I hear the door slide open and the boy in front of me step through. I can't hear anything else after the door closes except my own breath, which is so much quicker than normal. The door opens and Jack whispers for me to step forward. I can feel Jack's hand gripping my forearm as he guides me forward. His grip releases and I hear the door close behind me in the same moment the rough hands of the Executioner puts the rope around my neck. I'm not sure what I expected but the rope is smooth like warm silk. Perhaps it's warm from the crying boy who went first. The Executioner tugs the rope tight and it makes me swallow. My legs start to shake and I feel tears bubble in my eyes. I scream in my head:

I'm not going to wet my pants.

I'm not going to wet my pants.

I'm not going to wet my pants.

You can watch *Denounced* being executed on a special TV Channel. The Secular Authorities think it's a good thing that such events are broadcast to the mass population. It is supposed to deter people and to make them think about the consequences of their actions. It's a shame the people who watch the channel don't know about the corruption.

Or maybe they do and they don't care?

'Good riddance to scum,' the Executioner laughs in my ear.

I don't care what he says, I've had much worse said to me.

I hear an electronic snap.

Then I'm falling through the air.

Falling.

Feet first.

3

Falling.

Downward.

I smash into the floor and I hit my head on something metal. Pain bounces through my skull and I can't work out what's happened other than the noose is chokingly tight and the rope's length is coiled across my body. I'm stunned that I'm not dead or, I don't think I am, and it's the same old story. Nothing works as it should at the Holding Centre, and now this. A boy told me once they occasionally make an example of a *Denounced* for the TV. It's against the law but nobody cares and they do it for the Airtime Ratings, and it works. Now I'm going to have to relive my execution because I dared to show dignity. Next time, I'll pee my pants to get this over and done with, and I'll have the dignity of knowing it was fake fear and not real, so I still win.

I reach for my mask when hands grab my upper arms and drag me across the floor, as someone loosens the rope and slips it from my neck. My mask is yanked from my face, but, before I have time to focus, a hood is jammed over my head. What little light seeped through the edges of my mask is completely gone and the blackness and the hands and the sudden movement fill me with a new kind of fear.

'Stay quiet or I'll strangle you myself,' a man's voice says. 'Do you understand?'

I nod that I do.

'Stand,' he commands.

I try, but really, I'm pulled to my feet and marched at speed into a slow jog. I'm fighting to stay calm and I'm more panicked now than when I first saw my Executioner. Voices and the sounds of running feet flood my ears. Whatever is happening to me is happening to others. I'm pulled to a halt and it jars my knees. I recognise the sound of the security-cube doors opening and closing. It's like air being sucked from a room. I'm turned a half circle and forced into another jog out of the cube. Hands are on my arms, guiding me this way and then that. My breath is hot inside the hood and I continue to struggle to get my thoughts straight through the imposed urgency. Somebody kicks my feet from under me. I yelp out in pain as I fall backwards, but more hands grab to cushion my fall as I'm simultaneously lifted and lowered into a long box. The hood is snatched from my head and the lid of the box is snapped into place before I have chance to see who these men are.

I'm a snug fit and there are dozens of tiny holes in the top half, which allows me to breathe – that has to be a good sign for what is coming, right? My box is lifted and slid across a metal floor. I hear a door close and what small shafts of light I could see disappear. People are crying around me. I try to listen to see if one of the criers is the boy with the swollen face who was first in line. I can't tell, but I hope his rope snapped too and he's in this truck, which has started to move. I wonder if I'm being rescued. The thought gives me too much hope so I block it and there's nothing else I can do but try and relax, which is harder than it sounds. There's enough room for me to turn on my sides and there's even a foam block for my head that is more comfortable than the pillow in my cell. I settle in as best I can and I'm not worried any more, just flat-out exhausted.

It's the vehicle stopping that wakes me. I tense. The back doors of the truck are opened and I hear boxes being dragged across the metal floor. I count seven before the box

SJ SHERWOOD

I'm in is scraped forward and dumped on the ground in a loud thud that makes my head shoot up and hit the top of the lid. I count another twenty boxes being unloaded before I'm finally released. Night blinks back at me, and I glimpse a burnt-out tree and more boxes from a second truck before another hood is rammed over my head.

'Stand,' a man snaps.

It's the same voice who rescued me, although I'm not so sure about the rescued part any more. I'm helped to my feet and I go dizzy for a moment as I'm guided out of my box and walked a few paces and told to stand still. The air is warm and strokes at my skin and I'm sure I can smell the sea. All I can see is my white sneakers if I stare hard down, along with the tarmac road. We are told to jog on the spot to get our circulation moving. I do as I'm told, but I'm more focused on the sound of 'other' running feet. I counted twenty-seven boxes, twenty-eight, if you include mine, but it sounds a lot more than twenty-eight of us jogging.

It sounds like fifty, a hundred, but it can't be, can it?

We're handed a drink along with a food bar.

'Nobody lifts their hoods if they want to live,' the voice commands.

These people don't sound like Court Officials and something is telling me they are not going to take any defiant behaviour from someone like me, so I feed the straw under my hood and take a long drink of sweet lukewarm lemonade. I follow it with a bite of the food bar. I've eaten these at the Holding Centre and they're made of nuts and dates and sticky black syrup. They taste like dried straw but they fill you up and give you energy, and I haven't eaten since yesterday, which suddenly makes dried straw a delicious meal.

After I finish my snack, my empty bottle is taken from me and I'm guided back to my box. As I'm lifted into the truck, my eyelids go heavy and there's this feeling like a weight has been laid across my chest. The food or drink must have had something in them to make me sleep. I fight the tiredness, but I can't keep it up and the floating drowsiness makes me think of something I haven't thought about for years.

How different would my life have been had both my parents lived?

4

I'm confused and dazed and scared.

I'm being told to get up and move. *Move where*? I think, as a man grabs the front of my jumpsuit and drags me to my feet.

I blink through bright lights.

The sound of electronic whistles drills into my ears.

There are men pulling boys and girls from long boxes. There are more boxes than I can count, and I know we're all *Denounced* by the purple jumpsuits and zip ties. Everyone is staring at everyone else hoping for some kind of answer. The same shocked faces are on each of us, so mine must be all wide-eyed and slack-jawed, too. There's still a heaviness across my chest, like someone punched me, and I'm fighting with myself to get my legs and arms moving.

It's the drug, I know.

A man grabs my hands and cuts the plastic ties from my wrists with some kind of special shaped scissors. The ties drop to the floor and I rub at my sore wrists. He points over to my right and gives me a shove to move in that direction. The boy next to me has his ties cut and is shoved in the same direction as me, but he loses his footing and bangs into my side. He doesn't say sorry, but then why should he, it wasn't his fault. In the Holding Centre, I would have pushed him back, because you have to show face, but I let it go because from what I can tell no-one is going to notice and we've all got bigger problems than a bit of pride to protect.

'Do you know where we are?' he whispers.

I shake my head, thinking it's the dumbest question I've heard in a while – like how would I know? He's a big lad but his face is all crumpled with worry and his eyes are puffed from a whole lot of crying, so I step away from him. I've got this gut feeling that showing weakness around here is not going to do anyone any favours, and I might have enough trouble defending myself without the hassle of feeling responsible for someone I don't know.

I stop where the man shoved me to go. Everyone this end has had their ties cut and the crowd is growing bigger as more join. Nobody is talking and everyone is looking bewildered. I stare around and realise the ceiling is hundreds of metres high and curved like the inside of a football. The lights are piercingly bright, like a fake sun, and I have to turn away. All I can see is black spots for a minute. Behind me are dozens of buildings. They are mostly rectangular with flat roofs and no windows. The area we are stood in is open and, like the ceiling, I can't see where the walls start or end. The flooring is plastic and has tiny ridges built in so you won't lose your grip when you walk. It's then I notice the colour, or lack of it. Everything is a shade of grey, black or dark blue and spotlessly clean. It's the clean part that makes me fret the most. The rules here will be strict and rigidly enforced. The clean-freak Wardens are the worst of them all, and if this is a rescue it's not the kind I fantasised about.

A high shrieking bell sounds and everyone looks toward it.

'Follow me, quick and quiet,' a man shouts, waving his arm so we can see him, before he points forward. We fall in line and still nobody talks, and apart from the occasional cough, all I hear is the shuffle of reluctant feet.

The vastness of the space is overwhelming, and I'm not sure how long we walk for, but we finally come to our first wall. It's as tall as the side of a mountain and disappears into the haze of white light above my head without any real end in sight. We are herded through a door into what looks like an Assembly Hall. At one end is a stage and in the far corner are markings on the floor in tiny halogen lights. At the head of each section flickers the name: *Pod One*, *Pod Two* all the way up to *Pod Fifteen*.

We are shepherded away from the markings and it's then I spot the mixed-race boy and the blonde girl who were scheduled to be executed along with myself. It's a comfort to see them, something familiar in an unfamiliar setting. I catch both their eyes and give them a nod. The mixed-race boy nods back but the girl totally ignores me like I'm not here. At first, I think she didn't see me but I catch her giving me a second glance before looking away. She's playing tough and hiding it well, but I've seen enough fear in my life to spot hers at a hundred metres. I search for the other boy who was first in our execution line, but I don't see him and it's then I notice nearly everyone is either tall or well-built for their age. There's a toughness about everyone, even an air of menace, and the boy I'm looking for was small and thin and emotionally weak.

I get this overriding sense that his show of fear cost him his life.

'We're not going to have any trouble from you are we?'

I stare at the crowd to see who's stupid enough to make trouble. I'm mean, how brainless can you be!

'Oi … you. Yes … YOU … I'm talking to YOU.'

'Who me?' I say, surprised.

'Am I looking at anybody else?'

I realise what's happened. The men are corralling everyone into lines and I was so busy looking for the boy from the Holding Centre that I must have missed a command and he's come over to pick me out.

'I didn't hear. I'm sorry,' I say.

'People like you never hear. In line, now.'

I glimpse a couple of smirks. I want to kick myself. There are some golden rules to surviving a Community Home and number one is not to get noticed for as long as you can. You need to go *Invisible* and for my height and size, I've got it down to a fine skill, but I was slow to react and I'm now front and centre. The boy next to me gives me a knowing smirk. I stare him out until he gets the message, but he looks away not because he's scared of me, but because he's not going to pick a fight now. I drop my head but I'm keeping my ears open for any more commands. Nobody is talking and I'm too nervous to look around, but I can see some things around me.

The men and women who got us up-and-moving are all dressed in olive coloured track suits with stripes across their shoulders. Some have three stripes, some two and a few one. The man who pulled me up for not paying attention has four, and he's the only one with four stripes from what I can see, which makes me feel worse than I already do. They are all wearing the same black, thin-strapped watches and have electronic whistles hung around their necks. Every one of them is lean with muscular arms and legs and healthy tans. Around the edges I can see Guards, which makes it more like the Holding Centre than a Community Home. They are dressed in black short-sleeve tops and black trousers and military style boots. They are all carrying standard State issued electronic guns. The guns fire metal pellets that explode, encasing you in an electric arc. They can be set to *stun*, *wound* or *kill*. In their utility belts are handcuffs and electronic batons. The batons frighten me more than the guns. They can be used as crowd control to prod you in a certain direction or keep you at a distance. But more often than not they are used as a whip. I've seen the Guards at the Holding Centre use them for their own form of entertainment. If they are switched to their highest setting, the electric arc can cut you in half. I hate the weapon nearly as much as I hate Court Officials, I decide, as I spot the man with four stripes walk to the centre of the stage.

'Eyes forward, shoulders back. Stand straight, like you mean business.'

There's an audible shuffle as we try and stand to attention, which I think is what he's asking us to do.

'Average,' he snarls. 'But more of that later. For now it's time to meet your mother.'

5

His words shudder through me and temporarily make me forget where I am. My mother has been dead for a long time and I've worked hard to block the pain of her loss from my mind. She'd be fifty-seven if she were alive today. It sounds old to me, but it's not when I think most people live to be a hundred in our Secular World. I wonder what she'd look like today, and if age would have been kind to her? I hope more than anything that she'd be happy and fulfilled with her life, and that she'd be proud of me and my sister.

I can't tell what the others think but to me the Assembly Hall feels like it's contracted into a claustrophobic ball. I still don't have the nerve to look around me as the man with the four stripes attempts to pull me in with his stare. He's waiting for me to make another mistake so he can stamp his authority by making an example of me. I keep my eyes firmly down. I'm not going to risk goading him and forever become his whipping boy. That's the point about your dignity. They can't take it away from you, but you still have to pick your moments or you win the battle and lose the war. It took me a long time fighting the System to work that one out.

There's a sudden shuffle of noise that reverberates down from the stage and not looking will probably get me into the same trouble as if I had stared at the man. I glance up to check and sure enough he's gone, and standing in his place, sentinel style, are two Guards. Toward the back of the stage is another man I've not seen before. He is wearing the same combat uniform as the Guards, but he's much older than anyone I've seen so far. He's stocky and muscular with thick silver hair, cut into a flat top, almost shaved at the sides. His face is both tanned and lined, and there is something about his deep blue eyes that command respect before he's even spoken. I'm convinced I'm looking at the Boss until a woman struts onto the stage and there's something about the way she moves that tells me she's in charge and not him. She is all smiles in a sea of sullen faces, as she walks toward a central lectern, which is rising from the floor at the front of the stage.

She is, I'm guessing, our new mother, and I dislike her instantly.

She surveys us with a wide smile over straight white teeth. She is what you would call beautiful even though her smile is as false as the bright lights above my head. I'm not good at guessing ages but she must be about forty. She is slim and I can't tell if she's tall or not as she's wearing heels and because the stage is high in front of us. She is wearing one of those suits for women. The type they wear in Court but with trousers rather than a skirt, and it's black, not blue, and seems to fit her more tightly than the one my lawyer wore. Her hair is the same colour as the suit and it touches the top of her shoulders. It appears to shimmer under the lights and reminds me of a waterfall at night.

'Welcome to your new home,' she says, slowly opening her arms. 'My name is Ilse and in time I will get to know your names. I'm sure you have many questions but for now what is important is what I represent to you. I am your saviour; your leader; your one source of inspiration. I'm here to guide you on your next journey in life. Today is a significant day for all of you. You are free! The Secular World convicted you of being *Denounced* and was going to hang you by the neck until your life ceased. They were wrong in their assessments and accusations and they had little understanding of the precious commodities they had before them.'

She pauses as if waiting for a question. I'm not sure what to think. Her words don't make sense and I trust her less than I already do, which was close to zero anyway. I want to look at the others but I'm part mesmerised by Ilse and part too terrified to seem like I'm not paying attention. She continues, her voice softening.

'By bringing you here today, we have corrected that injustice. Powers – perhaps beyond your current understanding – have intervened and have demanded change.' She sniffs loudly and slips a handkerchief from her sleeve and dabs the inner corners of her eyes. 'I want to share a secret with you. You are the chosen ones who will achieve greatness in your lifetime. The Powers have bestowed a gift upon you. Your time to die has not yet arrived. You have been re-born. It is an opportunity to be cleansed. To be pure again. Free of the corruptions you have become accustomed to. Free of materialistic impulses. This is why I am your chosen *Mother* from now until you graduate. I welcome you, *my children*, into my home and heart with open arms.'

I hear a boy clear his throat and cough behind me.

I hope that's all it is but I tense, sensing it's going to be more.

'Where are we?' he asks.

I'm not sure Ilse heard it, but I did and so did most of the other *Denounced*. She smiles and steps around the lectern to the foot of the stage.

'I know you are all nervous but you don't have to be. We won't bite. Speak up, my Son. What was it you said?'

The boy coughs to clear his throat some more. I want to tell him that if they don't bite then why are they carrying guns and electronic batons? But I don't, and all I can think is that I'm glad the attention is off me, because the man with the four stripes is going to be staring at this boy from now on. Life in the System can be cruel. It's a fact. I've learn to live with it.

'I want to know where are we and why we were drugged?'

I realise it's the boy who asked me where we were earlier on. My chest tightens as I look at Ilse and wait for her reply. Her smile slowly broadens and then turns into a high-pitched laugh that vibrates across my teeth.

'Did you say drugged?'

She laughs even louder and turns to the man with the commanding blue eyes.

'My Son thinks I drugged him. Have you ever heard anything so ridiculous in all your life?'

The man with the silver hair starts to laugh as he looks at his two Guards on the stage who in turn join in the laughter. It spreads like a virus through the rest of the Guards and the men and women in tracksuits.

I'm not sure how to react and it's the first time I dare to look around at the rest of the *Denounced*. The same terrified uncertainty is stretched across their faces when a boy and a girl toward the middle of our crowd force a laugh. I spot a Guard nudge a few teenagers in the back to encourage them to start laughing. They join in and it soon becomes infectious, and I fake my laugh to make sure I'm not the odd one out. Within seconds, everyone in the room is laughing except the boy who asked the question. Tears are rolling down his flushed face. I'm caught between being angry at him for his stupidity and wanting to help him, but I'm not going to do anything. I can't. He should have kept his mouth shut. He's clearly never been in a Community Home before or, if he has, he's a *Newbie* to the System and he's about to learn a hard lesson – it's going to be tough to claw back from this mistake. Through the laughter, I spot hardened eyes of some of the other girls and boys who understand what's going on. I make a mental note of their faces and if I get chance I'll befriend a few. I might need them as allies. The mixed-race boy is one of them. He's looking at me, laughing, but I'm sure he is thinking the same as I am. I search for the blonde girl. She's over to my far left and she's pretending she can't see I'm staring at her, but she's checking me out in the way I'm checking her out. I can tell she already has her own agenda to survive this place and that's okay by me, but I'm not sure about her, and if she wants any help from me, she's way out of luck.

Ilse raises her hands to stop us from laughing. As we begin to quiet, she dabs at the inner corner of her eyes with a fresh part of her handkerchief.

'I think that is the funniest thing I've ever heard in my entire life,' she says, staring at the boy. 'I did answer your first question, but you clearly weren't listening. You are standing in your new home, surrounded by your new family. Now it's time for the serious work to begin. What do you say?'

She's asked the boy a question but he doesn't answer. I can see he's frozen with fear and he hasn't registered her words.

'I asked you a question,' Ilse says, her tone turning icy and clipped.

The boy is lost in his own panicked mind and could be at the bottom of the ocean for all he knows.

'Are you refusing to answer your mother?'

I spot a Guard step forward, snapping his electronic baton free from his utility belt as he moves. A second later, the electric arc crackles from the tip. He pushes past two girls and approaches the boy from behind, striking him across the back in a full sweeping arc. The boy didn't even know it was coming and he screams in pain, collapsing to the floor, the back of his jumpsuit singed with a long single burn mark.

Nobody moves to help him.

Nobody ever does in places like this.

'As I said, before we were so rudely interrupted,' Ilse says with a broad smile, 'it's time for the serious work to begin.'

6

All I can hear is the whimpering of the boy. I'm sure we're all too scared to look at him, or I am anyway, and I hope for his sake he stops crying soon. Either he doesn't understand how his actions will be perceived or he can't stop himself, but he's losing his self-respect and it's going to be hard for him to get it back, especially in a place like this – whatever this place is.

Finally, a man in a tracksuit runs in front of me, heading toward the boy. I snatch a glance and watch the man pull the boy to his feet and tell him he'll be in more trouble if he doesn't get himself together. The lad nods, doing his best to stifle his sobs as he wipes his face with the back of his hand. I knew by the sterile look what the rules would be and I'm sorry for the lad that he got to prove my point.

Suddenly, my attention is taken by activity on the stage from men and women dressed in brown overalls with white t-shirts underneath. The style of their clothes is similar to our *Denounced* regulation issue and I wonder if they are prisoners in some way, too? I can't decide, but watching them work, I notice they don't look as physically fit as the rest of the personnel, and I get the impression they are the *Workers* and the people in the tracksuits are like *Trainers* and, well, guards are *Guards*.

If I've got this right, then I'm observing the full authority structure. Ilse is the Governess and the man with the blue eyes is Head of Security. Then there are the Trainers in their olive coloured tracksuits and stripes denoting rank. The man who made me stand at the front is, I think, Head of this Group.

I was panicked I'd made an enemy for life, but it looks like the boy who asked the question is going to be our resident scapegoat. That's tough on him, but good for me. But why do we need *Trainers,* or even *Guards,* and Ilse mentioned something about Graduation. What are we graduating from exactly? I don't see this place as a Community Home where at eighteen you can graduate out as an Adult or go to College – either way, you're free of the System. From what I've seen so far, I wouldn't call this place a Holding Centre, but more like a prison, although a Holding Centre is a sort of prison with a Court attached. And who and what are *The Powers*? Are they like special Court Officials who have additional authorities which make them closer to a Judge? Or maybe they are more powerful than a Judge? And the way Ilse said it made it sound like they'd set us free, but I'd like to see any one of us try and walk out of here without being stopped.

Or whipped.

'Eyes front!' The Head Trainer growls at me.

I snap my head forward, keeping my eyes on the stage and I'm extra careful not to catch anyone's stare while paying full attention. I'm not going to get caught out again while I'm thinking what to do. The lights begin to fade and I buzz with a mild relief that I can return to being invisible. The wall behind Ilse turns into a giant screen as she is captured in the centre of the stage by a spotlight from above. From nowhere, a gyroscope of effervescent colours appears before her. It's suspended in mid-air and makes us all gasp, and I'm mesmerised by the magic of its unexpected appearance and constantly changing shape. Our Mother is enjoying the moment as she slowly inserts her hand into the gyrating mass of colours, like she's slipping on a precious glove.

'As your mother, I now give you your brothers and sisters.'

Her tone is personal and intimate, like she's talking to you in private, but I know she's not. I watch, mouth ajar, as her fingers close, her hand turning into a fist. She steals a second glance towards us, throwing a smile as she does. Everyone is holding their breath. I'm not sure any of us knows what she means or intends to do next – I don't. She pulls a handful of effervescent liquid from the centre of the gyroscope and holds it up for us to view. It dances in the palm of her hand like an erupting volcano. Then, she turns and throws the liquid at the screen. It busts into an explosion of light as it hits. The waterfall of colours sparkle in a second round of intensity before fading to reveal six names. There are four boys' names and two girls', each with their allocated Secular World IDs. More gasps fill the room and I'm stuck between being relieved and scared. Should my name be up on the screen or not? Or is it a bonus that I've not been picked? Ilse clicks her fingers and the names reshuffle and settle into a new order, tiered as you would see at the start of a motor race.

The first name is Taylor 8-2-2-7-8-0-1.

Without thinking, I look around me, wondering who and where Taylor 8-2-2-7-8-0-1 is. Two Trainers seem to know who to go to, and the other three boys and two girls are ushered to the first lit Pod on the floor I spotted when we stepped into this Assembly Hall.

Pod One has been selected, I realise.

Ilse repeats her lucky dip of names. Six more appear. This time it is three boys and three girls. One of the girls is stood to my immediate left and her name drops to number three in the re-shuffle.

Pod Two is complete.

Ilse takes a deep theatrical breath as she reaches in for a third time. She's enjoying the game she's created, but she's the only one. None of us know what these new groupings mean, and anything new or different in the System usually equals bad news for those involved. The dark enables me to turn my attention from the stage to the lit Pods. There are fifteen in total and each pod has six tiered lines, which makes a total of...

'Ninety,' the boy behind me says.

I'm not sure if he's talking to me or himself, but he's right. There're ninety of us and the ratio is more weighted toward the boys than the girls, maybe 60/40 or even 70/30, but it's definitely not a 50/50 split.

I unexpectedly begin to feel isolated as others around me peel off to join their new brothers and sisters in their designated clans. The boy who asked the question is in Pod Eight. He's at the back, but even he looks happier now he's part of something and not isolated. I wonder what the other five members think having the scapegoat forced within their midst? I wouldn't be happy, I would see it as an unlucky charm.

There are still four family pods to be filled. The mixed-race boy hasn't been picked and is staring at the floor, indifferent to the proceedings, which I don't think is a good idea. I check to see if the blonde girl has been picked. She hasn't. It's hard to read her emotions in this light.

Ilse throws another fistful of light at the screen and I find myself starting to pant, which I get under control as fast as I can. I've been gripped with a creeping fear that I'll be called last. It has the same connotations as being picked to go to the front. It gets me noticed and I was all about getting to eighteen and getting out of the System without being picked for anything other than a game of basketball, before I was convicted of being a *Denounced*.

The lights on the screen sparkle and wane and I hear myself gulp in the silence of the room. My name isn't up on the screen, so I'm going to be in the last pod – Fifteen. I knew it. I go to walk toward the designated area when a whistle is sounded and I'm pointed at to stay where I am. I nod a *sorry*. I was too overcome and forgot to think. My mistake isn't enough to get me whipped, but I feel the stare of the Head Trainer and I could kick myself for my second mistake.

The screen re-shuffles the names of Pod Fourteen and Rebecca 3-7-8-1-9-9-1 is the first name. The new Pod members jogs over to their designated spots. I glance at who is left. I knew it. The mixed-race boy gives me a smile like he knew it too. The blonde girl still looks ahead, like she hasn't registered that we were in the same Holding Centre together, went to the same Court, were set to be executed on the same day, and are now in the same Pod. I don't have time to register how I feel about that or to look at the other three members of my new family as I return my gaze to the screen.

All our names are up, but Ilse hasn't done the reshuffle.

'Don't worry, my sons and daughters, no-one here is the runt of my litter. Last is by no means least. You will learn that you hold your destiny in your hands.'

She clicks her fingers and our names start to spin. If there is such a thing as a premonition then I'm having it now. My heart sinks into my stomach. The back of my neck prickles with the heat of panic. Our names settle and my glimpse into the future becomes my new reality as the enormity of what has happened dawns on me.

The one thing I absolutely didn't want in my life, I now have.

I'm the Head of my new brothers and sisters.

We are four boys and two girls, and we are ordered into our Pod in the following order.

Me.
Rasa 4-3-4-2-7-3-1 (the blonde girl).
Spencer 3-9-4-1-2-3-7 (the mixed-race boy).
Diego 1-1-1-7-4-3-1 (never seen before).
Kuro 8-6-8-3-0-1-9 (never seen before).
Chantal 9-9-3-4-7-1-0 (never seen before).

7

I'm wondering if being dead may have been my better option. I've no idea where I am and what is going to be expected of me, but if I understand this correctly, I'm now responsible for five other people. Five people I don't know; have never met until today, and didn't have a say in picking. I feel sick at the thought. I wonder if there is anything I can do when the applause snaps me back into the moment. I'm the last to join in clapping Ilse off the stage as she waves goodbye, like she's the winning contestant in a competition. It's an odd departure when I take in what has happened and how we got here, but it's all part of her happy act. I'm not buying it. I can see, too, that my slackness has been noted by the Head Trainer, who I'm sure is counting how many breaths I take and if they are somehow in rhythm with everyone else. I ignore him as I watch Ilse leave the stage. I can tell some of the others think they're safe and that the worst is over, but they are fooling themselves. This place is worse than the Holding Centre, far worse, because at least there they had to stick to the Rules even if those Rules sometimes became corrupted.

Here, we don't know the rules.

A whistle is sounded and we are ordered out in Pod Order. As Pod Fifteen we go last; I'm guessing, this is going to be the norm from now on. In its own way being last is like being first and we're going to get noticed every day. Pod Eight or Pod Seven are the best Pods to be in for wanting to join the crowd, and my fists clench at my developing situation.

I feel more a prisoner now than I did before I was about to be executed.

Outside the Assembly Hall, I blink hard under the glare of the lights. The air tastes dry and the faint hum of an extractor fan sounds high above my head. I stare up to see if I can see it. I can't, but the noise reminds me there's a place outside of this giant grey prison, and I find comfort in that thought.

'Where are we going?'

It's the other girl from our Pod who's asked the question. Chantal is her name and she was last in our order. She has an accent that I don't recognise and her question bugs me. It's like the dumb boy from Pod Eight who asked a similar question. How would any of us know? We don't, and all she is doing is showing her weakness by letting everyone know she's not lived in the System before. Great, I think. I have a newbie to watch over. This is getting worse by the second.

'I said where are we going, Ned?'

I twist round and stare at her. I hadn't noticed how small and lithe she is compared to the rest of us.

'Shut your mouth.'

'Don't speak to her like that,' Rasa, the blonde girl snaps back.

'Yeah, don't tell me to shut up,' Chantal chips in. 'Ilse told us we were allowed to talk between ourselves and to get to know each other.'

I stop walking and grab Chantal by the front of her jumpsuit and yank her close to my face. She's so light I could probably pick her off the floor with one hand and toss her across this grey wasteland if I wanted.

'I'm telling you to shut your mouth for your own good. You saw what happened to that boy.'

'Ilse said we should get to know each other,' Chantal says, trying to push my hand away.

'Let her go,' Rasa says.

I shove Chantal off to my left and step in close to Rasa. She doesn't move or even flinch as I approach. I thought she was beautiful, but I was wrong. She has a cutting frown and small eyes like my executioner, and I can smell she's riddled with trouble.

'I'm not scared of you,' she adds.

'I don't remember talking to you,' I say, taking another step closer.

'Hey, Dude,' Spencer, the mixed-race boy, says. 'Ilse did say we should talk and introduce ourselves. We probably should, no?'

I stare back and look through the other Pods ahead of us. I know I tuned out at the end because there was too much going on in my head so I'm thinking I must have missed Ilse's instructions, but I don't see much talking going on in front of me.

'Talk all you like but don't count me in. Ilse asked that boy to speak up and look what happened to him.'

'But he asked a stupid question,' Chantal adds, all chirpy.

'That thing between your head is designed to keep you alive. You should remember that. Who else is talking? No one, but us idiots. Just my luck to be stuck with a bunch of hillbillies who've never lived in a Community Home before.'

I turn around and trudge on. I don't care if they want to spill their life's stories to each other. It will only come back to haunt them. You can't trust anyone but yourself in a place like this, maybe in the Adult World, too. I ache with a mild panic of having to deal with all these new thoughts. I stare at the other fourteen Pods and try and imagine what some of the others are thinking, what fears they're suffering. The thought pulls me up. I'm innocent of being a *Denounced* but I might be the only one here. I could be surrounded by eighty-nine others who wanted to destroy our Secular World. That isolates me even more than I already am and makes sense to why there are so many Guards to watch over us.

I'm going to have to be even more careful then I first thought.

We head on and in the mid-distance I can see the buildings I saw earlier when we first climbed out of our transport boxes, or were they our original coffins? I shudder at the thought. The small town is bathed under a halo of white light and I'm struck again how difficult it is to get a sense of distance and space, which only adds to the confusion building in my mind. I don't even know the time.

It could be morning or it could be night.

We eventually step into the crop of buildings and they are as plain as they looked from a distance. Few have windows and the ones that do are rectangular shaped cheap ones that are used in less expensive housing. The doors have electronic locks and I see the Trainer at the front of Pod One touch his watch against the electronic panel of the door to gain entrance. Pod One is ushered inside, followed by Pod Two. It doesn't take long before we are next. Inside is a huge storeroom and a Worker is handing out plastic crates with our names and numbers on one side from behind a counter. He has mine and Rasa's already on the counter top and is lifting Spencer's into view as I collect mine. Once I pick up my crate, I'm told to go right and Rasa and Chantal are shown to the left.

I enter a changing room and some of the boys have already changed out of their purple jumpsuits. Inside my crate is a two piece sky-blue tunic set. A set of grey loose lounge pants and a top that looks like sleepwear. Next is an all-in-one black workout bodysuit. I touch it and can tell it's made of the best materials for professional athletes that will wick sweat away, and keep you both warm and dry. The zip is under the right arm, and the knees and arms are padded, as is the butt. Underneath the workout suit is a pair of sneakers that fasten with Velcro. I check the size and they are a perfect fit. If seeing the Trainers wasn't a hint enough, this confirms that I'm going to be doing something which requires me to get fit. I'm strong for my age, but I'm not built for running and I hate any form of exercise unless it's a bit of basketball. Finally, there's a wash bag and a small First-Aid kit along with underwear, socks and a set of white t-shirts. I pick up the First-Aid kit and feel the weight. It's packed tight and heavy, but its presence alone depresses my mood further.

Why is it here and has anyone else registered it?

I doubt it, somehow.

Getting changed is the first moment of pleasure I've had since leaving the Holding Centre. The blue tunic is freshly laundered and smells of freedom. The t-shirt is soft on my skin and I get an unexpected memory flash of my mother putting her arm around my shoulder. I'd fallen down on the sidewalk and cut my left shin on some broken glass. I still have the scar. It momentarily makes me smile, but I shake the memory from my mind just as quick. Being sentimental in an institution is a form of weakness and I know I can't afford to either feel it or, more importantly, let it show.

Once everyone is changed and outside, we are walked to another building, but still nobody is talking between themselves. The girls' casual tunics are a soft yellow colour compared to our sky blue. We enter another building and it's the smell of hot food that starts the first mumblings of conversation. We're made to queue in a single line and, as we near the food, we're given a choice of starters, a main

SJ SHERWOOD

course, followed by dessert. I want to jump straight to the main course of chicken and chips, but I'm not allowed. I have to have a starter and I can't eat my main until my starter is finished. That is not going to be a problem. I could eat a week's worth of food in a single sitting. I go for the ham and pea soup with a slice of warm bread and butter. I get my main course, followed by the largest slice of apple pie and vanilla ice cream I've seen. They make me wait for the others in our Pod to choose their food because we have a dedicated table, and we have to sit down in our new family and eat together. The world *family* makes me want to rage. I had a family once but they are all dead or gone. These people aren't my family and never will be, and I refuse to accept them as such no matter what Ilse might say.

The noise in the canteen grows louder, but as a Pod, we don't talk, which is my fault. I don't care, I decide. I want to eat and then go to bed and worry about tomorrow when I wake. I start my dessert and get an instant reality check that stops me mid-bite. What if I'm stuck here for any length of time? I can't fight all five of my Pod members, and if they turn on me as a group, I'm going to have more trouble than I can handle. Chantal is already whispering to Rasa and they will have a natural bond being the only two girls. Everyone needs a friend in a place like this, even if those friends happen to be *Denounced*.

I let this thought take hold as I look around at the other Pods who have started to talk more freely amongst themselves. I'm not being smart, and I've survived the System this long by being smart.

I turn back to our table and remind myself that these people aren't my family and I don't owe them anything, but it's okay to get to know them.

'Look, I was a bit tense earlier, but I'm Ned 5-7-9-0-1-2-3. I was born and raised in Secular World Quadrant 1, North East, Section Two-C in what used to be known in the Old World as New York City, America.'

8

I might as well have vomited onto my plate by the look on the five faces that stare back at me. I smile as best I can and get a pang of guilt, because there're no genuine emotions driving my friendliness. I get this flash of the last time I saw my sister, Liz. She started on this weird story that if you're not part of your own agenda then you become part of someone else's. I didn't get it at the time, but it was her way of condemning me to the Community Homes' System. I get it now, and to survive this place, I'm going to have to play it on my terms and not those of the five people sat around this table. And I've just come to a simple conclusion. I've been given plenty of dud shots in my short life but maybe, just maybe, being made Head of Pod Fifteen is the best thing that has ever happened to me.

But only if I play it right.

Only if I think of myself first.

'I'll go first,' Chantal says all upbeat. 'Actually, I'm second as Ned went first.' She giggles at her own joke. 'Well, I'm Chantal 9-9-3-4-7-1-0 and I'm from Secular World Quadrant 3, North West, Section 10-S. I like this next bit. I've never done it before. So, in the Old World, that makes me from Paris, France, but as you know, I'm not meant to say that. It's illegal, you know.'

I knew where she was from the minute she asked me the question, but I was too hyped to register her accent. She's one of the smallest of all the *Denounced*, from what I can see – birdlike – and she gingerly moves from one foot to the other. It's not what I would call a walk, more a hop. She's the hyper-talkative type, and I bet she's an expert at knowing everyone's business. She's so not my kinda person, which is going to make my relationship with her tough to keep up. I decide she must be a real *Denounced*, I mean, anyone who's going to talk as much as her is bound to have slipped and criticised our Secular World.

'Thank you,' I say. 'It was good to hear where you're from.'

My voice sounds false even to me and I'm sure I saw Rasa roll her eyes. It's only a matter of time before we clash for real, but not now, and whatever she does at this table today, I'm going to ignore. I look at the tall lean boy with black spiky hair sat next to Chantal. He fidgets in his chair and pushes at the front of his black rimmed glasses, blushing as he absorbs five stares, his own gaze resting into his cupped hands.

'Er...yes...em...do you want me to go next?'

'If you want to, or you can go last if you want?'

'You should go next, because you don't want to,' Chantal says. 'It's fun to do things you don't like. Anyway, we're a family now and we have to get to know each other.'

I have the opposite thought, but I smile that he should do what Chantal suggests. He nods, pushing at the bridge of his glasses, his head dropping a touch as he completes his habitual movement. 'I'm not very good at talking in front of people, but here goes. My name is Kuro 8-6-8-3-0-1-9. I'm from Secular World Quadrant 4, South Central, Section 17-E. In the Old World that makes me from Tokyo, Japan. I hope I don't get into any more trouble for saying that. It's good to meet you all. Thank you,' he finishes with a small bow of the head.

His English has no accent whatsoever and if he'd not mentioned his Old-World roots I would have said he was from Secular World Quadrant 1, the same as myself by his voice alone. He strikes me as the intelligent and thoughtful type, but he's a born worrier, that much is obvious. Or maybe he's a worrier because he knows he's guilty and he got caught. I don't trust the shyness and lack of eye contact and, like Chantal, he must be a real *Denounced*.

I look at the boy next to him. The others follow my lead. His face shows the start of being an adult with his thick eyebrows, strong jaw and dark stubble sprouting from his chin. He'll be fully shaving in under a year. His hair is jet black and his skin is the colour of light mud, but his eyes are young and unsure, and he's nearly as wide as he is tall, like his body can't decide which way to grow.

'I'm Diego 1-1-1-7-4-3-1,' he says, between short nervous coughs. 'I was born and raised in Secular World Quadrant 2, Central, Section 1-A. In the Old World, I'm from near Mexico City, Mexico. I'm proud of my roots and where I'm from we always say *Tula* – the name of our village – and not Section 1-A.'

Immediately, I know his type. He was part of a large family before he was ripped from it, and I have a good idea why he was taken. It's against the law to speak in any other language except English, but by the strength of his accent he speaks his own tongue at every opportunity he gets. He's a real *Denounced*, but not in the true sense. His type don't ridicule the Secular World and want to live in a Quadrant where they can pray to a God, but they are passionate about their ancestry and heritage, and it causes friction within our Secular State. The Holding Centre was full of his type. I almost like him, but I've made a promise to myself – I'm innocent and I have to get through this, so I shouldn't waste my time making friends with those who are guilty.

I don't bother looking at Rasa, part out of spite and part because she'll talk when and if she's ready. I glance across at

Spencer and he gives us a big smile. His teeth are white and straight and he's comfortable within himself. He must get a lot of attention with how he looks. Maybe that was his problem and how he ended up being a *Denounced*. Our Secular World has issues with those who get themselves noticed and they don't like when people step above their station.

'Hi, I'm Spencer 3-9-4-1-2-3-7 and I'm from Secular World Quadrant 3, South East, Section 3-A. In the Old World that makes me from London, England, but I'm happy to say I'm from Section 3-A. I'm not one for causing trouble. Not much else to say other than this is one messed-up day, and if you have any ideas on what's going on then I'd love to hear it.'

He has an accent that makes him sound like he's better than everyone else, but that's just his voice. I don't think his personality is like that. He pretends nothing bothers him, but I know that's not true, either. It's a survival mechanism you learn once you enter a Community Home and he's been in the System for a while, of that I'm sure. We're fellow kin in that sense. He's tall and strong and he's lifted weights to build himself up. He's got a man's body with a boy's head. I'm more curious about his secret story than anyone else's, and he could be the ally I need. Others instantly warm to him, which they don't to me. I suddenly check my own need to like him. I've met enough people who are all smiles in the System, but will fillet you like a dead fish if they get the chance. Our Mother, Ilse, is such a person. Maybe Spencer is too? I wonder what he did to end up here? Like Jack, in another place, at another time, we may have become friends but there's nothing about him that makes me think he's not a real *Denounced*.

We turn to Rasa. She has her blonde hair weaved through her fingers and is picking at some split ends, like none of us are here. After a beat she lets her eyes flick into the circle. It's too cool and calculated for my liking, and she knows exactly what she's doing. For all her looks there's nothing about this person I want to know. I can't see her ever being on my side and that has nothing to do with us squaring up to each other earlier on. It makes it even more important I befriend and work the other three boys, especially as Chantal will be her natural ally, being a girl and all.

'I'm Rasa 4-3-4-2-7-3-1 and I'm also from Secular World Quadrant 3, East Central, Section 4-B. In the Old World that makes me from St Petersburg, Russia.'

We wait as if she's going to add some more, but she doesn't, returning her interest to her split ends. I remember once there was a Russian boy in my second Community Home and he always had some scheme on the go, some plan he was implementing. He didn't care what anyone thought of him and he often took a beating from the older boys, but it never deterred him from what he wanted to do. I swear he even liked it at times, like he fed off the hate. Rasa's cut from the same sheet of metal as that boy and whatever she did to get here, she did it with drive and determination.

She's a real *Denounced*, no question.

'Thank you,' I say with my new false smile.

She ignores me but it's okay, because I've made up for my earlier mistake.

I have four people who have warmed towards me and I honestly don't care about the fifth.

9

A female Trainer tells us to load our dirty plates onto the trays at the end of the room. We do as we are told and fall in line behind the other Pods. The movement and the close proximity of the other Trainers brings the chattering in the Canteen to a halt, the only noise is the percussion of cutlery. I absorb the uncertainty around me, oddly relaxed about what is coming next. Everyone looks exhausted and it has to be bedtime with no more surprises scheduled for today. It's then a thought smacks me in the face. Apart from the Holding Centre when I was in an individual cell, I'm used to sharing a dormitory with boys, but what if our Pod Structure holds twenty-four seven?

That means I'll be sharing my private life with two girls! Woo!

That will definitely be weird and scary, I mean, will I have to shut my eyes when one of them gets undressed? I can't believe they'll do that to us, and the idea of being stuck with Rasa all day and all night gives me a stab of indigestion.

Outside, I forget about sharing a dormitory as I start to doubt my memory. I'm sure a single path led from the Canteen to the Storehouse, but now there are two paths that both curve to the right, and the Storehouse is much further back and at a different angle to how I remember.

Or am I so dead tired that I'm imagining things and nothing is different?

It's possible, I think. It's been one strange day.

The female Trainer who told us to stack our plates starts to walk alongside our Pod. I wonder what she tells her family she does for a job and if they approve or not? I'm jealous that when she leaves us tonight she'll be going home where nobody will tell her what to do and how she should think. I want that to be me in a few years. Free to start my life, under my own rules, doing what I want, when I want. I'm Ned Hunter, not Ned 5-7-9-0-1-2-3. I'm innocent of being a *Denounced* and I deserve to be free. Or do I? Maybe I'm here because I showed dissent over my name and Number. And I questioned the rules in my Community Homes, and I pointed out the corruption to my Lawyer at every moment I could, maybe I really was questioning our Secular World and all its Laws. And most of my thoughts *are* about how to beat the bad things within the System.

We step into another flat-roofed building and like the Storehouse, the inside space bears no resemblance to the small block I thought I was entering. The corridor is wide and long with rows of doors on either side. Each door has the number of the individual Pods across the front. This is going to be our home and the real test as to whether we'll get on or not as a group. We are the last door on the left. I can see why they split us, because the first door on the right is Pod Eight, so the other seven Pods must be in the building next to us.

Our Trainer touches her watch against the panel on the door and the first thing I notice is the lack of a handle. This makes our sleeping quarters more a cell then a dormitory, not that I'm overly surprised. I'm told to step through first, followed by Rasa then Spencer. If this structural hierarchy is going to be observed going forward then that makes Rasa my official Number Two. I've been slow to work that out, but I doubt she has. Her coolness now makes sense and I realise she's already started to undermine me and is looking to be Number One as soon as she can. She's been around long enough to know that being Head is going to have its advantages and could be the one real ticket out of here.

Our cell is simple, but big and there's a set of bunk-beds on the left, a set on the right, and a set to the right of the door as you enter. We're sharing, no question. My day is getting even more worse than I thought it could. Each bed has our plastic crates placed on top of the mattress, and we're told to put our belongings into the small wardrobes by each set of bunks.

'When you've unpacked, put your crates by the door. Lights out will be in ten minutes. You can talk between yourselves if you want, but my suggestion is you shower and then sleep. You've had a long day and you'll have a longer one tomorrow. Everyone understand?'

We nod in unison, but none of us say anything. The Trainer isn't looking at anybody else, either, but me. I get it and so does Rasa. I'll take the fall for everyone if it goes wrong, but I'm guessing, I'll take the praise if things go right.

'Remember, you're personally responsible for your property. And if you know what's good for you, keep your room clean and tidy,' she adds, closing the door behind her.

It clicks and then locks, and I find myself staring at it for a moment, thinking about her going home and being free. I have to stop these thoughts as I'm only torturing myself. I have to deal with what is directly in front of me, and then my next problem, and the one after that and don't worry about the future if I can. It's the only way to get through. The System has taught me that, if nothing else.

I turn back into the room and catch Rasa staring. She looks away, like I'm not here. Between the two facing bunk-beds is a door that leads into a small hall and splits into two bathrooms with separate toilets. At least I won't have to shut my eyes when the girls get changed, and Rasa and Chantal share a bunk-bed, which separates them from us. I can live with that – not that I have a choice. The bathroom to the left is for myself, Spencer, Diego and Kuro, and the one to the right is for Rasa and Chantal. There are no windows but a single warm glow light in each room.

'I'm going to have a shower if nobody objects?' Spencer asks, reaching for his towel.

I shrug an okay. Rasa reaches for her towel and heads into the bathroom not consulting myself or even Chantal. It's no big deal because I'm never going to use the girls' bathroom, but in a way it is a big deal because she didn't follow the same protocol as Spencer, and we both know it. And I wonder if anybody else clocked it?

Spencer's quick and Diego follows him with Kuro going last. I should shower, but I can't be bothered. I've climbed onto my bunk-bed and, like the food, the mattress is better than it looks, and I've become too comfortable to move again today.

Kuro climbs onto his bunk-bed and a second later the light fades into a blacky-grey. It's enough to let you sleep by, but you could find your way into the bathroom or hunt through your wardrobe with no problem. I'm used to this lighting. I'm not sure I could sleep in the pitch black any more, not that I'm scared of the dark, just this lighting is the norm for the Homes I've lived in.

I watch Kuro trying to get comfortable until it hits me he doesn't like the night-time glow. He finally pulls the sheet over his face. It tells me he's never been in a Community Home before, so he's not an orphan like me. I glance up at Spencer who is above Kuro. He's spread eagled and snoring softly. I almost smile. This is home-from-home for him. I glance over the edge of my bunk at Diego below me who is curled on his side and has the blanket pulled tight under his chin. He looks uncomfortable, but comfortable at the same time. I guess he's used to sleeping in a room with others, but not in a Community Home. I imagine him with six or seven brothers and the same number of sisters. I see his family as a poor but tight group who'll stick together. He'll be a true and loyal friend if he likes you, but he'll sit there and watch you burn if he doesn't.

His trust and friendship will be hard to win.

I look across at Chantal. She has her blanket over head like Kuro. I knew by how open and friendly she is that she's not been in a Home before. She's got some tough lessons ahead and I have to be careful she doesn't become our weakest link. I'm undecided how to handle her and she's going to run to Rasa at every opportunity she can, which is going to add another layer of complexity. Or maybe it won't, and I just don't know how to handle girls, and she'll be okay, because she's such a newbie and will be easy to manipulate.

My eyes flick up a bunk and I rest my stare on the enemy.

She's picking at her split ends while I'm sure there're a thousand poisonous thoughts chopping through her mind. She's smarter than my lawyer, which isn't hard, and I bet I wouldn't be here if I'd had someone like Rasa representing me in Court. I don't think she's an orphan, but she's been in a Home, no question, and I wonder if she's been in pre-adult prison and she's progressed through that System before she ended up in the Holding Centre awaiting trial as a *Denounced*. If she's had that journey, she'll be tough and not only physically, but mentally, too. I've learned that girls are often tougher in the mind than boys. Just look at my sister. I never did understand all that stuff about opening doors and letting them go first because they're a girl. They say it's about respect, but respect is when two people are equal and there's nothing equal about opening a door for girl who's stronger in the mind than you. Maybe I missed something and I need it explaining to me again. I'm too tired to think about it anymore, and I close my eyes and drift into sleep, dreaming that Kuro, Spencer and Diego are standing in front of me, and Kuro is holding a Trainer's watch.

And I'm running into the sea.

And I'm surfing at a break point.

And I can see blue sky and clouds.

And…

10

'…don't move, my friend.'

It's Diego's deep voice that echoes in my mind loud and clear.

I open my eyes, startled, unable to move if I wanted to and I'm unsure when my dream of surfing turned into a nightmare. Diego has hold of my arms and I can tell he's using a fraction of his strength. Spencer has one hand over my mouth, with a single finger of his other hand rested against his lips. If this is a mutiny it didn't take Rasa long to work her charms. It's then I see a different reality, which sends a bolt of panic through me. Just like my dream, Kuro is holding one of the Trainers' watches and he's grinning like he's eighteen and about to get his digital credits to enter the world as an Adult.

Spencer removes his hand from my mouth and Diego releases his grip and I slowly sit, catching my breath. I snatch a glance at the girls. Chantal is sat on her bunkbed with her knees hugged under her chin. She's been crying and is fighting her sobs and I wonder how long the boys have been awake. Rasa is lying on top of her sheets, her legs crossed at the ankles, picking at the end of her split ends, like none of us are here.

'Where did you get that?' I ask Kuro.

A cock-sure smile spreads across one side of his face. It seems more pronounced on him than it would on Spencer, because he's the last person in our Pod I thought was capable of smiling with that kind of intent.

'It doesn't matter,' he says.

His voice is an excited whisper full of hope and danger.

'Yes, it does,' I say. 'It matters a lot.'

'We can escape,' Spencer adds. 'We can get out of this nut shop.'

'We can get into trouble, too,' I say. 'Painful trouble,' I add. 'You saw what they did to that boy from Pod Eight. Tell me where you got it?' I ask again, ignoring Spencer and looking at Kuro for my answer.

'When we were walking back from the Assembly Hall, I saw one of the Trainers stop to adjust his shoe. When he stood, it slipped from his wrist. Look, the strap's broken.' He steps forward and hands me the watch. Even in the low light of the room, I can make out the tiny holding mechanism which attaches the strap to the main body of the watch has snapped in two. I glance up at Kuro who is still smiling like he's won the top prize. That's the thing about people in the System – you don't know them until you know them. And it's not what somebody says that counts, but what they do that's who they are. Look at my sister, Liz. She said this and that about how she loved and cared for me, but when the critical moment came she left me in the System. It's the same with Ilse. She was all smiles and telling us how we are her children and she is our mother and how she'll protect us, but she's having a boy whipped in the same breath. And Kuro looks all innocent and the worried type, but I'm doubting my early assessment as I look as his stupid grin. Maybe playing weak is his way to skip under the radar and really, he's an expert slight-of-hand and one of those conniving types that's been in trouble all his life. It's how he ended up in the Holding Centre being a *Denounced*.

It's possible.

I know it is.

'Why didn't anyone see you pick it up?' I ask.

'I was at the back with only Chantal behind me and it fell directly in front of me. I just scooped it up. It was easy.'

I look across at Chantal. She's crying.

'I didn't see him pick it up,' she says.

And I believe her, I think, as Rasa says.

'It's too convenient if you ask me. It's a trap.'

'Nobody's asking you and, anyway, what do you know?' Diego says. The sharpness and aggression in his voice, surprises me.

'If you can't see it's a trap then you're a clown. I should whip you myself to teach you a lesson. That's what they do with clowns in our Quadrant.'

'You're a dumb blonde who does nothing but play with her hair. You know nothing. You should leave the decisions to the men.'

'I know you're an idiot and I know this is a trap, which is two more things than you'll ever know.'

Spencer looks at me and says. 'If we go to where they first dropped us then it shouldn't be hard to find the main entrance the trucks came through. If we can get past those gates then we'll be free. It's perfect and we have surprise on our side.'

'And what if you can't find the gates? And what if that key doesn't open the main door? And what if there are lots of Guards? And what if we're hundreds of miles from anywhere? And what if and what if?' Rasa says with a roll of the eyes.

She's right, of course, but I'm not thinking about them and the possibility of escape, I'm thinking about myself. If I was a real *Denounced* then why not try and escape because the Secular World wants to execute me anyway. On the outside, I could attempt to hook up with other escaped *Denounced* or *Doubters* and live in one of the underground groups to survive the Authorities. But if I escape, then I lose any chance of ever proving my innocence, because maybe, you know, just maybe, I could be one of those lucky ones that ends up being on TV and making millions of digital credits because I was wrongly accused and I got to prove it. It's not the fame or the digital credits I care about, but the freedom. I'm desperate to understand what it means to make my own choices in life with no one telling what to do.

'How are you going to find the drop-off point?' I say. 'I'm not certain I could remember the way back to the Canteen. And our Holding Centre had cameras everywhere so there has to be cameras here, too?'

'I've been looking for cameras since we arrived and I haven't seen a single one, and the main exit can't be that hard to find,' Diego says.

'Everything is hard for an idiot like you,' Rasa snarls from her top bunk. 'You boys have no brains. At least that stupid boy had enough about him to ask an intelligent question, even if it did get him whipped.'

Diego snaps round and steps toward her. Spencer blocks his path and calms him with a shake of the head, *leave it*. I'm sorry that he did because I'd like to see them fight then I'd know what they're both made of. But, I've learnt that Diego can't stand Rasa. That gives me at least one friend and probably two, because I'm sure Spencer's on my side by the way he keeps asking my advice.

'What do you say?' Spencer ask, looking back at me.

I glance back at Kuro. I twist the watch through my fingers knowing I have a problem. If I say no to the escape, I lose three allies, but I'm smart enough to know Rasa is smarter than me and if she says it's a trap I should contemplate what's she's saying.

'It's our first day here. We don't know where we are and we don't know what's beyond these walls. Why don't we sit on it for a few days and get our bearings and then plan our escape. This can be our secret weapon,' I say, holding up the watch.

'I'm innocent and I want to go home,' Diego snaps at me.

His words smash through and I feel my jaw slacken.

Diego innocent?

No way. I don't believe it, but I don't have time to register it any more as Spencer steps in close and says:

'We should try and get out while we can. There will be daily inspections and we can't risk them finding the watch. And once the Trainer knows it's missing, he'll report it and they'll cancel the codes so it won't work anyway. There's a chance he hasn't missed it yet, so we should go while we still can.'

'Finally, the boy connects with his common sense,' Rasa says. 'Of course he'll report it missing. He probably has already.'

'Shut your face before I make you eat your hair,' Diego snarls, his muscles tensing in his neck.

'I'd like to see you try.'

'Ignore her, Diego,' I say, wanting to ask him more about being innocent. 'If the Trainer has reported it missing it's not going to work anyway, then we have the problem of getting rid of it.'

'Rasa is number two in this family so her vote counts more than yours, Diego,' Chantal chips in. 'We should listen to her.'

'I don't see any one voting but it's a good idea,' Spencer says. 'I want to risk it. I don't believe the Trainer has missed his watch yet. Who's in?'

Diego nods, followed by Kuro.

'Losers,' Rasa snipes from the dark of her bunk-bed.

The boys stare at me waiting for my answer, but I can't get Diego's words out of my head. He's innocent and he wants to go home. If he does get back to his Quadrant his family will protect him – whereas I have nobody. My sister, if I could find her, would hand me straight back to the Authorities without a second thought. That's the problem with being an orphan. I have to rely on myself and my actions have more consequences for me than they do for him.

'It's a mistake to go. We should wait a few days. Work out what the Guards do; find out where the cameras are; get a map of this place in our minds. We should try and get an idea of what Quadrant we're in. If we get outside tonight then what? Where are we going to go? What are we going to eat and drink? How are we going to keep warm if it's freezing out there?'

I feel Rasa looking at me.

'I'm not sure I can take it here,' Spencer says. 'I've seen enough to know it's not going to be good for us. This could be our one and only break. Anyway, when they stopped to give us food on the journey here, it was warm.'

It's the first time I've heard the fear in his voice and I can see the crack in his nonchalant armour.

'Me too,' Diego says. 'I want to go home. If I get out of here, they'll never find me, ever. I'll die before I come back.'

I look at Kuro.

'I want to go,' he adds. 'This place scares me.'

I glance across at Rasa. She's returned to picking at her hair and I know what her answer is anyway. I glance down at Chantal.

'We should stay together as a family,' she says. 'It's our best hope.'

'We're not a family,' Diego says. 'I don't know you and I have enough friends back home. If you don't want to go then don't. It's the same for you,' he says looking back at me. He holds out his hand for the watch. I debate whether to give it to him or not. He's stronger than me, but he doesn't scare me; I'm sure I have a nastier streak if it really came to it. I glance across at Spencer. He's hyped and he's made his mind up. So has Kuro. I can't fight them all and I don't want to lose their respect either because I'll never get it back.

'Good luck,' I say, as I hand over the watch to Diego. 'I'm staying.'

11

I watch and wait, my mind a scramble of thoughts, most of them negative about this haphazard plan. I should be doing something to stop them, but I don't know what. So, instead, I settle into my mattress, with my legs crossed out in front of me and one hand perched behind my head, like I'm relaxed about the situation. I'm not, of course, and it might be nice and warm in the dormitory, but I'm cold and shivering inside. Diego was right about one thing. We don't owe each other anything, but my view on them has changed in these last few minutes. Diego's innocence has fuelled his passion to escape and blinded his judgement in the process, but it's proof enough that he's not lying about his conviction. Kuro is the last person I would have expected to attempt an escape and here he is about to touch the reader with the watch he found, or more likely stole. I like Spencer or maybe it's because I know his type better than the rest. He's institutionalised and it's made him a *chancer* who is not as tough as his easy-going attitude would suggest. I have always fought against institutionalisation, and I wonder if it was another element to me being singled out, contributing in some small way to my current situation.

The lock buzzes open and Spencer looks back into the room for any last-minute takers. I'm not moving and neither are the girls. He throws me one of his handsome smiles and I give them a thumbs up, because I don't know what else to do. Their minds are set and so is mine.

'We head toward the drop-off zone and then via hard right, which in turn should get us to the main gate. It's not much of a plan unless you want to do like Ned said and wait?'

There's no conviction in Spencer's last sentence and he's doing it to make me feel good and to free himself of the guilt about leaving us behind, even if it is our choice.

Diego shakes his head. 'No chance. I want to go.'

'Me too,' Kuro says, nudging his shoulder into the door.

It clicks open and a strip of dark light drops through the gap making my heart race even faster.

'Wait,' Diego says. 'We'll need these.'

He dashes to his wardrobe and picks up his First-Aid kit, followed by Spencer's and then Kuro's.

'Smart move,' Spencer says as he takes his kit from Diego, passing one on to Kuro.

'There's nothing smart about what you're doing,' Rasa says. 'You should re-think.'

Her advice, if that's what it is, sounds spiteful and her tone is laced with fear. They ignore her, as I knew they would, and Kuro steps out of sight first, followed by Spencer, the door coming to a gentle rest as Diego falls into their slipstream. I stare at the strip of blackness between the frame and the door that is left in their place.

All I can hear is my own breath and Chantal's stifled sobbing. I should get up and click the door closed, but I'm paralysed by uncertainty. In times like this I ask my father what advice he would give me. It's a game I've played throughout my life when I've needed someone to turn to and there's been no one, which is most of the time. My father had this job working at the Port doing something with computers that tracked ships and their cargos. It came with lots of responsibility and he was confident at making decisions, or so my sister said. I'm sure I get my stubbornness from him.

I glance at Rasa. She's stopped picking at her hair and is staring intently at the gap between the door and the frame, waves of panic dancing across her face. I'm nervous, but more for Spencer, Kuro and Diego than I am for myself. I've witnessed many boys and girls escape from Homes; some never return, so they must have got to where they wanted to go.

Or at least, I hope they did.

I decide to close my eyes, waiting for sleep or an answer to come to what I should do next. I will take whatever comes first.

I struggle to get comfortable and I can't shift Rasa's stressed look from my mind, which has triggered a hollow feeling in the pit of my stomach. Then a thought drops in. I snap open my eyes and stare through our simple room. We are ninety *Denounced* in total and we've been split into fifteen pods. The Pod dormitories are set up for six. The Canteen has its own dedicated Pod tables. The crates were ready and waiting with our names on the outside when we went to the Storehouse. I hear my father's voice saying it's not an accident that we are here and whatever plan Ilse has, it's not for fourteen Pods of six and one Pod of three. We've messed with her grand plan, or rather Spencer, Diego and Kuro have, but if they do get away then it's going to be myself, Rasa and Chantal who'll pay the price. We won't be able to play the *they escaped while we were asleep card*, which is what I was thinking to do.

An alarm shrieks, vibrating through my chest and out through my back, breaking my thoughts.

I sit up, startled.

The nightlight in the corridor switches to full beam.

I jump off my bunk-bed and grab my sneakers.

'Don't let the door lock,' I yell at Rasa.

I rush out of our dorm into the corridor to see the boy who was whipped dart out of the last door on my left and step outside. It takes me a few seconds to realise Pod Eight have managed to smash open their door and have made a dash for freedom. I don't know what they were thinking, because it's obvious to anyone that these doors would be alarmed after lights out and the only way to stop that is via the electronic key.

I don't want to over commit, so I stop at the main door to our sleeping quarters and peer outside. Guards are appearing along the pathways and darting between the buildings. It looks uncoordinated, but I'm sure their whistles sound instructions. I spot the boy who asked the question running left and away from me, but he's about to run straight into a Guard closing the net. This kid has no luck and I'm glad I don't have his Number, it must be doomed for sure. I see a girl trying to head back to where I'm stood, but a Guard is too quick for her and brings her down with a single strike of his electronic baton. Her mouth opens in a scream, but I hear nothing over the chaos of sounds that fill the space.

'Get back,' I hear Rasa shout behind me. 'You can't be caught outside our dorm.'

She's right and I'm about to turn when I see Spencer and Diego sprinting back toward the door. They see me and I point wildly for them to head to the next building to their right so they won't meet the two Guards running parallel to them. They react in the nick of time, ducking out of sight for a second, before heading straight for me.

'Where's Kuro?' I yell over the alarm at Spencer as he steps into the corridor.

He shrugs, fear and bewilderment etched into his face, his breath short and laboured.

'Ned, you have to come back,' Rasa bellows at me as Diego runs past her into our dorm.

Five is still not six and we'll be in as much trouble as Pod Eight if I can't find Kuro, maybe worse, because we had a key and they used brute force. I scan the immediate space. The Guards look like they have caught three members of Pod Eight, but not Kuro. *Where are you*, I scream in my mind, stepping deeper into the relative cover of our corridor when I spot him couched by a low wall. We lock eyes. *You have to risk it*, I'm pleading in my mind, when he reads my thoughts and does what I ask. He sprints to the next building and crouches low. I hold my hand up for him to wait. A Guard is close, checking the next block.

'Ned!' Rasa yells behind me.

'I'm coming.'

The alarm continues to shriek.

More Guards flood the space.

I don't want to get caught, but I don't want to let go of the door in case the system locks down and the watch Kuro has no longer works. I spot another girl from Pod Eight dash left and two Guards yell and point at her. It turns them away from Kuro and I urgently wave him forward.

He has to move.

Now.

This is his chance.

Our chance.

Run, Kuro, run.

His arms are moving fast. His legs are at full stride. He's quick. Quicker than I would be. Then a Guard steps from behind the building. I can't believe I didn't see him, but I didn't, and he's running towards Kuro, who isn't going to make it, which means we aren't going to make it. The hole in the pit of my stomach opens up and I see my own life swallowed whole.

'Hold the door,' I shout at Rasa.

'No,' she screams back, but she does as I ask and runs toward me and grabs the handle as I sprint out to help Kuro. The Guard smashes into him from behind and they skid to the floor in front of me. My anger toward my Conviction, my Court Official, my Lawyer, the Corruption and my sister all flash through my mind and I find my right leg connecting with the Guard's face.

Thud.

His head snaps back.

Pain ricochets into my ankle, and I'm not sure what I feel toward the man who's unconscious on the floor, blood spilling from his mouth. If Kuro and I can get back to the dorm, we're safe, because all the Guard caught sight of was the back of a boy and a white sneaker that could have belong to any one of ninety *Denounced.*

I grab Kuro under the arm and yank him to his feet. We sprint towards our sleeping quarters, the alarm loud in my ears. Kuro gets there first, me a beat behind. To my surprise, Rasa grabs him by the throat and rips the watch from his hand. He's overcome by the whole experience and he lets it go without a fight. She tosses the watch high and far out of the door and then slams it behind me as all three of us sprint back to our dorm, where we are once again...

Six.

12

I hear quick, heavy footsteps in the corridor outside our secured dorm. Normally, such a sound wouldn't wake me, but I've been up all night dreading this wake-up call. It feels like a repeat of when Jack, the Court Official and my Executioner came to my cell to carry out the sentence of our Secular State. Yesterday, I didn't care. Today, I do. I'm unsure what has changed between the two days other than I'm now Head of this Pod and oddly during the chaos of yesterday evening I had an unexpected glimpse of freedom, and it's dominated my thoughts since Rasa tossed the watch into the night.

I hear the buzz of the lock open and my heart pounds as the grey nightlight flickers to full beam. I blink through the glare, pretending I've woken from an untroubled sleep. Nothing could be further from the truth. None of us have slept or have even dared to discuss what we did, and I think that might be an error. Will our stories be consistent if we're questioned by the Trainers or Guards one-on-one, and can we even trust each other to protect us as a group? Or will one of us sell out? Apart from stealing the watch and the attempted escape, I assaulted a guard and Rasa now has a golden chance to take me down if she decides to point me out. My throat goes dry at the thought.

'You've got five minutes to get washed and changed into your Tunics. Move. Now!'

Our Trainer is different from yesterday and if he knows we tried to escape, his body language and tone aren't letting on. I leap off my bunk-bed and taste the fear in the air. We all need to keep our nerve. Rasa tells Chantal to use the girls' bathroom first. The boys wait for me to tell one of them to go, but I let Chantal step ahead of me and I then follow her in. She's spent the night swallowing her tears and her eyes are puffed and sore, and I'm scared how she'll be perceived once she's outside in front of everyone. When we are out of sight of our Trainer, I grab her arm and twist her to face me.

'Don't touch me,' she hisses, trying to push my hand away.

I don't let go and she's not strong enough to free herself.

'You need to clean your face up, and if you're asked, you'll say you've been crying because you're homesick.'

'Are you threatening me again?'

'I'm telling you what's good for you.'

'I'll be the judge of that.'

'We're in this together.'

'No we're not. You're out for yourself. I can smell it on your breath. You only saved Kuro to save yourself. What if you killed that Guard?'

She yanks her arm free and steps into the girls' bathroom, slamming the door closed, before I can answer.

'Watch it in there,' the Trainer's voice echoes from the other room. 'You've got four minutes.'

Chantal's words spin through me. The Guard was breathing when I left him, but the consequences for me are the same whether he's dead or not. She's scared and this is new to her, and she doesn't understand the importance of sticking together to survive. This is not the outside world, where the person who did wrong gets punished. The rules in these places always have consequences for anyone associated with the wrongdoer. I want to talk to her more to try and explain, but it's going to make it worse, so I wash my face and brush my teeth, and try as best I can to flatten my hair. I look tired, for sure, but I'm more scared I look guilty.

I step out of the bathroom as Rasa enters the small space, crossing Chantal in the process. We lock eyes as she tries to step around me.

'You need to talk to Chantal if you know what's good for you,' I growl under my breath, stepping out of the space and not waiting for Rasa's answer.

The Trainer watches me as I nod Kuro in next, pointing to Diego to go afterwards and Spencer to go last. I start to get dressed, aware the Trainer isn't taking his attention from me. If he's trying to force me into some kind of nervous error, I'm not going to fall for it. I may not be guilty, but I'm not a newbie either.

'You need to change, so you're ready to move after you use the bathroom. We'll run out of time if you don't,' I say to Spencer.

He does as he's told and I refuse to look at Chantal as I don't want to draw attention her way. I might be imagining it, but when Rasa comes out of the bathroom she appears to be using her body to block any direct eye contact between our Trainer and Chantal. I take a bit of comfort in this show of support, even if it's to protect herself and not really for the greater cause.

'Thirty seconds to go,' he says, as Spencer rushes out of the bathroom to put on his sneakers. We all stand and wait by our bunk-beds, military style. It's taking all my strength not to sneak a glimpse to see what the others are thinking, but furtive glances are only going to make us look guilty, or at least up to something. I decide I have no choice but to deny kicking the Guard in the head. Unless I was caught on camera, I don't see how they can prove it unless Rasa or Chantal sing my guilt and, even then, it would be their word against mine.

'Follow me,' our Trainer says.

I go first. Rasa falls in line followed by Spencer and the others. Our Trainer makes us slow jog along the corridor to the main door. The other Pod doors are open, the dormitories emptied. Pod Eight's door is closed, but you can see the lock's been smashed open and the frame damaged, and I wonder how they managed to do it.

I step outside and see the other Pods have gathered into a tight group. I can't see the boy from Pod Eight, but we're at the back and grouped so tightly it's hard to tell if he's here or not. In searching for the boy, I see nothing looks the same as it did yesterday. There is only one path, and not two, and it's double the width, you could drive two cars along it side-by-side. I'm definitely not imagining it, I know the difference between one path and two. The building I think is the Canteen is further back and the structures in general look closer together, more compressed.

The landscape has changed, no question.

A whistle sounds and Taylor is told to lead the way. I remember his name because he was the first boy's name to appear on the screen and physically he's hard to forget. There's a brutality and menace, and an arrogance in the way he carries himself. He has a scar that runs from under his left eye and it seeps into the edge of his cheek. I can imagine him as one of the alpha males in the Community Homes he's lived in. He'll be used to being a leader of a gang and if he hadn't been picked for the Head of Pod One, I'm sure he would have made it his position before long. It's another reminder, not that I needed one, to keep an eye on Rasa.

I'm expecting Taylor to be told to enter the Canteen and, by the way he's slowing, he's thinking the same when a Trainer shouts for him to up the pace. It has a ripple effect through the rest of us and soon the steady sound of running fills my thoughts as we leave the compressed block of buildings and enter the grey open wasteland. I stare into the vastness and try to guess where it all ends. Everything beyond a certain distance is obscured by ripples of hazy light. Guards dot the edges or perhaps they're Trainers, it's hard to tell. We jog past the transport boxes we arrived in and head for a wall of light that blurs into the Assembly Hall as we draw closer. The Trainers slow us into a walk and panting hard, I enter the Hall and take up my position as Head of Pod Fifteen in our designated area. I know why I didn't see the boy from Pod Eight. Their position on the floor is empty. It's like a gaping hole in the hull of a ship.

Two Guards walk onto the stage. Their guns are more visible and there's a seriousness about them that wasn't there yesterday. The lights dim and from nowhere, a spotlight picks out Ilse who is stood in front of her lectern.

'My children, it wasn't my intention you should be brought back today, but circumstances call for us to meet again. Your cruelty toward me is hard to bear. I've let you into my home; fed and clothed you, only for you to turn on me at the first opportunity.' Ilse dabs at her eyes with the corner of a handkerchief. I believe her tears as much as I believe the truth about my own *Denounced* conviction. 'It is clear you need to understand a valuable lesson in life. Any relationship without boundaries will fail and you have disrespected mine.'

I glance across to see the Head Trainer staring hard at me. My instinct is to look away, but for some reason I hold his gaze for a moment, before letting my eyes rest back on Ilse. I don't want to challenge this man as I'll never win, but I can't afford to look culpable, because the heaviness in my stomach is telling me something bad is rolling our way.

'Last night, we had an attempted escape. Why, I ask myself? You are not in prison. You are not in a Community

Home. You are not in the Holding Centre. You need to think of this place as a school. A School of Life and in good time you will be free, but for now you need to pay back the gift we have bestowed upon you by saving you from the gallows. As a family, there is a collective responsibility and I told you yesterday that you have the choice of what happens to you. Last night, Family Eight made the wrong choice.'

The lights change and the giant screen behind Ilse turns from opaque to transparent. I hear gasps and screams that echo through the room. I'm not sure if I react or not because I'm transfixed by six individual spotlights. I'm never going to know the stupid boy's name and I'm sorry I was mean to him when we first met. It wouldn't have hurt me to show him a bit of kindness. Now I watch him swing from the end of a hangman's rope, along with the other members of that Pod.

They are all dressed in their purple jumpsuits.

Denounced.

Or maybe they're not.

Maybe they're just like me.

Guilty of wanting to find somewhere they can call home.

13

The lights dim and a blast of air from the stage washes over me. If it's meant to cleanse me of what I've seen, it's not working. I thought it was impossible to hate Ilse and this place any more than I do, but my contempt has found a new depth. I want to run and hide, but it's impossible to do either of these things as the overhead lights snap back on. I blink through the glare to see the stage is empty, the screen opaque. There's nothing to indicate the horror I've witnessed other than everyone's silence. It's only day two and I'm not sure how much more I can take.

A whistle is sounded and I've been captive long enough to know it's our signal to move. We filter out of the Assembly Hall in Pod order. If Ilse had known about our attempted escape, I have no doubt there would have been twelve hanged today instead of six. I have to be thankful for our luck and try and not let what I've seen affect me too much. Those uncomfortable thoughts I've had about kicking the Guard unconscious have vanished. I did something necessary to save my life and that of our Pod's. I have no more concerns about Rasa or Chantal calling my name in. They've seen enough to understand they need to keep quiet.

'Hey… stop… leave her,' I hear Spencer say, his voice urgent and controlled. 'Stop it, dude.'

I turn to see Diego has Rasa pinned to the floor with his hand driving down into her face. She's struggling to get free, but he's too strong and Spencer's not strong enough to pull him off.

'Stop it! Stop it!' Chantal yells, drawing the attention of the Guards and Trainers. 'You're going to hurt her.' I glance to the front. The other Pods have started to peer over to see what all the noise and fuss is about, drawing more attention to us.

I run forward and grab Diego by the shoulders – Spencer has his right side, me the left. We pull in unison, but it's like trying to move a concrete block cemented to the floor.

'You threw our one chance away,' Diego snarls into Rasa's face. 'Who made you chief around here, because I didn't? You don't have to worry about getting hanged because I'm going to do it for them.'

He pushes her face further into the ground. Rasa squeals in pain, her punches missing, her jaw looking like it might shatter under the pressure.

Whistles are sounded.

I hear the soft thud of running footsteps on the hard plastic floor as I fight to get Diego to stop.

'Diego,' I whisper, 'this is not the time. You've got to let her go.'

'What do you care if I kill her?'

'You'll kill us all.'

'I'm innocent,' he says. 'I shouldn't be here and she's finished us off with her arrogance.'

'Me too, I shouldn't be here, either,' I say, without thinking.

He stares at me, pain and anger flaming in his eyes.

'You've got to let her go, my friend. You've got to,' I repeat, like I'm talking to a child, tugging gently at his shoulders as I do.

It takes a moment for his brain to make sense of my words. He looks back at Rasa, before releasing his grip from her face. Spencer pulls him away as Chantal bends to help Rasa to her feet. Her face is marked with the imprint of Diego's hand and she's shocked and hurt, and not looking quite so tough and moody all of a sudden. I've got my answer to who would win a fight between them, not that I had any doubts.

Our Trainer is almost upon us. I step forward and stand between him and Diego, hands up, nothing aggressive in my manner.

'Out of my way,' the Trainer shouts. 'Now!'

'He didn't mean it,' I say. 'He got a bit upset, is all.'

Our Trainer pushes me aside as two more Trainers descend upon us from different angles. They grab Diego by the arms, trying to get him into an arm lock. He's not having it and he starts to wrestle back. Mistake, I think, seeing for the first time how strong he really is. A Guard comes running toward us, his electronic baton high in his hand, the electric arc hissing in the air. Chantal is crying and making it worse, and I see my fragile existence collapsing around me, my freedom gone for ever. I look for the Head Trainer, who is watching with interest from the front. I don't know why I do it, but I point back at the Assembly Hall then point at Diego, shrugging at the same time. I'm trying to tell him as best I can, without being aggressive, that it's been too much.

All our nerves have been shocked.

Our senses, too.

What does he expect from any of us after less than two days?

Give us a break, I scream in my mind.

Just give us a break.

Then a tight smile breaks across his face before he presses his electronic whistle. The sound must be different to the other whistles as the Trainers holding Diego look straight over toward him. He nods for them to let Diego go. Like robots they do as they're told and the Guard re-houses his electronic baton into his utility belt. The moment enhances the man's power further in my mind and I'm bound to pay for this small show of rebellion at some point in the future. It's a risk I took and worth it, I think.

'Back in line,' our Trainer says to us. 'You – get moving.'

He shoves me forward before I can do as I'm told. Pod One is already jogging and the movement is filtering down through the rest of the Pods. I loathe running and I'm not built for it, but I'm glad of the distraction. My mind is full of conflicting thoughts, and I'm angry at myself for letting slip I'm innocent. I've given something away about myself for free and all I can hope is nobody heard me in all the confusion.

I'm not sure how long we jog for but I'm panting hard and struggling to keep up when I see Pod One slow to a walk. It cascades through the rest of the Pods and when we stop I have to bend forward, hands on knees, to catch my breath.

'Up and in there,' our Trainer says.

I lift my head to see the boys are being told to enter a building on the right; the girls a building to its left. That cold fear of uncertainty returns as I watch Rasa and Chantal peel off and join a different line to ours. Rasa's face is still heavily marked from Diego's hand and it's going to bruise. Last night, I thought it was a good move she threw the watch away, but I'm not convinced any more and I understand Diego's anger. I turn to check on him. He's staring at the floor, like none of us are here. He's gone somewhere else in his mind, lost to another world. He's seeing his family, comparing home life with here and trying to contemplate what's happened to him, driving himself to despair in the progress. I've learned over the years to block that kind of pain, but maybe it's easier for me as I'm an orphan and he's not. In his world, he has a place to go. An identity to hold onto and even a forbidden language to root him. It should be a strength, but in here it's a weakness that can push you over the edge. I thought Chantal was our Achilles Heel, but she's not – it's Diego. He's going to be a problem for all of us and that translates into a problem for me.

Inside the building, I strain my neck to see what is ahead, but the curve of the corridor makes it impossible to see. The boys at the front of the queue seem relaxed and if they're not worried then neither am I. We shuffle along, nobody speaking, until I hear the faint hum of electric clippers. I'm not surprised at what is next and I could have worked it out if I'd thought about it. My hair is short at the sides; longish on top and is swept to one side. Since I've been allowed, I've gone for the messy, surfer look – not that I've ever surfed. It was my promise to myself that it was going to be the first adult thing I did when I left the System. A celebration of my free life. When they took me to the Holding Centre my Lawyer said I should keep my hair neat and that I should drop the beach look. I did as she asked and look where that got me. I'm sure my father used to say you shouldn't try and please people too much. Or that's what I think he would say, anyway.

'I knew it,' I hear Spencer say.

I turn to face him. He has great hair. His tight afro curls go past his collar and frame his face. They add to his handsome looks that distinguish him from everyone else.

'Bye, bye hair,' Spencer says with a knowing grin.

'Be quiet back there,' a Trainer shouts towards us.

I let out my first genuine smile since I've been here. We're not going to get a choice of haircut and whatever they do you can't let it show it bothers you. With everything that's gone on since we've been here, I'd forgotten the basic rule of survival. Your dignity is yours to keep and you should never give it up.

EVER.

'Don't complain,' I whisper to Kuro.

'I said, be quiet down there,' a Trainer bellows at us. 'I won't tell you again.'

I look at Diego. He's still staring into the ground. His hair is cropped short and there's not a lot they can do other than shave it off and even that wouldn't bother him. Diego's not the vain type, plus he has more important things tramping through his mind right now. I just hope he doesn't start wanting to wrestle with the Trainers again once they sit him in the Barber's Chair. He got away with it once before, but he won't get a second chance. Not here. Not today.

We enter the small room cum-make-shift Barber Shop. There are four chairs and four Trainers with clippers and combs waiting for us to sit. Toward the back of the room is a small mountain of hair being swept up by a Worker. I sit in the first seat and the Trainer wraps one of the gowns around me, closing it tightly across my neck.

'How would you like it today, Sir?' he asks.

Of course, it's not a question and his tone is all sarcastic and vindictive. 'The usual, please,' I say, playing along, but making sure I'm not sounding rude.

'Short then?' he adds.

'Just how I like it.'

It takes him all of ninety seconds for him to match the top of my hair to my short sides. Spencer comes off the worse. His afro twists sit like metal springs on the floor. He's smiling like he doesn't care, but I can tell he's seething inside. The cut makes him look older and I would have said he was eighteen and not sixteen if I'd met him for the first time with his new streamline look. Diego gets a pass and I'm grateful we don't risk another flashpoint. Kuro couldn't have heard my advice and makes me think again he can't have been in a Home to understand how it works and, that maybe, he did find the watch after all and didn't steal it. He asks the Barber not to go too short and leave a bit on top. I thought the Trainer was going to have a heart attack from laughing and now Kuro is almost bald compared to the rest of us. His glasses are too big for his face and he looks like he's peering from the bottom of a jar.

We gather outside and Rasa is first to re-join our Pod. Her long blonde hair has been cut to the middle of her neck. Her split ends are gone for good. She doesn't look at anyone. Her mouth is clamped tight and her lips are quivering, and her cheek is showing the bruise from Diego's hand. I almost feel sorry for her, but I block that thought. I don't trust her and I'm a fool if I let her pain make me sympathetic toward her. Chantal leaves the building to join us and she's crying hard and making no effort to show her distaste at what they've done to her. The cut accentuates her long neck and hollow cheeks, and she look sickly to me.

A whistle is sounded and I look forward.

If I thought the day couldn't get any worse, I was wrong. One of the Trainers is holding a First-Aid kit and I instantly pulse with the heat of worry.

I glance across at Spencer.

'It's not mine,' he whispers.

'Or mine,' Kuro says.

Diego is staring at the floor as tears bubble into his eyes.

He doesn't need to say anything, more, because I know his answer.

We all do.

It's his.

He dropped it last night.

14

The Head Trainer calls for a Kit Inspection.

The two words echo through my mind as the buildings around me fall in and out of focus. I'm struggling to work out what is true or false; what is real or not. I'm standing still but I feel like being pulled backwards, my vision blurring at the edges. Kit Inspection means our attempted escape has been uncovered. Somewhere between the corruption of the Holding Centre and the madness of this place I had dared to hope, imagined freedom as a reality. I let myself believe my innocence would shine through and I'd be set free to continue into Adulthood. After all I've seen and known of the System, it was naive and stupid, and I hate myself for dropping my guard.

I jog on as I'm instructed to do. The Trainers and Guards want to punish the person who kicked one of their own unconscious. I can see it in the Head Trainer's face – he believes more than one Pod made a run for it last night and now he has his proof. It's not going to make any difference that I had no part in it. The First-Aid kit might as well have my name stitched across the front, because ultimately it belongs to Pod Fifteen. More fear heats my veins when I hear Chantal begin to cry. Why can't she understand only the guilty would act this way and if she cared to take a look, she is the only person crying in fourteen Pods. I have the urge to turn and shake some sense into her but it won't help me or the situation, only highlight us more. Diego's mind is lost to the terror of his mistake, compounding how he already thinks and feels. Rasa's eyes are as blank as Spencer's, and if I was inclined to blame anyone I'd be pointing the finger at Kuro for either stealing that damn watch or being stupid enough to pick it up. If he has a solution to the problem he's created, which I doubt, he's keeping it to his shameful self. If anyone is going to solve this waiting avalanche of pain, it's me, but I'm lost to my own self-pity as well.

The horror of seeing Pod Eight hanging by their necks and what's in store for us starts to make my legs grow heavy as we near the three-pronged fork in the path. The first seven Pods will soon divert right toward their dormitories and we will go left toward ours. My chances of proving my innocence and surviving longer than twenty-four hours are shrinking by the second. I glance up and across at our looming sleeping quarters, when I catch sight of three Workers stepping out of the building carrying what I realise are two plastic crates each from Pod Eight. I look back at the three-pronged path.

Then the Workers.

Then the path.

Then the crates in the Worker's arms.

Then the path.

The first seven Pods have started to via right. We will go left and the Workers will surely take the third prong, taking them hard left toward the Storehouse. If I pace this right, I'll reach the intersection of the three-pronged fork at exactly the same time as the Workers, with the last six Pods blocking our view to the main group of Trainers. An idea filters in and with it an unexpected calmness dilutes the panic that has been burying my hope. I calculate in my mind the distance between myself and the oncoming Workers. At this speed, I'll get there way before they do and my slim advantage will be lost.

I begin to slow my jog and Rasa clips my heels with her foot. A Trainer notices I'm slowing and he tells me to up my pace. I ignore his command, because I'm the walking dead and what can he do to me that Ilse isn't going to when she discovers Pod Fifteen made an attempted escape? The answer is nothing and he loses his power over me as I concentrate on the Workers who are heading my way.

'I said up the pace. It's your last warning.'

I stop running.

Rasa crashes into the back of me and Spencer crashes into her. I can't see it, but it feels like a falling pack of cards as Kuro must have knocked into Diego and Chantal into Kuro.

'What are you doing?' Rasa says, all surprised.

I snap round and stare at her.

'Let's see how smart you really are,' I snarl.

'Uh...what?'

I grab Rasa by her Tunic and spin her round. I switch one hand to her face and plant the other in the top of her chest, pushing her as hard as I can into the oncoming Trainer. I'm strong and I'm angry and I feel lawless so I use every bit of power I have. The back of her head crashes into the Trainer's face as I had hoped. I hear a dull thud and his nose breaks. They stumble together and he instinctively grabs her shoulders to stop himself from falling. I turn back to face Spencer. He's gawping at me like I've completely lost my mind, and maybe, I have. Maybe this place has sent me crazy and I didn't even know it, but terror and hope are pumping through my veins in equal measures.

I'm innocent.

I'm Ned Hunter.

I'm not 5-7-9-0-1-2-3.

I punch Spencer in the jaw.

Whack.

He staggers back and I step in closer, glaring at Diego as I do, flicking my eyes hard right. Diego glances beyond me as I punch Spencer again this time in the side of the face, making him stagger the other way. My hope is Diego's innocence and need to get home will override his self-induced catatonic state. Spencer is still stunned at what I've done, so grabbing him in a neck lock is easy.

I bend in close and whisper.

'Run me backwards if you want to live.'

I pull his head to my right side and hold it close to my rib cage giving him a clear line of vision as I fake punches to his kidneys. My evaluation of Spencer as a *chancer* needs to come true or this last-ditch idea is finished before it started. I get the subtle message I need. It's enough to spike my hope. I sense him wedge his shoulder into my waist. I relax into it making it easier for him to get primed as I continue to throw soft punches. He roars and I'm lifted from the ground, propelled backwards. I was right about his body. He is as strong as a man and he's using it well.

Whistles are sounded.

Trainers are calling for reinforcements.

We have seconds to pull this impromptu plan off. Diego's eyes sparkle to life and he's onto it straight away. He comes charging at us. Spencer can't see him, but I can. I prepare myself for the impact. It's a Gale Force Ten when it hits. Spencer's feet leave the floor and I'm thrown into the air. The power is enough to cover the extra ground and we smash as a group into the three Workers. I flay out my arms to make sure I catch at least one of them, but I get two. My fists are closed and I hit with hard knuckles across their faces. The Workers fall like bowling skittles and the crates spin through the air. I hit the floor first, winding myself, but I don't care. I roll on top of Spencer and I start to throw punches. They're not hard, but they're not soft either. This has to be real and ugly, and however bruised and cut we end up, it will be less painful than a rope around our necks. Spencer gives as good as he gets and I'm in the ugly scrap I wanted. We wrestle on the floor throwing punches and kicking at each other, and I know he gets it because we're moving toward a crate. Spencer springs to his feet which lets Diego join in. It's a three-way fight. Spencer shoves Diego who stumbles back, kicking a crate towards Chantal as he does. Spencer grabs me in a headlock and I pause to catch my breath, spotting Rasa out of the corner of my eye. She's got it, but I'm not that surprised. She's rolled on top of the Trainer and in pretending to be hurt, she's managed to entangle herself into him, keeping him pinned to the floor and out of our way. Spencer throws a punch and it catches me in the eye. It connects as it should. I wince with pain. I'm going have a shiner. Authenticity is the key. I duck another punch before we're both swamped with Trainers pulling us apart.

I keep up the act.

I struggle to push a Trainer away as I spit at Spencer.

'Not so tough now,' I yell.

I catch sight of Chantal passing the First-Aid kit to Kuro who stuffs it down the front of this Tunic trousers, sucking in his stomach to compensate the new bulge. It's too smooth and my first assessment of him that he's a slight of hand looks spot on. Chantal and Diego move sideways, bodies blocking my view, which means the main group of Trainers can't see Kuro, either. We couldn't have planned it better if we'd been real friends and a tight-knit group.

The Head Trainer pushes his way through the crowd of Trainers and watching group of Pods. He grabs my arm and yanks me within centimetres of his face. His grip is pure power and I smell bacon and coffee on his breath. The muscles in his jaw twitch. The bristles on his head are the same length that cover his face in a rash of black. His eyes fester with something I've never seen before. I'm not human. I could be a dog that he can use and do what he likes with and nobody's going to hold him accountable.

Nobody.

'Your type thinks you're better than us. You're not. Take him away.'

15

I offer no resistance – not that it would make any difference if I did – as I'm dragged between two Guards to an open-top buggy with three wheels either side, and a wire prisoner's cage in the central section. The vehicle is painted in waves of camouflaged greys, whites and blacks, and it hits me for the first time – I've been enrolled into Military School. The haircut should have given me the final clue and I feel sick at the thought as one of the Guards places his hand on the back of my head, stooping me into the prisoner's cage. The Head Trainer steps out of the nearest building and strides toward the buggy, not looking at me. He has a purposeful look in his eyes and he's talking into a handheld device in a language I've never heard before. He's a powerhouse of muscle with board shoulders, a lean waist and thick set thighs. We're about the same height but that's all we have in common. From the start, I promised myself I would stay out of his firing line, but circumstances have made that impossible and I now have an enemy for life. How long that life will be, I guess, is down to Ilse. I tremble at what trouble awaits me, but I'm going to keep denying my attempted escape, which isn't actually a lie if I think about it.

He climbs into the passenger seat and the driver addresses him as *Marcellus* before they slip into the same language I heard a moment ago. It's illegal to speak anything but English so this must be a special language designed for here, like a secret code, which excludes us. None of the words resemble anything I can relate to and knowing the Head Trainer's name only increases my apprehension toward him.

Marcellus points forward and the driver pulls off, jolting us all in the process. The vehicle is electric and apart from the hum of the tires running along the path, it is absolutely silent. A nervous bird wouldn't hear us approach. We move at speed; the Guards communicate in their secret code as the dark grey buildings fall away and we enter a vast open space with its rolling wave-like terrain. I get an unexpected image of hiding in the sand dunes with my sister. It's the cleanest vision I've had of her in years and I can see her green eyes and wide smile – it's my mother's smile.

The image of my sister triggers my thoughts about my so-called *new* family. I hope Kuro managed to get the First-Aid kit back in place. I have a feeling he did. He was too slick and controlled, and if I ever get to see him again I'm going to push him on how he *really* found that watch. He's not what he seems; maybe the others aren't, and maybe I'm not what I seem to them, either. I don't care what they think of me because I have to try and survive this place any way I can, but maybe I do care? It's a conflict within that I'm struggling to understand, and then there's this swelling of pride at our team work – we pulled off the impossible.

Marcellus doesn't know it was me who kicked the Guard, and our Pod beat the system which, in a strange way, makes this moment bearable.

My skin goose-pimples at a sudden change in temperature, breaking my thoughts. I stare forward to see we're heading for what looks like a rippling wall of electrified fog. It's a vertical storm locked within itself, alive and angry, like me. I've never seen anything like it and I wonder how our electric buggy will cope if we get any closer when I get my answer. A section in the amorphous wall begins to part, allowing us to drive through. Amazed, I stare up into the grey storm, thick sparks of white light dance around me, the wall folding gently behind us as we move forward. We enter the other side to an oasis of colours that my senses have been deprived of since I was arrested and taken to the Holding Centre. The road is still the same grey toughened plastic, but this time it's edged in lush green grass. There are trees and flowers, and fresh air tickles the inside of my nostrils. I take a deep breath and allow it to fill my lungs. It makes my whole body tingle with a pleasure I'd long forgotten. High above my head, there's a touch of blue, and I would swear I was outside if it wasn't for the distinctive hum of the extractor fans in the near distance. Directly in front of me is a glass tower that is supported high above the ground on a tripod of steel legs. Everywhere I look, I see Guards, Trainers and Workers. I notice the Guards aren't carrying guns and everyone appears more relaxed, talking amongst themselves in this language I don't recognise, and I'm suddenly not sure it even is a secret code any more.

'Eyes forward if you know what's good for you,' Marcellus says without looking at me.

I do as I'm told and begin to fret at what's ahead of me as we approach the Tower. Our driver pulls up tight to a bank of elevators and I'm guided out of the cage by a waiting Guard who touches his watch against the control panel next to the elevator door. Marcellus looks to follow me in, but the stationed Guard raises his hand, adding a shake of the head. I get another one of Marcellus's murderous stares, as if it was my decision he wasn't coming up. I'm told to step in and the moment I do, the doors close and the lift moves at an incredible rate, Marcellus and the Guards becoming unrecognisable below me. I get a heady sensation and a tightness in my stomach, before the lift slows, coming to a gentle stop. The doors slide open to reveal a giant room with a polished wooden floor that beams back my reflection.

Stood opposite, by the window, with her back to me, is Ilse. I wonder if this is her home and I'm too petrified to move, never mind talk.

'Come in, Ned,' she says, not turning to greet me.

Hesitantly, I step forward and see the surrounding walls to the office are made of glass, and I'm so high up, it's like I'm floating in the clouds, a free bird. I've never flown in a plane before but this is how I imagine the view to be. The room is split into two sections. There's a large office table in the middle with a monitor and a phone, and in the far corner it's more like a living room with leather settees and soft lighting. Sat in one of the long chairs is the man with the grey hair and blue eyes, dressed in casual clothes. He looks at home and he stares at me unblinking, like he's looking right through me and I'm not here. Marcellus does the same and I don't like it one bit.

I'm not a dog, I think.

I'm a real person.

'Closer,' Ilse says, still not turning to greet me.

I walk to the middle of the room and stop on a red checked rug that is soft beneath my feet, my hands behind my back, my fingers interlocked. All around me is a panoramic view of a City I don't know the name of.

Ilse turns to face me, and as she does the glass windows frost over with a single click that makes me jump. In their place appear works of art. Warm lighting above my head floods the room and it's a relief from the intense brightness I've started to become used to.

Ilse is dressed in the same black style suit as when I first saw her. I'm not sure what Quadrant she's from. Maybe the old Spain or Italy, or somewhere they once called the Mediterranean. Yet her skin is the whitest I've ever seen, like she's never been outside and she's scared the sun will age her.

She must be vain.

My lawyer was.

Ilse starts to walk toward me, her heels clicking on the wooden floor. My throat dries and my shoulders tense and I have to stop myself from licking my lips, a nervous habit I have when I'm under pressure. As she draws nearer, I see she's taller than I thought but not as tall as Rasa. She steps in close and grips my upper arms, squeezing them tightly, her hands cold, her breath mint fresh.

'You're a big, strong, boy, Ned. It's what we like around here. It's what we admire. We consider it a gift.'

'Thank you,' I say, staring at my feet.

'I bet you could kick a ball hard if you tried. Kick it so hard you could take the air from it. What do you say?'

'Maybe, but Basketball's my game. You don't kick a basketball.'

'He's scared,' she says, throwing a laugh toward the man with the piecing blue eyes. He says nothing. If it wasn't for his stare that is boring into me I would say he was disinterested in my presence. Ilse looks back at me and I see she's suddenly holding the watch strap in her hand that Kuro found and Rasa tossed away.

I flinch and I'm angry at myself for acting guilty.

This is a game I know how to play.

Even here.

'Do you know what this is, Ned?'

I start to shake my head. 'No,' I say.

I will deny it to the end, I think.

She nods.

'Of course you don't, why should you,' she says, her smile fixed. 'Ask me a question, Ned. You must have at least one question for your mother?'

I have hundreds of questions but none that I would dare ask.

'I don't have any questions,' I say.

'Oh Ned, don't disappoint me. I want you to ask me a question. It would give me great pleasure to share some of my knowledge. That's what I have over you. Knowledge. Come...come...you must have *one* question? How about... what are we doing here?'

I check my tone in my mind, making sure it's as neutral as it can be before I speak.

'This is Military School. We've joined the army.'

Ilse shrieks with laughter, clapping her hands. 'I told you he was a clever boy,' she says, pointing to the man sat on the long chair.

He says nothing.

'It is more than that – it is a place to cleanse. But tell me, Ned, do you know what *gravitas* means?'

I search my mind: *gra...vi..tas*.

I shake my head.

'It's something deep inside of you that makes you strong, Ned, and I don't mean physically. I mean in your mind. It makes you special. When you walk into a room, people can see it. They notice it. They expect things from you. All the digital credits in the world can't buy it. Even Presidents of Quadrants don't have it. It is a quality you are born with, but it comes with responsibilities, my son.' I nod, unsure what to say as I have no idea what she is talking about. Ilse continues. 'Did you do history at school?'

I nod again. 'Modern History,' I add.

'Ah…yes…*The Terrorist Wars*. We all know about those. I meant Old-World History?'

I shake my head from side-to-side. 'It was banned in my Homes.'

'That's a pity, Ned, because then you'd know about a famous warrior called Napoleon. He once said: *I have plenty of good Generals but I want lucky ones*! That's you, Ned. You're the lucky General-to-be. I have four more like you, but I think you're my number one. How does that make you feel?'

'I'm not sure,' I say.

'Of course you are not sure, because you don't know what you have. If you did, you wouldn't have *gravitas* but *arrogance*. But you will learn, Ned. I will teach you and then you will teach me.'

She starts to stroke the top of the watch with her thumb and I can see she is debating something in her mind when a thought makes me go weak. There must be an electronic log of where each Trainer's key is used, and the one in her hand has to show our dormitory door was opened after hours. Dread pumps through me as the smile drops from her face. She suddenly looks older, her eyes full of the experiences of life, something I don't possess or can't even contemplate because I'm only sixteen and only know the System.

'It's important you behave yourself, Ned – play by the rules. We all have missions in our life, including myself. I need you to be a success here. Do we understand each other?'

I don't, but I nod that I do, and I understand something else in this moment which confuses me even more. Ilse knows I've lied about the watch and that it was probably me who kicked the Guard unconscious, but she's letting it go, giving me a pass.

Something Pod Eight wasn't lucky enough to get.

16

I step from the elevator and to my relief Marcellus and the two Guards who escorted me here are gone. In their place is a smaller open-topped buggy without the prisoner's cage, and a different driver from the one who drove me here. The Guard at the elevator points me toward the buggy with a grunt and a stern stare. I step forward and climb into the backseat and the second I sit, he pulls off, nearly tossing me out. I grab for the anti-roll bar as the buggy squeals into a half-circle, skidding away from the Tower and heading for a main pathway.

This man doesn't speak or even acknowledge my presence, and he has a strange habit of rolling beads through his fingers as he drives. I'm tempted to question him about where I am and what he thinks. I doubt he'll answer, assuming I can even understand his language, and I bet talking to him constitutes a whipping offence. So I sit back and wait, a breeze starting to kiss at my face. I catch sight of a stream. This is how I imagine a summer's drive through a beautiful park would be. If I ever do get out of here, I'm adding owning a convertible car to my Wish-List along with learning to Surf and having a girlfriend. I suddenly catch my thoughts and cut them dead. It's dangerous to let yourself dream when you're in the System.

Nothing good ever comes of it.

We approach the Wall of Fog, which rises angrily in front of me. It's the greatest prison wall I've ever seen and I wish I had a camera to take its picture. I can't see the summit and I look back for the Tower, which has vanished, like it was never there. I take one last look at the array of colours, imprinting the gardens on my mind, knowing in a few minutes I'll see nothing but greys and inky blues, returning to a world of latent hatred and uncertainty.

I turn back and the fog door has already opened and we start to head through, not slowing, my mood crashing towards rock-bottom with each turn of the wheels. If I'm supposed to be relieved Ilse gave me a pass, I'm not. I didn't wilfully enrol into Military School and I don't know what she meant by me having *gravitas*. It strikes me like another burden that I'm going to have to endure, and I wonder if it has something to do with Marcellus hating me.

Well, he's more than welcome to have it.

I'll give it to him if he wants, if it'll keep him off my back and out of my life.

The journey home seems quicker and we soon reach the crop of buildings that has become my unwanted home. It's the darkest I've seen it and everywhere is deserted, a ghost town within a City that's within another giant structure, and maybe another one after that, for all I know.

The driver stops by a building and a female Trainer is waiting to greet me. I'm beckoned out of the buggy, and as I start towards her she touches her watch against the metal panel and the main door to my sleeping quarters opens. I wouldn't have recognised the building had she not been stood waiting for me. It's like I'm back in the Holding Centre having to go through the Security Cubes and in a way, I am, I think. I see Pod Eight's door has been repaired and you wouldn't know it had ever been smashed open.

I'm escorted to my dorm. I step through and the door clicks shut behind me. I'm greeted with silence. I've no idea of the time, but I'm hit with an unexpected hunger pang so it must be late, or my nerves have settled enough for me to think again about food. If I was expecting a rush of concerns or even congratulations – I'm disappointed.

Nobody even looks at me.

Nobody says a word.

It's like I'm here on my own. A newbie in a fresh Home on his first day, needing to prove himself. I shrug to myself. I've been to enough Homes to have learnt it's best to ignore the silent treatment and get on with your own thing. People will either come to you or they don't, and if they don't, you generally don't want them anyway.

Everyone is in their sleepwear and has climbed into their individual beds. The night lights are on but none of them are asleep. I grab my sleepwear from the wardrobe and walk into the boys' bathroom, deciding to take my first shower. The water is powerful and hot, and it's an unexpected pleasure. I stay longer than I should, trying to block the pain of this prison from my mind and wonder what Ilse meant about being cleansed. I soon begin to feel guilty about spending too much time in the shower. In any other Home I've stayed in, I would have been in trouble by now for being indulgent and wasting the water. The steam has built up so much it's like I'm driving through the Wall of Fog all over again, only this time, I'm alone in my own cocoon.

I wish.

I switch off the shower and towel dry and return to my bunk-bed. For all the harshness of the new regime and the constant air of vindictiveness and the threat of hanging, the facilities are comfortable and clean, and the food is excellent.

It's another paradox of my new life, which is something else I don't understand.

'I thought you'd drowned in there,' Chantal says, breaking the silence, as I come out.

'Thanks for coming to rescue me,' I say with an edge of sarcasm.

She huffs and I wait for one of the others to chip in, but nobody does. I decide I'm too tired to care, and what concerns me most is this *gravitas* thing and what it means now Ilse has pinned the label to me. I settle into my bed and close my eyes trying to put some sense into my meeting with her.

'Who is it?' Spencer says.

His deep voice bounces off the walls. If the question is aimed at me, I ignore him. I don't like his tone, and why is he asking me a question when he should be telling me about the Kit-Inspection. It must have been a success. Ilse knew about the watch, but I don't think she or the Trainers knew what we did today and the true reason behind the fight. We should be celebrating, not sulking or picking on me.

'Like, that is it? You're not going to tell us?' he adds.

There's an added annoyance in his voice and I froth with anger toward him, toward them all. I sit up and glare at Spencer across from me.

'What's your problem, dude?'

'What's my problem! What's your problem?'

'Where have you been?' Rasa snarls at me from her bunk-bed. Her voice is full of confidence and I like her new tone even less than I liked the old one.

'Minding my own business is where I've been.'

'I told you it'd be me,' she says to Chantal.

'I'm sorry,' Chantal says. 'You don't deserve it. It should be him.'

'You don't deserve what?' I say.

I could kick myself for asking Rasa a question. If she wants something from me it's up to her to ask. I lie back on my bunk, staring at the ceiling – I managed to get us

97

out of trouble and this is the thanks I get. I close my eyes, wanting today to end. It doesn't. The boy from Pod Eight flashes through my mind. I realise he never had a chance here. There was something about his personality that didn't work for surviving the reason we are here. If it wasn't the failed escape, it would have been something else. Maybe that was true for the whole of that Pod as well?

'You have to tell us who it is,' Diego says from below me. 'It's only fair.'

His voice is heavy and full of sorrow. He sounds like he's aged ten years in the three days we've been together – we probably all have. I lean up and rest on my elbows.

'I don't know what any of you are talking about.'

'They took you to see Ilse, no?' he asks.

'Yeah, they took me to see her?'

'What did she want?'

'I don't know.'

'You're lying,' Chantal says.

I stare at her, knowing she's not one to hold in her honesty, before I look at each of them individually, suddenly feeling jealous. I sense they've bonded somehow in my absence, making some kind of pact that I'm not part of.

Even Rasa has snaked her way back into favour.

'She had the watch Rasa tossed away. She asked me if I knew what it was and I said no. That was it.'

'You've been gone a long time for a short conversation,' Kuro says, all mature.

My instinct is to ignore him, but I can't. It's five against one – odds I'd struggle to win against at the best of times.

'There's another part to this place. It's inside like here, but it's outside too. I can't explain it any better than that. But it has trees and flowers and grass, and a blue sky. I even saw water. It's full of Guards and Trainers and Workers. And they talk in a code so we can't understand what they are up to. Ilse told me we've been enrolled in Military School. I don't know why, so go figure it out for yourself, because she didn't tell me and I didn't have the guts to ask. I bet none of you would have had either! I don't give a crap if you believe me or not. She had it and I denied I knew what it was. And…oh…yeah…while it's on my mind. Thanks for letting me know about the Kit-Inspection. It must have been okay seeing as no one is dead. And, one other thing while it's on my mind.' I stare at Kuro in the bunk-bed beneath Spencer. 'I don't believe you found that watch. I've seen your type before, and if you put us into that kind of trouble again you're going to have me to deal with and you can decide yourself if you can handle it or not. And that goes for any one of you.'

I lie back down, staring at the ceiling. I'm shaking inside, part anger, part fear. I should tell them Ilse knows that it was us, but I'm not sure I understand why she let us off and it'll sound like I've struck some kind of bargain with her, which I didn't.

Silence.

'Thank you,' Chantal says, after a long pause. 'I guess, we owe you that for what you did.'

'Forget it. I didn't do it for you. I did it for myself.'

More silence.

I should regret saying those words, but maybe I don't. It's true. I don't want to die, not here, not over a stupid watch-cum-electronic key that I didn't even want and knew all along would bring nothing but trouble.

'Who is it?' Diego asks again.

'Who is it what?' I snap back.

'Marcellus said that if you come back tonight, it's because you made a deal with Ilse.'

I almost laugh as his words sink in.

'What kind of deal?'

'Instead of you getting punished for starting the fight, as Head of this Pod you get the privilege to nominate someone else.'

'It's four strokes of the electronic whip for boys, three for girls,' Chantal adds.

I sit up and look through the room, my eyes finally resting on Rasa. If that was true, I'd have no problem nominating my punishment taker.

'If Marcellus said that, then Ilse didn't. I haven't nominated anyone. And I won't. And I won't because I've lived in this environment all my life and I know when you have to take your own punishment and when you don't.'

I turn over and face the wall. If it's true, maybe Marcellus will make me choose in the morning, but I won't do it. I won't do it, because I have to live here and look at another seventy-eight faces, all of whom will know I pointed the finger. It's another way Marcellus is trying to destroy me. How different my life here would be if only I'd heard his original command to look forward at the stage. I hate these small mistakes in institutions that define your life.

I take a deep breath and try to relax.

Four strikes of the electronic whip will be hard to take, but I've had two before and survived those, so how hard is two more?

I can take it, I think.

I have to.

To survive this place, I have to.

17

The door to our dormitory slams open and the lights flash on. I would have been startled had I not been awake, dwelling on what Ilse is going to teach me and even more concerned about what I'm supposed to be teaching her. That thought alone is almost beyond my comprehension. I'm suddenly glad of the noise and energy that has barged into our dorm, it's a welcome distraction. Throughout the night, my mind has been a tangle of its own thoughts and I've been fighting with myself from spiralling into a desperate mindset.

I kick the blankets from my body and jump down from my bunk-bed. I'm wise enough to know that some things will never change and it doesn't matter if I'm in a Home, the Holding Centre or now Military School, from now on this kind of start will be our morning alarm. Kuro, Chantal and Diego all looked dazed from the abrupt wake-up. Spencer and Rasa are like me – taking it in their stride – or are at least familiar enough with the System to understand the game.

Stood by the door, with her hands on her hips, is a female Trainer I've not seen before. She has hazel coloured eyes, like fresh tree bark, a high forehead and a fierce stare. It's the default look of our captors, I realise. Her hair is scraped back into a tight ponytail and the muscles on her arms are more defined than Spencer's. Sprouting from beneath the sleeve on her right arm is a cobra tattoo that curls around her forearm and wrist.

'You need to change into your training clothes. You've got five minutes,' she says, looking at me.

She steps out of the room, leaving the door ajar, not addressing anyone else. I watch her go before turning to the rest of our Pod.

'You heard her,' I say.

'Do you want to use the bathroom first?' Kuro asks, looking confused.

It takes me a moment to get what he's really saying. He's looking for direction, obeying the new rules of the House.

'No, you go first then Spencer and Diego, I'll change last. The girls can decide between themselves. We've got four-and-half minutes. Let's not be late.'

I'm surprised at my own surge in energy and it's odd to hear myself issue commands. My voice sounds loud and out of place, but I almost like it at the same time.

Kuro grabs his change of clothes and dashes into the boys' bathroom, Chantal heading for the girls'. The rest of us stare at each other saying nothing, as the carry-over tension hangs heavy in the room. They still think I'm going to pick one of them to take the punishment. I'm not, although my decision would be easy, as Chantal comes out of the girl's bathroom and I watch Rasa disappear from view. She did her part in keeping our Trainer preoccupied when I pushed her into him, but I'm not kidding myself. She was looking after number one – Rasa with a capital R, our self-proclaimed hair-preening Queen Bee. She going to stick it to me at the first opportunity she gets. I know her type inside out and upside down. Maybe I'm going crazy or have gone soft in the mind to even contemplate taking four strikes of the electronic whip when I don't have to take any. Apart from Rasa, in a day or two, it would all be forgotten, so why take the pain when I don't have to? It's not like any of the other *Denounced* scare me, apart from – maybe –Taylor.

And Rasa hates me anyway, so I'm not losing anything there.

Maybe she should take it after all?

Diego comes out of the bathroom and I rush in and get changed, hearing a whistle sounded from the corridor as I finish cleaning my teeth, fastening my shoes in the next beat.

'Ned,' I hear Spencer shout.

I dash out and we fall in line, heading into the communal corridor of our sleeping quarters. The other Pods are leaving their dormitories and it's a small relief to know we're not last or running slow. We are part of the mass for the first time and that's a good place to be, I decide. Being anonymous is key to surviving. Once outside, we are ordered into three lines. There's a Trainer with two stripes waiting to address us and Marcellus is sat in a road buggy at the top of a ridge, overseeing the start of our day. I'm sure his attention is focused my way, but I keep my eyes front and try to block my paranoia. Rasa is stood to my right, but she's kept an extra space between us. I don't care about her, but the isolation I felt last night from the others has seeped into my morning, and I don't like these new thoughts of insecurity. I'm not used to feeling like this, and I wonder if this is what happens when you have to worry about other people outside of yourself.

'Good morning, everyone,' the Trainer bellows out.

Nobody says anything.

'I said...*Good Morning, Everyone*,' he repeats, shouting out his words.

'Morning, Sir,' we say in unison.

He begins to walk along the front line, pushing chins up and forcing shoulders down, before marching back, front and centre.

Military School has started.

My sour mood deepens.

'In order for you to graduate successfully, it's required you obtain a Level One Physical Fitness Certificate. Therefore, each morning we will start with a run, followed by breakfast. After breakfast, the agenda for the rest of the day will be set. You won't know until each day what that agenda will be. This is part of your education over the coming weeks. We are testing your ability to handle the unexpected and how you deal with new challenges thrown at you. A core skill requirement is for you to develop the ability to think on your feet. Are there any questions?'

Core skills.

Running each morning.

Level One Fitness.

Weeks of Military School.

All rumble through my mind in painful jolts.

'Any questions?'

There's the odd cough, but no questions. Like anyone is ever going to ask a question again.

'Good. We are one day behind because of Pod Eight which means there is one day to make up. You will be tired. Your muscles will ache. Some of you won't like what happens, but I need you to remember the alternative before your Mother gave you a second chance. Therefore, prepare your minds and the pain is less. Is everyone clear?'

Silence.

'I'll take that as a *yes*. The objective of this morning is to keep pace with the lead runner. If they go quicker then you go quicker. If they go slower then you slow. Any questions?'

Silence.

'Good. We lead off from the right, starting with line one. Give it your best shot. You're being watched. Your performances are being marked.'

He sounds his electronic whistle. The female Trainer who woke us is the pacemaker for the morning. Her ponytail bounces behind her and I can see straight off that the pace is going to be too quick for me over any sustained period.

I'm hating this before I've even started, and…

I'm being watched.

I'm being marked.

His words haunt me as the lines start to peel off in Pod Order. I take a big breath and push off into a jog. It doesn't take long before we find our natural rhythm and eighty-four *Denounced* soon sub-divide into three distinct groups: *Fast*, *Not So Fast* and *Crap*. To my surprise, Chantal is leading the *Fast* group. Her bird like walk appears to generate additional energy as she springs from one foot to next in the lightest of bounces. Kuro is not far behind. He has the physique of a long-distance runner and slight of hands are always quick in my experience – running away is an essential asset. Spencer and Rasa are in the *Not So Fast* pack, and Spencer is keeping an easy pace alongside Rasa. I have no doubt they could both be in the *Fast* group if they wanted, but they're smart enough to save their energy and not show off for what is sure to be a gruelling day.

Suddenly, I see them share a private joke and I spike with unexpected jealousy.

I take my first bend, stitch starting to burn in my lower left side as I come out into the straight. Diego is struggling worse than me and he's locked at the back of the pack. The laggers are all built like him. Short and strong for their age. Bulls in the making in adult life, but no chance when it comes to running distance, especially at pace, not that I'm doing much better myself. My running technique is flat footed and heavy, and I'm losing more ground with each new stride. I'm panting harder than I ever though was possible. I want this to stop, but there are Trainers at the back and one of them is carrying an electronic baton.

I'm being watched.

I'm being marked.

I concentrate on ignoring my stitch and trying to find a comfortable running style, my mind flicking to what Ilse said about five of us having this *gravitas* thing.

If I'm one of them, then who are the other four?

Taylor, for sure. It's a no brainer. He carries himself like he's the co-leader alongside Marcellus. That leaves three more. I've noticed a black girl who is Head of Pod Nine. I heard a boy call her Suki. She doesn't smile from what I can see and she's Rasa's height, but twice as muscular. Her skin is so dark it shines under these bright lights, and there's something about her I can't quite decide if she's okay or not. I saw her shove one of the boys in the Canteen who stood in her way. He didn't bark back and their Trainer ignored it. That's not a good sign. She's pacing herself in the *Fast* group, but at the back, making it look easy, and she has the look of someone who's used to getting their own way. If that's three of us then who are the other two? I look through the runners ahead of me. No one stands out, but I'm going to keep looking. I guess I want to know who the competition is – if that's what Ilse meant, which I'm sure she did.

I realise that the pack I'm in is falling further and further behind and I don't know how much more I can take. I'm struggling to breathe and the muscles in my legs are burning worse than my stitch. I'll drop before I stop, because I'm too scared of the consequences, but it's me, Diego and three other boys who are bookending the other Pods.

'I didn't nominate anyone,' I pant out to Diego as we fall in line, side-by-side.

Diego is sweating hard than me; his face as red as a Stop Signal.

'I…don't…believe…you. Why didn't Ilse punish you then?' he manages to spit out between breaths.

'It was weird and I don't get it, but she didn't talk about punishments.'

'It doesn't make sense if she had the watch,' he gasps out. 'Did you make a deal?'

I surge with anger and I want to lash out, but I can't, and I wouldn't if I could. I get it now. The silent treatment and the suspicious looks all make sense. They think I'm a favourite and, in a way, I am, if I understand Ilse. But I'm not a favourite in the way my Pod thinks that I am. I haven't sold anyone out. I didn't ask for *gravitas*. I didn't ask to be Head of Pod Fifteen. I didn't ask to be here. I hate how small things come back to eat you alive in places like this. And whatever I say to Diego, or any of them, it will only make it look worse.

We run another bend and I see that the *Fast* group has stopped and the *Not So Fast* group is slowing as it reaches the same end-point. Spencer and Rasa glide to a stop, talking between themselves as Chantal and Kuro walk over to join them. I realise my absence last night has been the catalyst of their new-found bonding.

Diego and I finish the run joint-last. I have to bend forward to catch my breath, fighting for an answer with my thoughts about what I need to do next. I take another deep breath, fighting the urge to be sick, when I hear a Trainer's whistle. The sound is sharp and angry and I glance up, wondering what's wrong this time.

The Trainer who oversaw the morning's run is jabbing his finger in my direction. Pods have lined up in their Pod Order to enter the Canteen. Spencer, Rasa, Diego, Kuro and Chantal have joined the end of the queue and I'm stood on my own, away from everyone else. I head toward our Pod trying to show I knew all along what was happening. Marcellus is smirking and I bristle with embarrassment at being both isolated and unexpectedly finding myself at centre of attention as everyone looks at me.

Marcellus drives off along one of the many roads that make up this jungle of grey. I hope I never set eyes upon him again. I doubt my wish will come true, but I have bigger issues to deal with than worrying about him.

I'm the outcast within my own Pod and although I usually wouldn't care, this time…I do.

18

I jog to the front of our Pod while criticising stares come at me from all angles. I recognise these looks, because I've been on the other side. I'm toying with trouble again and it scares people. They're either worried they'll get dragged in if they get too close, or they think I'm a loser and it's only a matter of time before they have the privilege of watching me implode. Either way, they'll keep their distance and after yesterday's fight most of them know who I am, which is more than I do them. Considering my life's ambition is to live in the shadows and go unnoticed until I'm adult, I've done a terrible job since coming here.

It's a problem I need to address – and fast.

I give it a couple of minutes then I turn and stare at Spencer who shrugs back, like it's my fault I got left behind. His show of innocence isn't working. Yes, I was out of breath and bent forward, waiting for my stitch to subside, but they knew what they were doing and what they think of me has shifted a gear.

'Sorry,' Chantal mouths, suddenly looking ashamed.

I ignore her.

She made her own choice, like the rest of them.

I twist back to face the front, my anger creeping up a couple of notches now my embarrassment has ebbed. I have no choice but to deal with the growing dissent from within my Pod. I've seen what happens before at other Homes if you don't. Next, I'll lose what respect I have and then a mutiny will hurtle towards me when I least expect it. It's all about positioning yourself to survive, and they think by cutting me out it will work to their advantage. But they're wrong. There are no rules to follow because Ilse is going to make them up to suit her needs. What's good today, will be wrong tomorrow. We have to stick together or we die.

I get it.

They don't.

And I'm not sure what to do.

The Trainers go into the Canteen first, leaving us to ourselves with a few Guards keeping watch from afar. The hard line we've kept slowly breaks its ranks and conversation begins to dim the noise of the extractor fans above our heads. The lack of Trainers and the thought of breakfast is driving this new energy. I turn back to face my Pod but they stop talking, waiting for me to speak. I have nothing to say, or not now, not here in front of everyone else. I was going to try and join the conversation; feel part of the group; hope that my fears are just of my own making, but their sudden silence tells me they're not.

I turn back and shuffle along, smelling fresh cooked sausages, as the chat behind me starts again.

I'm isolated.

An island between my own Pod and the ones in front of me; trapped in a city within a city.

My frustration and anger towards all fourteen Pods, including my own, starts to pound. Everyone is laughing and joking because they're about to be fed like cattle. Like we're supposed to be grateful for eating when we shouldn't be here in the first place. We've been kidnapped and I'm innocent. Ilse hung Pod Eight because they tried to escape. They didn't even get a second chance. No warning, no first strike, no lesser punishment – nothing. One mistake and they were gone, and it's like everyone has a short memory because they can smell fresh bacon. I saw something in Ilse's eyes last night that I thought before when the boys tried to escape and it's now confirmed in my mind. She has a grand plan for why we are here and anyone who doesn't take it seriously isn't going to live. There's a lurking evil danger about this place that the other *Denounced* are ignoring.

I need to warn my Pod.

I turn to face them and they stop talking again, mouths ajar, like I'm the intruder. I get it. I've met with Ilse one-on-one and that elevates me, maybe even makes me a traitor in their eyes, and Marcellus has done a great job of poisoning the air around me. I could live with not being trusted if I was somewhere else, knowing I was counting down my days to becoming an adult. That isn't going to work here, and I have to do something that I'm not good at, that I think none of us are good at, which is to work together. Be a team. I don't know how to do that and I don't know how we compare to the other Pods, but my instinct is we're crap. Chantal is the smallest person here and has zero strength from what I can see. Kuro and Spencer are lazy and Diego's lost within his own confusion. Rasa is Rasa and she is going to cut loose at the first opportunity she gets. We're in danger of being four groups within one. There's me as the Head who they won't include and will stab in the back. I can see Rasa and Spencer being a clique. The perfect couple. Both too beautiful to let anyone else in. Diego's too angry to make any friends. Kuro and Chantal look like they'll tolerate each other and form a friendship out of necessity, with Chantal always looking to Rasa for her point of reference. Whichever way I think about it, not one of these cliques will help us to survive.

Unsure what to say or do, I step inside the Canteen and I eye my choices of food. I take a bowel of porridge, followed by a plate of eggs, bacon and some hash browns. I'm waved on, but not before I grab a plate of pancakes soaked with thick maple syrup. I get a look from a Worker, like no chance I'll ever finish all that, but he doesn't know me or how hungry I am. I still have room to squeeze an orange juice onto the corner of my tray before heading to our Pod Table not bothering to wait for the others.

Like they waited for me.

The moment I sit down, I gulp a spoonful of porridge into my mouth. It's made from milk and not water, and it's creamy and honey sweet. The pleasure of food does what it is supposed to do and temporarily takes my mind off my troubles. The portions are big, we're being fattened up for something, I know it. Rasa and Spencer sit down together, and she gives me a disapproving look as I scoop more porridge into my mouth, my spoon held like a shovel. Diego joins us next with Kuro and Chantal sitting down in unison, a moment later. There's enough of a gap between everyone, including myself, to confirm my suspicions of a growing disconnected group who will struggle to bond as a unit.

We're dead, before we've even started, I think.

I finish my porridge and then lean across and flip Kuro's plate into his lap, followed by Spencer's. Before they have time to react, I tip both Rasa and Chantal's orange juices into their plates of food, floating their eggs like rubber ducks.

'What the heck!' Kuro says.

'Why did you do that?' Chantal moans, her mouth gawping like a fish. 'You've ruined my food.'

'You think you're so special, don't you?' Rasa says, her voice cold and full of venom.

Her instinct is to come out fighting.

Well, so is mine.

I don't flinch.

'I'm not scared of you,' she snarls, her jaw clenched tight.

'So you've told me once before. But you should be scared of this place and you're not – or not enough.' I look through the rest of our Pod, slow and deliberate. 'You've had a run and you get some hot food and everything is forgotten. If you want to leave me behind and make an example of me then go knock yourselves out. I ain't gonna stop you, but if you think you're going to survive this place without me, you're more crazy than Ilse.'

'You've an inflated opinion of yourself,' Rasa says.

'I don't know why Ilse took me to see her, but I saw enough to know we need each other if we want to survive. I wish I didn't have to bother with any of you, but I have to. We all have to.'

'Everything alright, over here?'

Chantal's eyes dart down as do Diego's and Kuro's. I look over my shoulder to see our Trainer walking toward us, sipping coffee from a large mug.

'Yeah, everything's alright. Our table has a wobbly leg. We need to be more careful next time.'

She takes another sip of her drink, pushing the table with her other hand. It doesn't move. It's as solid as a mountain. She looks at me and I smile back, ignoring the floating eggs and piles of food that litter our table. 'The kitchen closes in ten minutes. You've a long day ahead of you and you'll need to stay fuelled.'

She doesn't wait for an answer and heads back to the Trainers' Table, taking another sip of her coffee as she goes.

'I'm not hungry any more,' Chantal says, pushing her plate away – food, laced with orange juice, spilling over the rim's edge.

'You shouldn't have done that,' Diego says.

'What? Lied to the Trainer?'

'You know what I mean.'

'How long are you gonna sleep in your own tears? Get over yourself. You're not the only one around here who's innocent.'

'Don't tell me what to do or what to think.'

'I just did and what are you going to do about it?'

He starts to stand and so do I.

'Don't fight, please,' Chantal says, putting her hands up as if she's a referee. 'We can't afford to get into any more trouble.'

'What we did with the First-Aid kit is a waste of time. We might as well have thrown our hands up and admitted it was ours.'

'Keep your voice down, Ned,' Chantal whispers. 'They'll hear you.'

'What do I care? You guys left me to the rats.'

'Sit down,' Spencer says. His eyes dart from side to side as he checks if anyone is listening. 'We shouldn't have left you, Ned. Sit down, please.'

I stare at Diego and wait.

I'm not moving first.

'Diego!' Spencer says, his voice trembling.

Diego starts to sit and I follow a beat behind him. I have everyone's attention and I'm about to speak when Chantal says.

'I'm innocent, too.'

Her words take the tension out of the air and replace it with a different kind. Tears start to dampen her lashes as she stares into her hands. 'My parents were divorced and I was living with my father. He died at work from a stroke and I had to go back and live with my mum. She was always drunk, which is why my father left her and why he was looking after me. She had started to drink more and occasionally fell into trouble with the law. One evening, the Secular Police came to our home and said I needed to come to the Station as my mother had been accused of being a *Doubter*. When I got there, I was put into a cell. In the morning, a Court Official turned up and said the Police had a witness who had seen me talking to an escaped *Denounced*. The witness said he heard me plotting with the escapee on how to spread anti-Secular propaganda to incite a new Terrorist War. It wasn't true, but if my mother had been willing to confess to being a *Doubter* then I would have been let go. She told me there was nothing she could do. She didn't even come to Court.'

Her tears flood down her gaunt cheeks, before she uses the inside of her sleeve to wipe her face dry.

'I'm innocent, too,' Kuro says.

We turn to look at him.

'I am,' he repeats.

'But you stole the watch,' I say.

He nods.

'I didn't mean to cause all this trouble. I wanted to get out and try and get home. I never thought Ilse would do…you know…what she did…'

'How did you end up here?' Spencer asks, his voice full of surprise.

'My parents were *Doubters*,' he says quietly. 'Please, don't hate me.'

We steal a quick stare amongst ourselves, while Kuro looks on expectant.

'We don't hate you,' I say.

He nods, a weak smile creasing his face. 'They live in one of the *Doubter* Communes in my Sector. I was born there and didn't know any different. Like most of the boys, we're taught how to steal so we can live. The Quadrant gives you next to no money and the Police hassle you all the time. Even here is luxury compared to where I was born. I was arrested, but this is the crazy thing, I hadn't stolen anything for over a year. There was this program whereby kids like me who were born into *Doubter* Communes could go to an Assessment Centre and look to be rehabilitated into the Secular World. You have to take test after test, and if you pass you get to live in a Home, like you're a real orphan. You have to disown your parents and you can never communicate with them again. My dad told me to do it. He told me if I was clever enough to pass the exams then I should take my chances for a better life. I was at the Assessment Centre getting ready to take the final exam when the Secular Police came and arrested four of us. They said the tests proved I was faking it and that I was skilled at spreading anti-Secular digital messages, designed to start a War. It's not true, it's not my fault I was born into a Doubter's Camp. My parents don't even know I'm here because they think I passed and have gone to live in the Secular World. They think I'm happy and safe. I didn't even get to go to Court. And now I'm here. We're all going to die.'

'Shut up,' I say.

'Yes, shut up,' Chantal says. 'We're not going to die. None of us are.'

'I'm sorry, but we are. We're going to end up like Pod Eight,' Kuro says.

19

The fragile sense of togetherness is shattered by a whistle and our moment is lost. We are told to stack our plates in the Collection Area, Diego mumbling he's still hungry. I'm tempted to point out he has enough body mass to feed himself for a month, but seeing as it was me who spoilt his breakfast and we've clashed once this morning, I keep my joke to myself.

Outside, I count fourteen buggies with drivers waiting for us. These ones don't have the prisoner cage in the central section like the one I travelled in yesterday, and seeing them creates a wave of excitement through the other *Denounced* that I don't understand.

This is going to be a trip we don't want.

We're ordered to climb aboard with three in the middle section and three at the back. I expect our Trainer to sit next to the driver, but she gets into a designated vehicle at the front. The relief that my every move won't be watched, is soured by my concern about what's in store for us at the end of this road. I've never been one for surprises, especially the ones I've witnessed here so far. I'm full of dread and have nothing to get excited about.

Once everyone is settled, we pull off in convoy. Guard buggies bookend the long train and we snake our way out of Base Town and head into the grey wilderness beyond. Our driver interlaces a set of beads attached to a thin piece of string through his finger. It's the second time I've seen this habit and I wonder why he does it. Ahead of me, fingers are pointing and heads are looking left and right as others attempt to grasp the vastness of the rolling space I encountered yesterday. I notice Taylor is pretending to be indifferent, like he's seen it all before, and it tells me a lot about his character. I look away and wonder if we'll pass through the Wall of Fog. I doubt it. Seeing those colours and smelling the cleaner air was an unexpected bonus, and it's probably a secret they want to keep from the others. If I brag about having been to the oasis where Ilse lives, it'll come back to haunt me. I can almost hear the whispers in the air:

He's Ilse's pet, you know.

He's got privileges.

But what does he do to get those privileges?

What stories does he tell?

Who has he grassed up today?

'I'm innocent, as well,' Spencer suddenly says, breaking my thoughts.

Like a choreographed unit, Myself, Kuro and Chantal turn. Spencer's sat in the middle of Rasa and Diego who have turned to look at him as well. He likes the attention, which makes me doubt him slightly, but there's a stiffness in his posture I've not seen before and fear in his eyes that I have.

'My parents died when I was three and I can't remember anything about them. I don't even know what they did for a living and how they even died. The last Home I was in, the Warden didn't care much about what we did as long as we kept out of his way and our grades were above average. He was getting ready to retire and he had a big house in the country where he kept horses, and it's all he ever talked about. I ran with this crowd and we used to sneak out at the weekends. You know, go into the local town and get into clubs if we could. I don't know why I did it but one of the older boys, Joe, talked me into breaking into this house. It was stupid, I know. Just boredom. Anyway, we found this box of marijuana. Looking back on it, Joe must have broken into the place before and knew it was there. I smoked my first joint with him but passed out, waking up in a police cell. A few hours later, my Warden – Mr Ewan – turns up. He's all smiles and it's like I'm not in as much trouble as I thought I was. I say I'm sorry, and I was. He tells me sorry is not enough and he asks me if I know what they do with horses who break their legs. I tell him they have to be put down because they are never the same again. He says that's right and that's what is going to happen to me. I'm all confused, wondering what he means when he stands up and jabs his finger towards me. And he's spitting as he's shouting and it's like I'm looking at someone I've never seen before and his face is puffed and red, and he looks at the Policeman and says: "This boy wants another Terrorist War. He hates our Secular World. He is a *Denounced, a Denounced, I tell you*".' Tears bubble in Spencer's eyes and he brushes them away as quickly as they appear. 'Every night in my dreams I see his face twisted with disgust. I asked Joe to tell them the truth, but he denied it all, said I was making it up to get him into trouble. Then it unfolds so quick and before I know it, I end up in the same line as Ned and Rasa all because I smoked a joint. And this is the crazy thing – I don't even smoke and I don't even know why I did it.' He shrugs and attempts a half smile. 'My record is clean and it's not fair I wasn't given a second chance. I don't want to be here.'

'None of us want to be here,' Diego says.

'Why are you here?' Chantal asks, nodding toward Diego.

Her question is blunt and honest, like Chantal, but it shifts something in Diego. He looks at me and I'm waiting for his answer when he says,

'Why are you here?'

Everyone switches their attention to me, but I'm okay with it this time. It feels personal and not intrusive. I shrug, more to myself than the others. I could talk about my Number being unlucky or about my face not fitting in, because it has never fitted in any place I've been, and it couldn't be truer for here. The truth is I don't really know what happened, unless having negative thoughts and debating the odd injustice about our Secular World is enough to become a *Denounced* – which maybe it is – but I'm not going to tell them that. I've lived in six Homes. Two were good, and I almost liked them. Two were strict, but fair, where there was a lot of emphasis on education. I stayed out of trouble for most of the time, although I can't say I made many friends, but I did feel safe and I was good at my studies. I've never known why I've been moved from one Home to another, but that's the System. It's secretive by nature and you only ever know the result and not the process. Two of the Homes have been cruel and oppressive places, and the last one changed me and not for the better. I saw another side of life, and I spent every day having to defend myself while I dreamt of being free. Just like here. I tell them about the email and my sister and the Court Official and my Lawyer, and I know I'm looking at Rasa for most of the time I'm talking. I suddenly wonder if I hate her so much because she reminds me of them, particularly my sister. Or is it because I genuinely don't trust her? I don't know, and I don't tell them I'm scared of dying in this place before I get to do some of the things I wanted to do, because what's the point.

I finish telling them about Jack and the boy in front of me who wet his pants, and seeing Spencer and Rasa and nobody says a word. I can't decide if that's a good or bad thing, or does it even matter? My circumstances, like everyone else's, are what they are, and I don't think I should be here, either, but I am. I start to turn back to face the front when Diego breaks the silence.

'I have eight brothers and six sisters and many aunts and uncles. We live in the same village and farm the land. We keep to ourselves and we talk our ancient language when we can. We occasionally get hassled by the Secular Police, mostly on Market Day, but generally they ignore us. One night, there's a raid on our village. It happens now and then but this time they rounded up and arrested more than thirty of us, including myself. They said we were part of a syndicate that spread anti-Secular materials to the other villages in our Quadrant. It was all lies. We're proud farmers, nothing more. My parents were doing everything they could to get me, two of my brothers and a sister, released. During the night, there's a riot and several police cars are burnt and a policeman has his legs broken in a fight, and another one is knocked unconscious. He died later in hospital. Someone tells me my father is the ringleader, which I don't believe. He's a quiet man, tough, but not a trouble maker. Then in the middle of the night, I'm moved to another location along with my brothers and my sister. The next day, I'm accused of being a *Denounced*. I haven't seen my parents or my brothers or sister since that day, and I don't even know which Court or Sector I was tried in. My trial lasted less than forty minutes and all they talked about was the policeman who died and the wife and baby he left behind. The Judge ultimately blamed me for the death of the policeman.' He looks at me. The seriousness I associate with him returns. 'And what about the family I've left behind? They could be dead, so don't ever tell me to get over myself again.'

I flush with shame.

His story is unique to him, but I've heard similar in the Holding Centre dozens of times.

I want to apologies for what I said in the Canteen, but a whistle is sounded and the convoy of buggies begin to slow and the chance is gone. 'What are they?' Chantal says, pointing at a crop of derelict buildings in the near distance.

I don't know but the design worries me. The space is a replica of a bombed-out town, the centre of a war-zone, with shell holes, rubble and dust. I hope it's fake. It must be – it has to be, I think, because this, after all, is Military School.

Led by Taylor, Pod One is ordered into one of the derelict buildings, disappearing from view. Pod Two does the same and the caterpillar effect takes hold. In the few days of being here, we've already become brainwashed into moving this way. You start to become what they impose upon you and I have a natural urge to rebel against it. I wonder again if this makes me a *Denounced*? I don't know but I ache so badly to be free.

I turn the corner and I suddenly get what's ahead of me. It's an Obstacle Course. I sigh long and loud at the forthcoming pain. We are told to fan out in a semi-circle and the Trainer with the two stripes stands in front of us. I look for Marcellus. I don't see him, but I sense his watching presence.

'Look at the size of that climbing wall,' Diego groans. 'I'm never going to get over it.'

'Silence over there. Let me guess – Pod Fifteen! I don't want any trouble. DO YOU HEAR ME?'

'Yes, Sir,' we say in unison.

'Good. Everyone, eyes forward, this is a long and complex obstacle course that won't be mastered today, tomorrow or even next week. This is also not an individual test. We want to see you work as a group. In your families. Families look out for each other, even bad ones. Those looking for individual glory will not get it. DO YOU HEAR ME?'

'Yes, Sir.'

'Then follow me.'

The Trainer jogs to the wall that Diego groaned at. I'm one metre eight-eight and one of the tallest boys here. The wall is over four metres, if not higher. Diego grumbles again under his breath at the task ahead and I don't blame him.

'The object of this exercise is to get all six of you over the wall in the fastest possible time. That's done by teamwork and technique. Each group has different strengths and heights. You have to use what you've got. You take the best of each and it compensates for the weak links you have. You,' he says, pointing at me. 'Who's the strongest in your group?'

Everyone turns and looks at me.

My throat tightens.

The base of my neck grows hot.

'Diego,' I say.

'I agree,' the Trainer says. 'But could that be a problem to you in this situation?'

I look at the wall then back at Diego.

'Diego's not tall, Sir.'

'So what do you do?'

Everyone is looking at me and Marcellus has appeared, his hands on hips, his judgemental stare on full beam.

'Get someone who is strong, but who is able to get to the top of the wall first, then they can help the next person up.'

'That's correct. Did you get that everyone?'

'Yes, Sir,' echoes around me.

'Look at your sizes and strengths within your Teams and then decide on who should go first and last.'

We huddle. It takes us less than two seconds to agree an order and I get a lift at our sudden brisk, functioning communication.

'OK, Smart Boy. Let's see what you've got.'

The Trainer gestures me and the rest of our Pod over to the obstacle wall. I nod at Spencer and we speed up and turn and lean into the structure, cupping our hands to make a step. Chantal runs up next. She is full of energy. She plants her right foot into our hands, and as she springs toward the top of the wall, we simultaneously propel her up. She's as light as a sheet and she makes the top no problem. Next is Rasa. She weighs more, but her athletic ability compensates for her extra weight. Next up is Kuro. As he runs towards us I'm worried, but I shouldn't be. He's as good as the girls at making himself light, and he's up on top of the wall, no problem.

Three down, three to go.

We put Diego in the middle so he'll get both strength from the bottom and the maximum help we can muster at the top. He starts to run and he plants his left foot between our hands. His technique is the opposite of Chantal's. All his energy drives down rather than up and he's leaned towards Spencer, so his balance is skewed. Spencer and I groan as we try and defy gravity, by pushing him up. Rasa grabs Diego's hands but she's straining to hold his weight. Kuro and Chantal each grab an arm, but he's still too heavy for the three of them. I don't need to hear the sniggers to know it's started to look comical. Diego's feet are skidding against the face of the wall, like he's cycling an invisible bike. In his attempt to get traction, he's twisted and it's adding to his problems. I look up and see the veins in Rasa's neck start to protrude, her face reddening, and I catch sight of Marcellus smiling.

He wants us to fail.

I have to do something.

I turn my back to the wall and cup my hands. Diego is directly above me and if he falls he'll break my neck. Spencer places his foot into the centre of my hands and springs up, pushing on Diego's feet in the same movement. For a split second, I'm supporting all of Spencer and Diego's mass and my lower back ricochets with pain. I can't see above me, but there's no more sniggering and Marcellus's face has returned to its menacing scowl and I want to smile.

Diego has made it.

Spencer jumps down, takes two steps back and runs towards me, planting his foot into the centre of my hands. He uses his athletic technique to spring up and it makes him almost as light as Chantal. I watch him scramble over the top before I run forward, turn and take five big strides toward the wall. I jump up, placing my right foot as high as I can go, reaching up for Diego's hands at the same time. I feel the power in his fingers wrap around my wrists, and he yanks me onto the top of the structure with the ease I expected.

We did it and I buzz with the hit of victory and turn to the others to hear Rasa whisper to Chantal that she's innocent, too.

I don't believe it.

It can't be true.

Rasa?

Innocent?

No way.

I must be hearing things.

20

A whistle sounds to bring an end to our day. There's been no change in the surrounding light and I have no indication of the time, other than I'm close to collapsing, having been on my feet for hours. Along with the others in our Pod, I trudge back to the buggy, my shoulders slumped, my head heavy. My back still hurts from taking Spencer's and Diego's weight and I hope like crazy the pain will be gone after a good night's sleep – this is not the place to be carrying an injury.

I climb into the buggy first, followed by the others, grateful that I can sit down finally. Nobody talks on the way back and I must have nodded off as I can't recall large sections of my journey home. We're dropped on a side path to our sleeping quarters and I immediately recognise the Canteen in the near distance. It's the first time I've had a genuine fixed point that I could trust since we've been here, but even now, the space between the paths and the Canteen and our sleeping quarters looks rearranged. I'm too exhausted to work out exactly what the differences are, other than I'm more convinced than ever that the layout changes when we're not around. It has to be part of the training program, but what it means and why, I have no idea.

Like everything else around here, I don't trust it. We're ordered into three lines and there's a quick Roll Call before the trainers herd us toward our sleeping quarters and ultimately our dormitories. It's the first time I think of my First-Aid kit in a positive light. I have the start of a blister on my heel and an even bigger one on the ball of my left foot.

I'm confident there'll be something in the kit to ease the pain and hopefully some painkillers for my back as well.

Our female Trainer stands by the door and counts us in. I get a sense the attempted escape from Pod Eight has worried them more than they are letting on, and these constant counts and Roll Calls, like the ever present use of whistles, is going to become the norm.

It's part of their brainwashing and it's why I hate the System so much.

'You've got fifteen minutes to shower and change. Leave your workout kits by the door. Fresh ones will be delivered for the morning.'

The door sucks shut and locks behind her as she leaves. I don't move or say anything. I can't recall ever feeling this tired in my whole life and our day isn't over. We still have to eat, and as hungry as I am the routine of the Canteen is something I would pass on if I was given the choice. Wearily, I climb onto my bunk and remove my shoes and examine my blisters. They're bigger than I thought and just looking at them seems to make them sorer. I'm tempted to pop the one on my heel so the water can escape and it'll heal quicker, but I'm sure you're not supposed to. Or maybe you are? Chantal walks over and hands me her First-Aid kit. It's an act of kindness that catches me off guard, but she turns and heads for the bathroom before I can thank her. Nobody is looking at me and the tension from this morning has returned with all its force. It's got nothing to do with the fact our day isn't finished and we have all this to do again tomorrow. They're convinced I still have to pick one of them to receive the punishment for the fight I started. A fight that saved us from being hanged, I'd like to remind them, but I don't. I see now our small victory at the Obstacle Course was hollow and the cracks within our dysfunctional Pod have returned.

When my turn comes to taking a shower, I turn the water to as hot as I can take it and it helps with my tired muscles and sore feet. I would like to stay longer and then climb into my bunk and dream of surfing and being by the sea, but my internal clock is ticking and telling me I'll get into trouble if I indulge for much longer. I dry myself off, change and head back into the main dorm to see the others waiting for me. I'm not sure what, but I want to say something when the door opens and our Trainer enters, glancing through the room and checking the pile of dirty workout clothes on the floor, before nodding us out.

It's bright and white inside the Canteen and the smell of garlic and chips float in the air amongst the clatter of cutlery. It's the obligatory three courses and I go for pea and ham soup again, followed by steak pie and a large slice of banana cake, which I've never eaten before. I don't see any banana, but it must be there somewhere. A Worker checks I've taken the minimum required. It's not a problem and never will be as I've always had a good appetite and I'm sure I could eat for two, plus the food is good. There's so much physical work ahead of us they are going to make sure we have enough fuel to complete each day and no-one is going to have the excuse of being exhausted from lack of food or water. I don't know why, but I think again of cows being fattened for the slaughterhouse and I shudder at my own morbid thoughts.

I hope I'm not slowly losing my optimism, because I don't know how I'll cope if this place sucks me dry of the last thing I have.

My dignity.

As a Pod, we eat in silence. I glance through the rest of the other Pods and there's not much conversation going on with them either. Everyone is flat tired, but that's not our reason. It goes deeper than that. We finish eating and wait for the signal to stack our plates and head outside. We do another Roll Call and I'm hoping this is the end of our day, but the heaviness in my stomach is telling me another story. The inevitable whistle is sounded and Taylor and Pod One lead the way. We've never spoken but I don't trust or like him. He acts like he's enjoying it here. At least we're allowed to walk, but we're heading along a new path, towards another nondescript rectangular building, when I'm hit by a bad memory. At my fifth Community Home, punishments were dealt out on Sunday evenings after last meal and before lights out. It was meant to cleanse us for a fresh start to the week ahead. I hated those days and the week was mostly full of dread. The countdown to Punishment Day began on Wednesdays with gossip about who was in trouble and who wasn't. It festered like a virus amongst us. On Sunday, the whole of the Community Home would gather in the Punishment Room and those in trouble would be made to stand while their crime was read out. It wasn't like Court where you got the chance to defend yourself, or at least your Lawyer could – if she could be bothered. If your name was called, then you were guilty and everyone else would watch the punishment. It was the first place I'd seen the electronic baton. Girls would get fewer strikes than the boys but not always. Everyone cried and the welts could take days, even a week, sometimes, to go.

'Who are you going to pick?' Rasa asks me.

I know by her tone she must have stayed in a similar Home to the one that has just danced through my mind as she knows what's coming. I want to tell her again that Ilse never mentioned any punishment, but she won't believe me, in the same way I don't believe she's innocent of being a *Denounced*.

'It's okay if you want to pick me,' she adds. 'It's best to get this over and done with.'

She falls back a step and before I can respond, Diego slides up on my left side and leans in close.

'You know I'm the strongest of us all. I can take a couple of those electronic whips. On a low setting, they don't hurt that much. I'll cry out more, like it hurts. Play it up a bit. You can nominate me if you want, and better it's one of us than the girls or Kuro.'

I get an unexpected pang of jealousy and insecurity wrapped into one. He's willing to support Rasa and the others, and I feel like I've been tag-teamed against as well as stabbed in the back by him. Spencer doesn't volunteer his pain services, but it doesn't matter. Diego decides my mind for me, although my mind was mostly made up, anyway. If Marcellus tries to force me to pick a member of my Pod in front of the other *Denounced,* I will refuse. I can't lose face or seem to be weak, because I'll be eaten alive by the other *Denounced* when the Trainers aren't around to protect me. I will take any punishment that is coming our Pod's way, and hope the pain doesn't last too long or interfere with tomorrow's physical activities.

We slow and I watch Taylor step into the building first. As the other Pods enter, a bubble of excited voices echo back. I step through the threshold, unsure what to expect and half anticipating to see Marcellus dressed as a Head Judge, but I don't.

'What's this?' Chantal shouts, pushing in front of me.

I want to rub my eyes.

I can't believe what I'm seeing.

We are in a games room.

With music!

'Woohoo!' Diego says, high-fiving Spencer and not me.

'I love pool,' Chantal says, running across to one of the pool tables and picking up a cue. 'Come on. Hurry!' she says to Kuro, picking up a second cue and a square of chalk. 'I bet I'm better than you.'

I scan the rest of the giant room. Everyone's mood has changed, even mine. We've all been energised, the physical activity of the day a distant memory. In front of me is a large annex room with a TV and a six-seater central leather chair with more chairs circled around it. In another annex, there's a refreshments area with fizzy drinks and crisps and chocolate cake. I count three pool tables and two table-tennis tables. There's a basketball hoop and half a court marked out. There are footballs and soccer balls. Baseballs and bats and gloves. In another area are TV screens with Gaming Consoles, and some of the boys have already run over and started playing. There's even an old-fashioned Pin-Ball Machine, which I've only ever seen in pictures. Everyone is smiling and some of the girls have started to dance to the music. It's like we've forgotten where we are. It's like Pod Eight is a distant memory and it makes my anger return, the smile dropping from my face.

Ilse is playing us all and everyone is falling for it accept me.

I turn to see Rasa walking toward me carrying two fizzy drinks. At first, I think the second drink must be for Chantal or even her new best friend, Spencer. But it's not. It's for me. It doesn't come with a smile, but I'm nearly as shocked by the act as I am at being in the room and the fact she protested her innocence. I take the drink and mumble a *thanks*, catching sight of Marcellus looking over toward us. I'm sure he's talking about us to our Trainer, whose smile is growing by the second.

I get it now.

He was playing his own game.

Testing our Pod.

Testing me.

Seeing if any of us would crack.

'I was serious. If you have to pick someone later on, you can nominate me,' Rasa says. 'Just don't choose Chantal, she's too weak to take the electronic whip.'

'The punishment is never going to happen. It was a test.'

'How do you know?'

'Because someone wants us to fail. Or me, anyway.'

21

What I nearly said, but stopped myself, was: *Marcellus wants me to fail and I know why.*

But I didn't say it because I don't totally understand what is happening to me. I made a mistake with Marcellus on the first day by not listening to his instructions in front of everyone, but it must go further than that. It's become personal with him. There was a bite and frustration in his eyes when the Guard stopped him from getting into the elevator in Ilse's Tower. Then another driver drove me back to the dorm, and I keep getting this image of Marcellus being dismissed, so I'm starting to suspect he's somehow jealous of me. It's a crazy thought to have about our Head Trainer and all the power he has here, but that's how it looks and feels. And if I'm right, it's not just me who will suffer, but the whole of our Pod.

So, do I tell them or don't I?

And if I do, I'll have to try and explain *gravitas*, which I can't really, and then talk more about my meeting with Ilse in a way that I don't understand. Then after I've fumbled through it all, I'm sure it will only add to the divisions that have seeped amongst us. I almost wish I was still at the Holding Centre and I could talk to Jack. He was full of good advice, and he had a way of making things simple. He had a phase that went something like: *how does this look when it's simple?* And I kinda understand what he means but I can't do it for *gravitas*, or not yet. He told me once, he didn't have children and it was one of the reasons why he'd asked to be transferred from an Adult Prison to the Pre-Adult Holding

Centre. In his own way, he could be a mentor of sorts to hundreds of boys and girls that needed guidance, and I will never forget his kindness over the chocolate cake, and even the delicate touch he used to place the mask over my eyes when I thought my end was here.

I walk into the TV Room and there's a film on with a car chase and loud police sirens. Some of the boys are cheering at the action. The best view of the screen is from the six-seater style settee with thick arm rests and cup-holes for drinks. On the central arm of the two middle seats is a glass touch-screen panel. There's a choice of films, but I notice at the top of the panel it says Pod One.

Taylor's Pod.

I'm wondering if it means we have to wait 'fourteen' rest evenings before I can enter Pod Fifteen and pick the films we want, when I'm hit with another reality.

We're being watched.

We're being marked.

Maybe, if you include the run this morning and then the Obstacle Course, Pod One have scored the highest overall mark of the day? I twitch with insecurity that we'll never get the best seat in the house. I can't see Taylor, but the other five members of his family are enjoying themselves. Would our Pod look as pleased with themselves if we were sat down? I bet Taylor picked the film without consulting the others then left to do something else. That's so his type. Stamping his authority from the onset, making sure he's number one.

Maybe I should learn from him.

Maybe he's going to survive and I won't.

I wander out of the room, my mind full of mixed thoughts about this Games House and its hidden meanings when I spot Diego and Spencer playing table tennis. Diego is surprisingly good. He's quicker on his feet than he realises, because his mind is on something else. It's good to see him laughing and smiling, and I wish I could do the same. It's the first time I've seen him laugh, and it suits him. I recognise a mutual trust between them that I've not spotted before, and I once again feel jealous of Spencer's easy and likeable charm.

Chantal is talking to a group of girls. They are sat on the floor, cross legged, in a semi-circle. One of them has found a short pair of scissors and is attempting to fix another girl's haircut. Chantal is busily giving advice and being her usual chatty self. She's a nice girl in a not so nice place. I hunt for Kuro and see him playing on one of the Gaming Consoles. He's chatting with another boy with glasses as they kill aliens, and he looks more relaxed than I've seen him. I can't see Rasa, but I spot a red-headed boy who is the same size and shape as Diego. His name is Sean. He has so many freckles across his face and arms it reminds me of scales on a snake. He was in our group on the run with us this morning. I hadn't over noticed him before, but I recall Spencer saying he is Head of Pod Eleven. He has a confident swagger I've seen in Taylor and Suki. He's playing pool, but he's nailing every shot. He has the walk, like he's good at most things, except running. He pots the black, the white ball spinning on the spot for a few seconds afterwards. He high fives the boy he beats. He tosses the cue on the table and then struts off towards where the fizzy drinks are stored. He stops and starts to talk to one of the girls near Chantal. The girl's body language tells me they haven't spoken to each other before, but she likes Sean's confidence. They flirt. He's not the best-looking boy in the room, but if he wanted to talk to Rasa, her surly face wouldn't put him off. Maybe Sean's the fourth person with gravitas.

So who is the fifth?

I turn to see if I can work it out when Taylor crashes into my right side, nearly knocking me off my feet.

'Hey…sorry…bro…I didn't see you there.'

He's holding a basketball and is sweating hard. He's a long way from the marked court and he's made it look like he's run out for the escaped ball, but he's not kidding anyone. He meant to do what he did, and it hurt. My shoulder throbs and it's jarred my back further, and had we been anywhere else, I would have been forced to defend myself, or I would have been his whipping boy going forward.

'Easily done,' I say, looking at the ball.

'Taylor,' he says, holding out his hand for me to shake. 'Boss of Pod One.'

'Ned – Head of Pod Fifteen.'

We shake hands and he squeezes harder than he should, forcing my knuckles together. I ignore the pain, the half smile across his face telling me he's trying to provoke me further. I get a flash of Ilse giving him the *Gravitas Speech* and he's doing what I've been doing and trying to fathom who the other four are. In that way, Taylor and I are the same and it's probably why I distrust him so much.

'What do you think?' he asks.

I shrug.

'Come on, don't give me that, bro. Of this gig? Freaky stuff with that Pod Eight getting…you know,' he laughs, then pulls a fake rope by the side of his neck, tilting his head to one side as he does. 'Let's be honest. It's crossed all our minds to try and escape this freak show, no?'

'It may have crossed your mind but it hasn't crossed mine,' I say with a smile.

He laughs.

'Yeah, yeah, bro, whatever, toe the line and all. So you guys like to get into trouble? I like your style. It keeps us all entertained. I hope you don't stop.'

'We aim to please.'

He laughs again then bounces the basketball through his legs. I can see he can play and that's he's probably good.

'Wanna shoot a few hoops?'

'Too tired. Another time.'

'You don't look it, but no problem, bro. I love this physical stuff. Can't get enough of it and it beats being locked up at the Holding Centre. So, where you from? I recognise that accent. It must be North East, Section Two-C. In the Old World that would have been New York, no?'

'Secular World Quadrant 1.'

'I'm close. Section One-A – Boston area in the Old World.'

We're smiling at each other, but really we're weighing each other up. I'm a touch taller but he's fitter and I can't tell who is the strongest, but he possesses a viciousness I don't have.

'You've got a nice blonde in your family. What she like?' he says with a wink.

'Bad tempered.'

'Of course she is, she's hot. All hot blondes are bad tempered. What's her name?'

I feel my anger and jealousy start to mix and I don't need a mirror to know it's showing on my face.

'Hey…sorry, bro…I didn't mean to step on your toes…that's why I wanted to run it past you first. No offence, intended.'

'You misunderstand. Her and Spencer…you know…they are like…together.'

'You mean that dude with the stupid accent?'

'Yeah him.'

'Well, if it's okay with you, I might try and do something about that?'

'You heard Ilse. We're family now and we have to stick together so it might be a problem…if it gives him a problem.'

'The girl can speak for herself and I'm asking you if it's okay to step in?'

The smile has gone from his face. He's leaned in, the basketball is aimed at my chest like a rocket. He's not asking, but telling, and he's spoiling for a fight, playing the odds, thinking we'll get the blame – Pod Fifteen causing trouble again.

Suddenly all the lights go on and the TV screens die and I'm seriously thankful of the distraction, as a handful of Trainers run in and fan out along the walls of the room.

'Two minutes, lights out. We have an early start tomorrow. Do you HEAR me?' a Trainer yells.

'Yes, sir,' we say in unison.

'You didn't answer my question, bro,' Taylor growls under his breath.

'Yes, I did,' I say, walking off, looking everywhere for Rasa.

I finally spot her with Chantal sitting by the wall. I recall the first time I saw her when I tripped on the step and it was Jack who caught me from falling on my face and embarrassing myself further. The truth was I'd been distracted by her beauty and looking at her now, even with her short hair and hard stare, I can see that she's the most beautiful girl in here.

Actually, I'm wrong.

She's the most beautiful girl I've ever seen.

22

'Congratulations my children on completing *Phase One*,' Ilse says.

Her voice booms through the speakers, crisp and clear, filling the Assembly Hall.

I find her every action insincere and I would be rolling my eyes and showing dissent if I were anywhere else. But I'm not anywhere else, I'm here. I smile broadly and fake nod at all the appropriate pauses, as her presence continues to chill me to the core. I wonder what the others in my Pod really think? We've never spoken about her as a group because we are too scared we'll be overheard, but I'm confident they feel the same as me. Personally, I've never been as petrified of anyone as I am of this woman. Her unpredictability keeps me on edge and worse, makes me fearful for my life. Even though this is the first time I've seen her since I was taken to her apartment in the Oasis, her twenty-four seven.

'I know that I've been absent from your lives with other important business matters. For this, my children, I am deeply sorry and I will make this up to you with a gift from my own heart.' She places her hands across the centre of her chest and drops her head in mock unhappiness. Marcellus and the other Trainers are watching intently for our reactions. I'm extra careful I don't show any disdain, nodding my understanding, expressing sympathy for whatever important business kept her at a safe distance from us. 'Rest assured you have been in my deepest thoughts. I have read your progress reports with the utmost interest and compared them with the originals when you arrived on day one. I have watched – albeit from a distance – with pride and fascination at your growth and development. Many of you have surpassed the expectations that we had set for you, and it fills us with a sense of pride that you have achieved what you have so far. You are magnificent! Exemplary! It's an honour to be in your presence.'

The screen behind Ilse comes alive with a flurry of exploding fireworks as the words *PHASE ONE COMPLETE* flashes amongst the digital display of colours. I'm dutifully looking at the screen but I'm not seeing the special effects that are designed to lift my mood and tell me I'm good at something I never wanted to be part of.

All I'm seeing is Pod Eight swinging by their necks, their lives gone from their bodies, for no other reason than to be made an example of.

It's an image that is indelibly printed on my mind and will stay with me for as long as I live.

Ilse turns to the man with the blue eyes and throws him a smile, asking for reassurance on her performance. He nods his approval and she feigns coyness, but it's all part of the act, and it's not fooling me, although I'm sure it's fooling some of the others.

I notice Marcellus has moved far right of the central lectern and starts to applaud as he moves into the light. Some of the other Trainers have spread amongst us and around the edges. They begin to clap and without hesitation we join in, turning it into a rapturous applause. Ilse keeps up the embarrassed persona as she steps from behind the lectern, taking a short bow. I'm clapping so hard my palms start to smart but I'm not going to stop. I'll clap for an hour and more, if I have to. Finally, Ilse raises her hands for us to stop. On the screen behind her, the firework display fades and our Pod structures appear on the screen. Pod Eight is still listed, but the names are gone. Again, the memory of that day blasts through my mind as I notice that each Pod has been allocated another number.

Pod One: two-hundred and seventy.

Pod Two: two hundred and ten.

I scan all the Pod names and corresponding numbers, comparing each one with our score as the knot in my stomach twists tighter. Rasa says what my mind refuses to accept.

'Our number is the lowest,' she says.

I do a quick re-take and sure enough – it is. Our number is one hundred and seventy-two, the lowest of everyone by a big margin.

'What does it mean?' Diego whispers.

'It means we're in trouble,' Kuro says from the back.

'We're always in trouble,' Chantal says with a croak in her voice, like she's about to cry.

'Dude, it's always us,' Spencer says. 'Why?'

'No one react,' I hiss. 'Chantal, don't start crying. Not here. Not in front of everyone.'

She nods and I turn back toward the screen. Ilse gives a single loud clap of her hands and music is pumped through the speakers. The screen flashes a mixture of colours then an ordered list appears, confirming my fears.

Pod One: 270
Pod Nine: 256
Pod Eleven: 248
Pod Twelve: 243
Pod Five: 231
Pod Three: 228
Pod Fourteen: 227
Pod Ten: 224
Pod Seven: 221

Pod Thirteen: 212
Pod Six: 211
Pod Two: 210
Pod Four: 209
Pod Fifteen: 172
Pod Eight: 0

'Oh dear,' Ilse says with theatrical surprise. 'It would appear that one Pod didn't even get two hundred points.'

Loud sniggers reverberate around the Assembly Hall. Taylor looks over his shoulder and gives me a wink, mouthing: *thanks for the entertainment*. I get a flash of being one of the Guards and having an electronic baton, dishing out my own idea of entertainment, before I let the image fade in my mind. I smile back at Taylor and then glance up at the screen, doing my best to calm my embarrassment. Through the quiet laughter that is surrounding me, I wonder if I've got my answer to who the fifth leader with *gravitas* might be?

Taylor is the Head of Pod One and they are currently ranked top of this leader board. Suki is Head of Pod Nine and they are second; Sean is Head of Eleven and they are third. All three of them I'm sure have this *gravitas* thing and are using it to drive their Pods to success. My theory would be laughable as we are last, but Ilse said herself that I have it, so I must be the fourth one, despite our pathetic Ranking. I look across at Pod Twelve. They are fourth on the list. It's the group with five girls and one boy. The Head is a girl named Arianne. She has dark hair and a plain face. She's around one metre seventy tall and looks more like one of the Trainers than any of us with her muscular shoulders and thighs. I've not noticed it before, but she has a quiet confidence and the other four girls will follow without too much questioning. The one boy in her group is more like Kuro and I'm not sure he has the character to challenger her authority. I've heard a few sniggers from the other boys that they would like to be in his dormitory, especially after lights out, but I'm not so sure they would. I bet he doesn't get much of a say, and I hope for his sake the other five girls aren't as aggressive and surly as Rasa or he'll be hanging himself long before Graduation ever comes.

'The scores you see before you are your current standing and will eventually go toward your Graduation's final score. There's another purpose, too. It enables us to assess your strengths and weaknesses, letting us guide your individual progress. It's important you don't come last, but one Pod will have to fill that space and I'm disappointed that Pod Fifteen is ninety-eight points behind Pod One, which is the largest gap we've ever seen. You have a lot of work to do, Pod Fifteen.' I hear more sniggers. 'However, I have great faith in Ned to pull his family back into the competition. Let's hear it for Ned. Let's give him a round of applause to encourage him and his family to improve and get back to winning ways.'

Ilse starts to clap.

Everyone joins in.

I see Marcellus smirking at me as he slow claps out of rhythm.

I want the floor to open up and swallow me whole.

It doesn't and eventually, Ilse raises her hands to bring my pain to a stop. 'With *Phase One* complete, then what is *Phase Two*, I can hear you asking? Well, I will let you into a secret, my children. It is more of the same with an increased focus on excellence. I hear your internal groans. I hear your internal doubts. But do not let it be a problem. *Phase Two* is something you should embrace. You have innate skills and are learning new ones that will assist you on your journey in this School of Life. You have already proven that you have the aptitude and, most of all, the desire to succeed. Embrace the second phase and let your desire to succeed shine. I want you to think of *Phase One* as your acclimatisation and *Phase Two* as a significant step towards completing your days here. I'm sure you've all debated within yourselves and your families what does Graduation mean? We will come to that in good time, but I want you to see it as a *Mission* of the utmost importance, which has been determined by the Powers who saved you. Therefore, I ask you, my maturing children – my adults-in-waiting – to step forth and claim who you are. You *can* do it. Pod Fifteen can raise themselves from the floor. Pod Four can be number one if they want. Pod One can lose points if they don't concentrate and keep up their hard work. All of it is possible and it is all determined by your attitude and commitment, because Graduation, if you play it right, means your FREEDOM.'

Ilse shouts the last word and everyone around me roars and claps, stamping their feet, the word

Freedom!

Freedom!

Freedom!

rings around me as our Governess walks off stage, waving us goodbye.

I watch her go before I glance up and try and spot one of the extractor fans I hear so often, wondering if there really is a world outside of this place.

My own thoughts scare me, because I'm starting to doubt there is.

23

I'm beginning to see that I'm trapped twice over.

Once in the world I've been kidnapped into – Ilse's world – and then into my allocated Pod.

As a group, we've fallen into a routine of tolerance that's a hidden danger to us all. Rasa and Chantal stick together when we're in our dorm as do Diego and Spencer, Kuro hanging onto their coat tails with myself watching from afar, wishing on one level I was more included, equally happy I'm not. It's become easier to pretend we're friends than it is to fall out, when maybe falling out is what should happen. We are last in the Rankings and thirty-seven points from the next Pod. With no one knowing how the scoring is attributed, I don't know if thirty-seven points is a big number to make up or not. I'm concerned we've fallen too far behind to ever make up the difference.

And with all this talk of Graduation and Freedom the Pods have become focused on the training, enjoying it, believing the end's in sight and around the corner. I even sense Rasa believes it, too, and she's the one person I thought would see through it like me. She is wrong, they all are. There's danger lurking in every corner. The Guards and Trainers watch our every move and I spotted the first camera monitoring our run today. Doors are locked behind us each time we enter and leave a space. Even the Games Room doors are bolted shut once we enter. Our dormitories are nothing more than comfortable prison cells and we're been force-fed to make us strong. I've heard the odd whisper that some of the other *Denounced* were wrongly accused and are innocent like me.

This confuses me even more as to why we are here, and that's it about our Pod.

We don't talk.

We're incapable of communicating, having, I think, unquestionably settled into Ilse's grand plan. We're all innocent, but we haven't mentioned it since it came out, like it's been forgotten – *innocent*, a dirty word. When I look at the top four Pods they have leaders at their helm, someone pushing them on. I hate Taylor. He's as vicious as any of the Guards and his Pod is scared of him, but my Pod isn't scared of me, and one of us is last and the other first. Ilse said it's important a Pod doesn't come last, but everyone, including us, has forgotten her warning.

We're not safe.

I know in my heart of hearts, in the deepest part of me, that something bad is waiting around the corner. And we are heading straight for it without a care to what it might be.

We might as well be Pod Eight, I think.

'I still can't believe she said…freedom…you know… like…*freedom*,' Spencer says, as he pots the number ten ball into the centre pocket.

He's mentioned it three times in as many minutes, and still shakes his head in disbelief each time the word leaves his mouth. *Freedom* is something you don't dare talk about when you're in the System. It is something that only happens when you get to eighteen and sometimes not even then, as it's said some never get the chance to leave. Not talking about it is just an unwritten rule we follow, yet here it is dangled in front of us, driving everyone to strive harder and harder.

I hate it.

And I hate I'm the only one that can see it.

'She definitely said it,' I say, watching Spencer chalk the end of his cue for another shot. There's no enthusiasm in my voice and if he's picked up on my negative tone he's not letting on.

'Freedom, dude! And, after being a *Denounced*. Amazing. Can I let you into a secret?' I shrug a smile. He smiles back and continues. 'I don't know what I'm going to do when I get out. I've had someone tell me what to do for so long that what if I don't know what to do. Crazy, no?'

'You'll know, trust me.'

'Do you think?'

'Do you think she's telling the truth?'

Spencer looks up from the pool table, a frown creasing his brow.

'Yeah...why not?'

'I'm just asking if you believe her or not?'

He stands up and stares at me. 'They're making us work hard to pass out. If they want me to pretend I'm a soldier I don't care, I'll pretend. I'm enjoying getting fit anyway, and look how much effort's gone into this place. I admit it looks weird, but it could be worse. I thought it was a prison at first, but it's not. We're the elite. We're the lucky ones. I get it now. We've been handpicked and we should be proud of that.'

I nod my agreement.

I want to cry inside.

'If we're innocent why can't we go home and choose if we want to play soldiers or not?'

'Dude, you're an orphan, like me, you don't have a home to go to. This *is* our home. You know how it works – any place we stay in is our main residence for the period you're there. That's it.'

'Diego's not an orphan, neither is Kuro or Chantal.'

Spencer lets out a short, sharp sigh.

'Look, it's not my first choice, but compared to some places I've been, it's good here. Anyway, how bad can it be?'

'They can hang us for looking the wrong way. That's how bad it can be.'

The second the words leave my mouth, I regret it. I can see in his face he views me as the 'problem' and not this place or Ilse's regime. I'm the negative voice, the one who might get us hanged if I don't toe the line and stop causing problems. Because, if I really think about it, and it hurts to think this way, causing problems is how in our own separate ways we all ended up being *Denounced* in the first place.

I wish I could pull back my words and say what I meant to say in a different way, that we shouldn't trust Ilse, and we need to concentrate on the main problem of not coming last, rather than dreaming of Graduation and Freedom, and the next slice of chocolate cake.

'Rasa's right. You should chill more. Let your hair down a bit. You're always on the edge, watching, judging us. You're like one of those Guards. It's arrogant, is what it is.'

I reel inside at his words, or are they Rasa's words really? Has she finally undermined me as I always thought she would? Spencer racks up the pool balls and I look through the Games Room waiting for him to finish, knowing something has changed between us. I'm the outsider within our Pod, maybe within all fourteen Pods, and maybe in life itself. It's what the judge called me, implying the world was a better place without me as he passed down my sentence.

Trouble is what he said.

I spot Rasa watching two girls playing on the Gaming Consoles. It looks like she's part of the action, part of the fun, but she's like me – stood on the edge watching, a periphery person, pretending she's part of something she's not.

'Winner stays on,' Kuro says as he bounces over.

'Sure,' I say, handing over my cue. 'Where's Chantal?'

'She was drinking a Coke with Diego last time I saw her.'

I nod and smile, more insecurity growing in me at my inability to integrate myself into our Pod. Spencer breaks the pack and the number seven spot shoots into the top corner pocket. He gives Kuro a smile as he pots the two spot, followed by the one spot. Kuro laughs and mocks giving me back the cue before he's even taken a shot. Spencer joins in the fun and I have to force myself to find the moment funny, like I'm one of them, one of the boys. I'm not and I can't bear myself that I can't fit in.

'I'm going to get a drink. Anyone want one?' I ask.

They both nod and I walk off, but not toward the snacks, straight for Rasa. I'm still a good ten or twelve steps away, coming up from behind, but she spins round, her claws out. Her survival radar is on high alert and it pleases me to see her will to survive hasn't been dulled by this place. If anyone here knows we're being duped other than me, I believe it's her.

Or at least, I hope so.

'What do you want?' she says all unfriendly, like she can read my mind.

'Is it true, you're innocent?'

'What's it to do with you?'

'Nothing, but I'm asking.'

'What if I don't want to tell you?'

'Your choice, I guess.'

We stand there and stare at each other. It's a stand-off and I'm fighting with myself not to walk away. I want to, but I don't. I don't because as much as I hate Taylor, he's taught me something about myself when he mocked me in the Assembly Hall. He's a leader and I'm not. I can't lead through violence and fear because it's not me. I know that much about myself, but maybe I can lead through reason and understanding. Jack, at the Holding Centre, told me once I was sensitive to situations, but not in a soft way. We laughed about it at the time and I was sure he was trying to prepare me for my end, but I don't think he was, I think he meant something else.

'I'm an orphan like you and Spencer. My parents died in a car crash. A lorry veered across the central reservation. I was in the back seat with my little brother. He's in a Home too, but one with learning problems. The accident damaged his brain. I was four years old and didn't even have a scratch. Tell me again how many Homes have you been in?' she says.

'Six, plus the Holding Centre and here, so that's eight in total.'

'Twenty-four,' she says. 'Twenty-six if you include here and the Holding Centre.'

'Woah...I think you like trouble.'

'I think you're arrogant and cold and only looking out for yourself.'

'You're wrong.'

'And so are you about me.'

'Twenty-Four Homes is a lot.'

'It is not my fault male teachers sometimes like me. Like me in a way that makes it tough. And they always have a get-out clause if you don't like them back. They can say you're anti-Secular and you want to incite a War.'

It takes me a few seconds to get what she's saying. Then it smashes through me and her aggression and self-protection make a whole lot more sense than they did a few moments ago. I nod, because I don't know what else to say, and I'm definitely not going to say sorry, because I hate it when people say sorry to me after bad news, like when they knew I was going to be hanged. That's what I liked about Jack.

He never used the word on anyone at the Holding Centre when bad news came their way. I respected him for that. I respected him for a lot of things. But mostly I respected him for his integrity. It's not often seen in our Secular World.

'You punched a lot of teachers?' I ask.

She shrugs, 'I stabbed one in the leg. They said he was lucky not to have bled to death. I wish he had. At least being here would have been worth it.'

'Is that when they accused you of being a *Denounced*?'

She nods, 'I had the same lawyer as Spencer. I saw you once in the Holding Centre and a few times in Court. I thought you were arrogant there as well.'

I turn to look at Spencer playing pool with Kuro, embarrassed at my own paranoia that I thought somehow Spencer and Rasa were...like...a couple...and about to gang up on me. I wonder why he never mentioned it, but that's how it works when you have the same lawyer. You become pseudo friends and compare notes to see what they are saying for the other person that they might not be saying for you, like it's going to make a difference on the final outcome, but it never does.

Ever.

Because the System's corrupt from front to back.

'We should be friends,' I say.

'What if I don't want to be friends?'

'I can live with that, but I still need your help.'

'What if I don't want to give you my help?'

'I tell you what. If you believe Ilse is going to free us then let's agree to tolerate each other for the sake of the others. If not, we need to help each other. Let me know.'

I turn and walk way, feeling vulnerable in a way I'm not used to. Spencer throws me one of his handsome smiles and shrugs as if to say where are the drinks. I turn toward the

Refreshments Area, my mind trying to see Rasa in another light, like I thought she was this person, but maybe she's not. But maybe, then again, she is, and she's lying about the teacher being over friendly and she'll stab me in the leg or the back at the first opportunity she gets. And have I just given her that opportunity on a plate, by offering my hand of friendship?

I fill three cups to the brim with Coke. I load the cups onto a tray as I stuff a soft piece of chocolate cake into my mouth, heading for the main Room.

Suddenly, I'm hit with a rush of energy coming straight at me.

I hear *fight, fight, fight*, egged on by Taylor.

Trainers are running toward the crowd.

I'm not surprised, tensions were always going to spill over between the Pods at some point. It happens in places like this. It's when I see the anguished expression across Spencer's face that I stare between the crowd to get a better view of who is fighting.

I feel my jaw drop, followed by the drinks from my hands.

Rasa has Suki by the hair and is pounding her head into the floor, Marcellus struggling to pull them apart before another Trainer assists him and all I can think is…why us?

Why is Pod Fifteen front and centre once again?

24

The shadows in the room make Rasa's empty bunk look like a freshly dug grave.

I can finally sympathise with how the others must have felt when I was taken to Ilse. Apart from the obvious loss that has left us feeling lopsided, it has driven a wedge of insecurity between us that I didn't expect. My mind has struggled with the same question that haunts the others – will Rasa trade information about us or the other Pods to lessen any punishment coming her way? I wouldn't, but that's me and not Rasa or anyone else. Despite my best efforts to calm our Pod, since lights out, the memory of our escape and the deaths of Pod Eight have lingered, making us retreat into our shells, which chips away at everyone's fragile confidence.

The consensus of the Pod, according to Chantal, is that Rasa got jealous about Suki and Taylor's supposed relationship and lashed out. I have my reservations about Chantal's interpretation, but I did see Taylor speak with one of the Trainers after the fight, who in turn spoke to Marcellus, which appeared to influence the decision to take Rasa away and not Suki, so maybe it's true, after all. Taylor, the rising nemesis in my life. He's a problem that I'd hoped would go away.

He won't.

My eyes drop to Chantal's bunk. She's fallen into a restless sleep. I've grown to like her, admire her in my own way. She can find something to like in everyone, even me. I thought she was our weakest link, but she's not by a long stretch. I'm the winner of that prize. She's too honest for a place like this, but she has a positive energy and a determined strength towards her problems I didn't think she possessed. For all her lack of physical strength she doesn't duck a single challenge that's been thrown her way, and she's always in the top group of runners.

I look across at Kuro.

He's still scared of his own shadow and I know why. He harbours the belief that this place is somehow linked to the tests he was going to take to get his new start in life and leave the *Doubters' Camp*. He's wrong and his over politeness grates, but he's way smarter than he makes out. I'm sure he has skills, beyond his ability to pickpocket, that we could use if we worked better as a functioning team.

Spencer purrs a soft snore, taking my attention.

He never struggles getting to sleep, no matter what's on his mind. I wish I had that ability. My opinion of him hasn't changed other than he doesn't think things through enough, and I'm disappointed he's bought wholeheartedly into the training program in the belief it will gain his freedom. Maybe I'm being too hard on him, but he questions nothing, and if you combine it with his *just enough effort attitude,* he's adding to our poor scoring more than he realises.

Along with myself, he's a big part of our problems.

I glance under my bunk to check on Diego. I'm never sure if he's awake or not, because he never moves. Of all of us, he's improved the most. He's lost weight and he's stronger than when he first came here, which I didn't think was possible. If his life depended on running he'd be dead, but he looks to have finally accepted he's here and not in his village. His change in attitude has a lot to do with his new belief in Ilse's Graduation story – a day I don't believe is ever going to materialise. In his own way, he's marking time, waiting for that day to come because he's following his hero,

Spencer. But he, too, doesn't understand that he's adding to our problems.

I look back at Rasa's empty bunk. If she hasn't sold us out and she's not a believer in the Graduation story then I need her help to shake our Pod out of its lethargy. She was the enemy and now she could be the true ally I need. If she's more of a natural leader than I am, I should consider letting her be Head of our Pod and stepping down.

The thought hurts my ego, but I have to consider it.

I wake from my recurrent nightmare of thirty-seven points, Ilse, my sister and Rasa as Head, to see our Trainer in full attack-dog mode. Over the last couple of weeks, she'd bordered on friendly as she'd got to know us, but this morning it's back to her old intolerant self. Rasa isn't in either and no one in our Pod can bear to look at one another as this implication of her continuing absence escalates through our minds. Our Trainer points to fresh workout kits within a basket she's brought, before pointing to bathrooms, reminding us to make our beds and keep the dorm spotlessly tidy. Her cobra tattoo looks alive on her arm as she waves at our mess.

We jog out for the Roll Call and I'm expecting the usual morning stretch, followed by the run, where myself and Diego will start another day coming last. But instead, we're steered towards a building in front of us that I've not seen before.

I sigh.

New buildings usually mean new punishing tasks.

'It'll be okay,' I hear Chantal say from the rear, trying to inject some of her ever-present positivity.

It should be me saying those words, but somewhere between going to sleep and this morning, I've lost a part of me. My energy has been depleted, my focus diverted.

Are these the first signs of losing my dignity?

Or have I lost what little hope I had retained, and have Ilse and the System finally beaten me into submission?

And is Rasa dead?

Taylor leads the way and we file through in Pod order. There are few advantages to being last, but I've learnt that on each new assignment the reaction of the Pods in front of me is an indication of what to expect. It acts as a thermometer, giving me a few brief seconds to mentally prepare. The shocked silence rolling toward me makes me look over my shoulder to the rest of our Pod for some form of reassurance. It doesn't come and instead I see that I am worrying them even more.

It should be me reassuring them.

I snap back around and enter a circular shaped room, which is more like a theatre. Stood in the middle of two Guards with her hands bound in front of her and her head bowed is Rasa. At least she's alive. She's still wearing her yellow down-time Tunic from last night, but it's ripped along the right arm and across the front of her shoulders, scuffed everywhere with what looks like floor marks. I think of the story she told me last night of the teachers liking her too much. She's fought back and not just with Suki. I'm looking at something that I'm sure was done after she was taken from the Games Room. The Trainers make us spread out and form a giant ring around Rasa, taking the natural shape of the room.

The door we entered through opens and Ilse is escorted in by two Guards and her Head of Security. They stop on the edges with the Trainers as Ilse continues into the centre of the circle, coming to a halt by Rasa, before turning to address us.

'I can't say this is a surprise. It would have been a surprise if this had been Pod Ten or Pod One. At least you make our lives interesting, Ned, I will give you that.' I say nothing as I stare at the floor. Ilse continues. 'I'm sorry that your celebration for completing Phase One was spoilt by Pod Fifteen. No one believes that it is right and a fit punishment is due. Would you all agree?'

'Yes, Miss,' echoes through the room, Taylor's voice the loudest of them all. He glances over at me, his face stern, his eyes mocking.

'Yet a punishment without learning is wasted. Wouldn't you agree?'

'Yes, Miss,' everyone shouted out again.

Ilse walks toward me and stops within a few centimetres of my face. I can smell soap and perfumes as her presence invades my air.

'It's a weakness not to look at me Ned,' she whispers. 'You know better than anyone here that weaknesses won't be tolerated.' I let my eyes come up and stare into hers. If it's true eyes are a window into somebody else, then all I see is empty cruelty. 'You've given me a problem, Ned, but I'm beginning to understand that is who you are. It's the curse of gravitas. It's your challenge and maybe even mine. You are better than you think and hopefully you will live to understand what that means.' She turns back to face the circle. 'Envy is an insidious emotion, an emotion that lives within us all. Nevertheless, it is not something we at Cadet School will tolerate. Envy destroys families. It causes rifts that simmer for years. As your mother, it is my duty to stamp such evil from your minds. Harmonious Pods are our goal.'

Ilse turns back toward me and steps in close for a second time. 'I won't tell you again to look at me, Ned.'

I do as I'm told.

'A member of your family attacked another family member, because she was jealous of a potential union. A union that had nothing to do with her and was motivated by personal satisfaction. What am I to do, Ned?'

My eyes dart to Rasa before coming back to Ilse.

'You have to set an example.'

'That's right, Ned. For the greater good of us all I have to set an example. It is my duty to purify everyone's soul, including yours. Yes, Ned – *The Soul*. It is no longer a prohibited word. You are free to use it.'

The word attacks me from all angles and I'm sure I flinch. Its use is prohibited, but the *Denounced* at the Holding Centre chanted it as a show of defiance after lights out. I never joined in, not even saying the word in my head, because I was innocent. And I'm not sure my mouth can even shape the word to make the sound. I don't want to say it.

Ilse walks back toward Rasa, turning to face us.

'Violence is no way to satisfy emotions you cannot handle. As the Head of Pod Fifteen was unable to control one of his own, we give him the right to punish that member, and to remind the others of the importance of structure and command. Therefore, it is right and fitting that Rasa 4-3-4-2-7-3-1 be subjected to four electronic charges administered by the Head of her Pod.'

Gasps echo out and I have to take a small step forward to steady myself as what I'm about to do sinks in. I don't bother to look at Taylor, Suki or Marcellus. I know what to expect from them and I'm raging inside at what I'm sure is an injustice toward Rasa.

It's the corrupt System turning its wheels again.

A Guard shoves me in the back, forcing me forward into the centre of the ring. Rasa is having the ties cut and is fighting back her tears. When the silence returns, a second

Guard enters the circle carrying a box of four silver oval shaped electronic grenades. I've seen them on the News, but I've never seen one up close. They are mostly used by our Secular Police for crowd control. You throw them like you would a stone and they explode in front of the person or persons, catching them in an electric arc. If used effectively by trained personnel they can keep an angry crowd penned in and under control. Much depends upon the settings and the accuracy of the throwers, but even at a low setting, four electronic grenades are going to leave Rasa badly shaken.

They say you have to be careful for what you wish for.

A few week ago, I would have been first in the line to throw one of these grenades at Rasa and now it's the last thing I want to do.

Rasa also has another problem apart from the grenades.

Me.

I've always been strong in the shoulders and I've played Community Homes' Inter-League Baseball as the first pick pitcher. I'm good at throwing balls. Very good, I think, when a thought drops through me at hammer speed. Spencer said he was proud of being picked and saved from his death. Proud of being one of the elite to have been chosen to come here.

But how did they pick us?

What was the criteria?

Ilse could have given me an electronic baton to administer four lashes of the electronic whip but, no, instead, I have to throw these four grenades. It's like she knows that throwing a ball is a skill of mine.

But who told her this?

Where did the information come from?

'It won't be good for your Pod if you deliberately miss. Do we understand each other, Ned?'

I nod.

'I said, do we understand each other?'

'Yes, we understand each other.'

I reach into the tray and remove the first steel ball from its foam protective cup. The oval shape is a good size, slightly smaller than a tennis ball, with grips etched into the longer of the two sides. I expected it to be cold to touch, but there's a light warmth generated from the hum of the charge that is pulsing into the cup of my palm.

'We don't expect you to stand there and get hit,' Ilse announces with a chuckle in her voice. 'I give you permission to attempt to escape Ned's throwing ability. If you do escape one or all of them then I would consider that as part of your training and a worthy way to mitigate your intended punishment. Good luck,' she announces to us both.

Marcellus and the Trainers start to stamp their feet.

Everyone quickly joins in and the beat and the fear and the frenetic energy vibrate through my chest.

The circle splits at one end and the lights are dimmed. The back wall where Rasa has been moved to brightens. She's thrown into silhouette, her face indistinguishable, like she's wearing a mask. I contemplate tossing the grenade at Ilse, I'd hit her no problem. A second Guard trots into the centre and stands next to me. He has an electronic baton in his hand, primed to go, the message clear enough. I'll get whipped if I look like I'm not trying, or dare to throw one of these grenades at anyone else but Rasa.

I glance up across at my number Two. I can't see her face, but her stance is defiant as ever. A whistle is sounded and the punishment, or is it entertainment, begins.

Rasa darts right, then left, and looks to duck low. As she comes up and darts right again, I hit her square on the thigh with the first grenade. It explodes in an arc of blue electric light, encasing her in a web of pain. She screams and collapses to the floor, writhing in pain for a few seconds. She didn't stick a chance. I wait while she picks herself up from the floor. I've never hated myself as much as I do in this moment. The Guard presents a second grenade for me to take. Hand trembling, I pull my arm back and curl it in with speed, hitting the top of her left arm. It knocks her sideways, wrapping her in another net of electronic agony. I have two left. I can curl the next one close to her neck and it should miss enough to give us both a pass. I pull back my arm and take aim, waiting for her to move before I let fly. She ducks right and I throw the grenade, crying inside, because I've learnt something else in this moment as my missile hurls toward her.

It's the worst pain in the world when you hurt the person you love the most.

25

I take a deep breath, aim at Rasa's right calf, then let fly with my last punishment grenade.

A second later, Rasa buckles in pain, collapsing to the floor as she grabs at her leg.

It's over.

That makes three direct hits and one miss. Of my three connects, I've deliberately caught Rasa in non-vital areas, and at the edges of her body. At any other time, I'd be patting myself on the back for four brilliant pitches, but I'm just thankful it was me throwing and not Taylor or Suki, or one of the Guards. I tell myself, I have to chalk this moment as victory for our Pod. Ilse would lose face if she punished us further for an infringement of her rules and she's not going to do that. To the uninformed, I have carried out Ilse's instructions to the full, but I've twisted them to our advantage and lessened the pain of one of our own.

The final sparks of the electric charge die from the room, the crackle replaced by an eerie silence as if the world has stopped spinning. Then the lights come on and a different urgency rushes into the void. Kuro, Spencer and Diego sprint across to the far wall to help Rasa. It's an outpouring of emotion I didn't expect. Chantal gallops across and throws her arms around me, hugging me in front of everyone. She lacks any self-consciousness when it comes to her feelings and her show of affection catches me by surprise. It's the first hug I've had in years, never mind a public one. I tense like a tree stump and once I've unfrozen myself from the initial shock, I gently push her away, although I secretly like her even more than I already do. I see her more and more as a key member of our Pod. She's our barometer, a guide to how we're functioning as a family, with an honesty I trust completely.

The boys guide Rasa into the centre of the room. She's dazed and unsteady, but she's doing her utmost to hide the pain, not only from ourselves, but from everyone who is watching. She knows better than any of us the importance of keeping how you feel locked inside. All my pent-up rage and hatred towards her has been extinguished. I'm seeing a different person to the one I saw twenty minutes before. We're the same person, I think. We've both been in the System for most of our lives; let down by everyone around us, including close family, with only ourselves to work out how to survive. We've had to discover our own moral compass. Throughout this constant upheaval, we've been strong enough to keep our independence. That's what I've hated about her and I don't any more. I saw it as a threat. We haven't been institutionalised in the same way Spencer and, in some ways Kuro, have become. Chantal and Diego haven't been entwined in the System long enough to become affected that way, but they are dealing with the shock of being here in ways I don't agree with. Chantal has hung her hopes on staying overly positive and ignores the reality, while Diego has latched himself onto Graduation and the carrot of Freedom. I've viewed their outlooks as negative, but maybe I shouldn't any more?

Maybe I should play on their expectations and, with the help of Rasa, we can improve our overall Rankings in Ilse's secret Table of Doom.

Head of Security, Ilse and Marcellus are nowhere to be seen. As I look around for them, I catch sight of Taylor and although his face is solemn, like the rest of the Pod's, his eyes are still mocking me. It's part of his campaign to be the alpha-male amongst all eighty-four of us and it's giving me a growing problem. He sees me as a threat and he's not going to let up until he wins, and I can no longer continue to let him undermine me. The System has taught me that his mocking smirks will soon turn physical, then continued bouts of violence. The bump with the basketball was his litmus test, the start. He's forcing me to show my hand, waiting to see what I'm made of. It's been his game from day one and I've been ignoring my own instincts, hoping I was wrong, hoping it would go away.

It won't.

It never does.

And we're trapped in each other's space, and his personality won't let the two of us co-exist. He sees life in winning and losing terms. It's a blinkered view of the world. Compromise means weakness and that's something he can't contemplate.

We head to the Canteen after another pointless Roll Call, like any of us have had the slightest opportunity to attempt an escape since the last count. I don't think anyone would risk their Graduation even if a genuine escape presented itself.

I'm not hungry, but I'm not allowed to move to our table until I take a full breakfast. As Rasa approaches, I shuffle across the bench to make space for her to sit. It's my first open gesture of kindness toward her and the others clock it immediately. She sits next to me. None of us speak, but it's more to do with the hubbub in the Canteen taking longer than usual to build to a level we deem private enough to talk between ourselves.

Once it does, I'm about to speak when Rasa says, 'Thanks for not hitting my face.'

I shrug.

'I was saving it for the next four.'

It drags the edges of a smile to her face and it reminds me how beautiful she is, more so, with this pained expression within her eyes.

You're not allowed to date in the Homes, but everyone does. I had a girlfriend once and we'd kiss in secret, but I didn't like the attention it drew once people found out we were dating. It's hard to operate and keep your reputation when everyone is gossiping behind your back, so I broke it off and promised myself I wouldn't date again until I was free. I remember she cried and I struggled with those emotions. I also remember the warmth of our relationship, and the confusion it gave me, having to trust someone outside of myself.

I wonder if I could ever trust Rasa that way, what with everything that has gone before us?

'Is there anything I can do?' Chantal says, genuine concern on her face. She leans in and puts her arm around Rasa's shoulders. Rasa acknowledges the gesture with a smile before gently shrugging herself free. 'Yes, you can,' she says, bringing us together with her stare. 'Ned has something important to say. Tell them what you told me,' she says.

I feel myself flush as my throat dries. I want to hug her myself, but I don't, of course. I just nod back, a tight smile held within. I gather my thoughts, as I check nobody from the other Pods or a Trainer is within eavesdropping distance. I'm safe to talk as long as I keep my voice low.

'I don't have any proof, but I think the Pod that comes last isn't going to get out of here, maybe none of us are.'

'What! Are you saying we're not going to survive?' Spencer snaps back, louder than I would have liked.

I instinctively glance around me, making sure nobody has caught his words or his tone. The hubbub continues and nobody is looking over. The nearest Trainer is five tables away.

'We have to be up in the top group to stick any chance of surviving, because if this place was a genuine second chance then it would have happened in Court and we wouldn't have been snatched from the rope. We are here because we're dispensable. People who are dispensable don't get their freedom after what will be a fake Graduation.'

'Don't say that,' Diego says. 'Why would Ilse lie? Once you get over the shock of this place and what we have to do, it's okay. There are plenty of Military Style Homes for those who constantly get into trouble.'

'How often were you in trouble before they accused you of being a *Denounced*?

Diego purses his lips then looks away.

The answer is *never* and he knows it. It's the same for Chantal and Spencer, and even Kuro to a degree.

'There's nothing okay about being here,' Rasa says, her voice soft but direct. 'Ned's making sense.'

'You're just angry because of what just happened to you. When you calm down, you won't think he's making sense,' Spencer says, defensively.

'Last night a Guard told me that when this was all over, he was going to come looking for me to have some fun.'

Her words and its implications swirl around our tight table. There's a moment's silence then the Pod comes to an unspoken agreement.

'So what do you suggest?' Kuro says, looking at me.

'First, we need to move up the Rankings and take some of the heat off us.' I check nobody outside our Pod can hear me then I turn back to face our table. 'We then make a plan to escape. A real one.'

'WHAT! Have you forgotten what happened to Pod Eight?' Spencer says, the anger in his voice simmering close to boiling point.

'You've gone crazy,' Diego says. 'There's no way I'm putting myself through that again. Not a chance. Don't count me in.'

I look at Chantal. Her arms are crossed in front of her chest, tears starting. 'My dad used to say that if something was too good to be true then it probably is and I should watch out. I would like to know more about this *Mission* and how it ties into our Graduation. Do we get some certificate that says we're no longer *Denounced*? I keep wanting to ask, but I'm too scared to.'

Nobody says anything and I look at Kuro for his answer.

He shrugs and pushes at the front of his glasses.

'The whole Mission thing scares me but I agree with Chantal. Is our record scrubbed clean? They'll hang us if they catch us even planning an escape. You know that, don't you?'

'We're lying to ourselves if we think being here is an accident and that being in these Pods is some random event.'

'What do you mean by that?' Diego says, glancing at Spencer for some buddy support.

'He means we've been picked and profiled for this *Mission*,' Rasa says, her tone sharp and uncompromising.

It catches Diego off guard, all of us, really.

'How are we going to get up the Rankings?' Chantal asks, getting to the point.

'We have to stop pretending we're a working Pod and start being one.'

Rasa nods her agreement.

Chantal wipes her eyes, then nods.

More despondency rakes across Diego's face, before he gives a solitary agreeing nod.

Spencer sighs, dropping his head into hands.

'I just wanted another chance.'

'We all do, but we have to make it ourselves and not rely on Ilse,' I say.

I glance across at Kuro waiting for his answer, because I need all five of them to buy into what I'm saying. Even one unsure member will eventually poison the rest.

'I'm not sure if this helps, but I know a way we can cheat at the Obstacle Course and make up some points.'

26

When I first became an orphan, it didn't take me long to work out that dwelling on my dead parents and the *"what could have beens"* was destined to ruin me. The System let me grieve and cry and hate myself, but after a certain point it churned its gears and confiscated my physical memories, before doing its best to eradicate the ones stored in my mind. Their job was made easier, because I bought into their brainwashing as it gave me a form of peace I was unable to achieve on my own. But I knew from the off that I was being brainwashed and I promised myself never to become institutionalised. And I haven't, even after my sister, Liz, turned her back on me.

But that's all changed since I've been brought here.

Each night when the lights go out, my mind begins to unravel threads of memories I didn't even know existed.

Like tonight.

I've woken in a cold sweat, convinced I'd been talking to my father. He was upbeat and playful as ever – my mother, the more serious and thoughtful of the two. They say opposites attract and looking back on their dynamic, her worrying and his playfulness balanced them out. He loved her, I know that by the way he touched her and looked at her and listened to what she had to say with genuine interest. All things I've never experienced in the System. When he was bothered by a problem that showed on his face, it worried me more, because if my father thought it was serious then it must have been – not that he ever confided in me. I play my internal game of asking his advice, but it's changed. It's me who is

169

doing all the talking and he's staring at me in a confused way, like I might not even be his son. As a kid, when I went to him with a problem, he would listen, a constant smile on his face, and when I'd finished, he would ask me what I thought. I would roll my eyes and pretend it was a big issue before telling him how I would deal with whatever was playing on my mind, like a mini dress-rehearsal to fix the problem.

It was our little game, because he would always answer me in the same measured way.

That's a good idea Ned, but have you thought about this…

And then what I wanted to hear would come.

As it should.

From father to son.

The natural order of growing up.

But, I'm getting to the same point each night and I wake before he finishes his sentence. His advice is getting lost between my dreams and my waking up. It's like he's dead all over again and has let me down. I know his dying wasn't his fault or my mother's, but I sometimes blame them, which is wrong and I can't help it, especially when I get frustrated. Like now.

Or what if it's not him at all, but my question?

Now that I'm older, maybe I have to phrase it differently; ask him from a fresh view point. Perhaps I have to make my question more sophisticated, like an adult would?

But I can't, because I don't know how to, and all I can hear in the background is my sister's doubting voice and my mother's irritability, as if she was too busy and I caught her at the wrong time with any questions I might have. *Ask your father*, she would say. And I'm trying and I keep asking the same question, because I don't know how to phrase it any other way. And it's this.

Why am I here?

I would ask another *Denounced*, but they're not interested in thinking about it, because they're all suffering *Graduation Fever*, except Rasa, who had it inadvertently beaten out of her. I can see in her scowl that she's dwelling on the same question nearly as much as me. That's another important fact about the System. Once you get accustomed to being in it, your problems become the rules they've imposed upon you, and you spend all your time working out how to navigate them. Rather than asking the most important question of all.

Why is it I have to do this?

It's the one question my father forced me to ask all the time, and it's the one question that will get you into the most trouble if you're not careful.

Especially here.

I sigh.

I'm tired of thinking and uncomfortable from the growing pain in my lower back, which I damaged on the Obstacle Course when I took Spencer and Diego's full weight. I've not mentioned it to any of the others as I don't want to worry them, but I'm sure it's getting worse. I've two painkillers left from my First-Aid kit and if that's not enough to see me through, I don't know what to do. None of the Trainers have mentioned a doctor being available and I'm too scared to ask. I ignore the dull ache and glance across at Rasa. She never moves in her sleep. I never gave her stillness a second's thought until she told the story of the Guard. Her death-like mask is the opposite of what's happening inside. She's alert, the lights are on and she's subconsciously listening, waiting for trouble, watching out for someone to creep up on her.

When this was all over, the Guard was going to come looking to have some fun, is what she said.

I know her well enough to know she wouldn't let that lie, but what she said and did, she's kept to herself. I'm convinced it's how she got the additional rips across her Tunic. I'll never know the full story. She's not the type to talk about how she feels. But, since she's shown her support towards me, we've bonded as a Pod beyond my expectations. I hadn't foreseen how cautious Kuro, Spencer and Diego were of her, and how my personal hatred was creating the divisions I blamed the others for. Kuro and Spencer are physically wary of her, while Diego has never met a girl with her personality, which is why he's kept his distance.

All together it's been a disaster for bonding and it's why we've been such a dysfunctional unit and are bottom of the Rankings.

I push up from my bunk-bed, swing my feet over the edge, and gently leap down. I get an unexpected jolt into my lower spine which forces a half buckle in my knees to compensate for the movement, as I let out a silent wince. I check I haven't woke anyone. I haven't. Diego's easy snore has become another comfort to me, like the sound of the extractor fans. It's familiar. A sound that represents normality.

I quietly pad into the boys' bathroom. I want to wash the heat from my face and stretch out my back. I've discovered that if I can twist the muscles in the opposite direction, it eases the pain. I run the tap until the water is ice cold and splash my face. I'm convinced my skin sizzles as I let Kuro's plan to cheat at the Obstacle Course beat through my mind once again. The others don't want to risk it just yet or, I should say, Chantal, Spencer and Diego don't want to try. Rasa's in, as am I, and Kuro wants to go with the majority, even though it was his idea. He blames himself for the botched escape and the death of Pod Eight, so he's careful not to push his ideas in case they backfire onto him.

I always secretly thought Kuro was sneaky and not to be altogether trusted. I was wrong and it was short-sighted of me. He's slim and wirily built. He's not a warrior like Rasa. He's lived his life in a *Doubters' Camp* where he's had to learn to steal, and live on his wits to survive. He's developed speed over strength for both his mind and body. It's natural for him to assess the Obstacle Course and to spot where he can outwit it. I've been looking at the Obstacle Course from my own viewpoint, knowing I can use my strength to improve my time.

But who is the wiser?

Maybe Kuro.

Chantal is a natural athlete and the most physically efficient person I've ever met. I've viewed all her attributes as weaknesses, when I should be looking to use what she brings. I'm sure she could teach us a lot about energy preservation. Diego's a good guy, he processes information slowly, yet he's unbelievably strong. When he pinned Rasa to the floor, two of us couldn't shift him and it was only reason that won the moment. I'd like to bet he's stronger than many of the Trainers and even some of the Guards. The thought brings a smile to my face.

Our secret weapon.

The hammer within our Pod.

Spencer's lazy and it's always annoyed me. In the back of my mind, I blamed him more for our order in the Rankings than any of the others, but again the problem is mine, not his. I've missed the power of his easy charm. People instantly warm to him and they often feel obliged to tell him things about themselves and other people. When we're not together as a collective Pod, even the Trainers relax around him and don't seem to associate him with Pod Fifteen, the perpetual losers. We should use him to harvest information about this place and especially the other Pods. There's even an old trick I learnt the hard way but we could use him to spread stories to suit our needs. He's another secret weapon we've left lying around unused. It's the same for Rasa. She's way smarter than all of us put together and she has this ability to take a glimpse into the future, it's like a sixth sense she keeps locked inside. We should be using it to get a first advantage move. If I can, I need to coax those thoughts out of her.

Maybe if I can't then it's a job for Chantal?

That leaves me.

I'm clueless to what I bring to this Pod other than having successfully nosedived us to the bottom of the Rankings. I'm sick of debating what Ilse's *gravitas* means and how it can help our Pod. I see Ilse's faint praise as nothing but trouble and I wish she'd never told me. I hate it, whatever it is.

I dry my face and step out of the bathroom, springing back like a startled cat, lucky to stay on my feet.

Stood in front of me, a scowl chewing into her face is Rasa.

She puts a finger to her lips and points me into the girls' shower room.

27

I glance toward the main dorm, expecting to see the others. I don't and Rasa's made a point of closing the inner door, which only adds to my concern. I step into the girls' bathroom, picking up on Rasa's urgency. She snaps the door shut behind us, then steps across me to the walk-in-shower and turns the taps to full-blast. The noise from the water hitting the tiles and the extractor vents combine to make an explosive echo around us.

'What's going on?' I ask, trying to sound more in control than I actually feel.

'There's a camera in our main quarters. It's new, I think it's only been there for the last few weeks. If there's a camera, there'll be a mic. I haven't spotted a camera in the space between the two bathrooms or our bathroom,' she says.

'WHAT! Slow down...Camera...Listening to us?' I say, glancing around me, seeing nothing but light-green tiled walls and the mirror on the wall above the sink, which is beginning to steam over.

'The bathrooms are clear, but I don't know how good the microphones will be. Probably excellent, if the rest of this place is anything to go by. The noise from the shower and the fan should muffle our voices, but keep your voice to a whisper. You shout sometimes, especially when you get nervous.'

I look around the bathroom again but with a more discerning eye, as steam fills the room. The only place there could be a camera is behind the mirror and I lean in to get a closer look.

'It's not two-way. I've checked it more times than I can remember,' Rasa says with an air of authority.

I nod, then we stare at each other, each waiting for the other to speak. The truce we'd slowly cultivated has gone and all my insecurities about her have flooded back.

Why has she chosen now?

Why this approach?

I'm not a person who likes unexpected dramatic moments. They break my rhythm and put me on edge for days. The System likes to play with you in this way. It's to make you worry; to make you think they know best, when really they don't. It's done for no other reason than control, just another way to undermine you and have you behave in a way you might not if you knew all the information.

Like now, perhaps?

'I don't go loud when I get nervous,' I say in a whisper.

'You do. It's how I know you're nervous.'

She smiles.

I don't.

'What's going on?'

'Are you serious about escaping?'

I tense some more. On my hate list after Court Officials, Electronic Batons and Unexpected Surprises are questions answered with questions. In my experience, people who do that are rarely honest. Like my Lawyer and my sister, and most of the Wardens I've had. The new question ends up deflecting your question, and if you're not careful, you get tangled in new thoughts and you never get the answers you wanted in the first place. And to make it worse, the answer she wants could get me hanged for just thinking about it so my lips are suddenly glued.

'I'm tired and I want to go back to bed. Let's talk in the morning.'

I move toward the door, but she steps across me and leans in, blocking my exit. I'd have to manhandle her out of the way to get out.

I pause because I've got the home advantage. She came looking for me and not the other way around.

'We can't talk tomorrow, because we won't get the chance, or not in private. Are you serious about escaping?' she says.

'You first...what's going on here?'

She sighs, impatient.

'Above the frame of the main door as you step into our dorm is a camera. You can spot it for a split second when the lights get snapped on in the morning. It's behind a glass panel, which is the same colour as our walls, but the sudden change in light is a second too fast for the glass to react. Check it out in the morning, but don't make it obvious, because the angle of the camera can take in the whole of our dorm. Except it doesn't. It's only ever focused on one thing. You.' She pauses and what she said takes hold, making my stomach turn. 'They must be hearing everything we say, which isn't much, so we've lucked-in there. I'm telling you this, because if you're serious about wanting us to escape and getting the others to fully co-operate then don't have the conversation in there. It'll get us killed.'

'Why didn't you tell me before.'

'It didn't matter before, because unless you talk about escape it's just hot air and no-one outside the Pods is going to care.'

I chew on that thought before I say. 'So are you in or out?'

'In, but I want to know what you really believe, not what you've told them,' she says, dropping her hand from the door and nodding toward our dorm.

'What if this place isn't Military School but Gladiator School? Have you thought about that?'

My words slice at her like tiny razors, nicking at her skin. She sees some element of truth in what I've said. *Phase Two* has begun to get more intense and our Trainer has hinted twice that hand-to-hand combat training is soon to be added to our schedule.

'I saw a look in Ilse's eye when she made you take the grenades. She's disappointed in you. Disappointed in a way that bothers her. What did she say to you when you were taken to her? You never did tell us.'

'Does it matter?'

'To me it does.'

'She told me something I didn't understand. I still don't understand.'

Rasa looks at me, waiting. Her eyes burning with a fierce intensity.

'She told me I had *gravitas* and that it was important I was a success.'

'Important that *you* were a success or *we* were a success?'

I think about this for a moment, looking away, my clothes starting to soak up the steam from the shower. I'm beginning to feel the heat and the damp against my skin and it's not all from the hot steam.

'The Pod,' I say. 'But me, too. She had the watch-key that Kuro stole.'

We stare at each other. She doesn't need to tell me I lied to my Pod by withholding the information, although I'm not sure what I would have gained by telling them. The conflicting emotions I feel for Rasa confuse me further: *anger, love, hatred, warmth, kindness, spite*, all colliding through me.

'I guess she's right.'

'About what?'

'Do you know what gravitas means?'

'No...yes...kind of.'

'Everyone's a bit scared of you, Ned. Even Marcellus. It's why he gives you a hard time.'

'He shouldn't be and you're not.'

'How do you know?'

I say nothing.

'Suki started a fight with me because she wants Taylor, but Taylor is always looking at you. He knows you're a threat, even though we're last in the Rankings.'

'What's that got to do with you?'

'You can be so naive sometimes. It's because of the way you look at me. If Taylor destroys you, then Suki has to destroy me or she loses Taylor. It's how it works in clans.'

I feel a wave of heat flood into the base of my neck. Even through the steamed over mirror, I see my own cheeks flush. I look down trying to hide my embarrassment.

'I didn't mean nothing by it,' I say. 'I'm not like those other people who stare at you.'

'I can't help the way I look, Ned. I sometimes wish I looked different. You know, life might have been easier. No one is ever interested in who I am on the inside or what I have to say.'

I nod.

'As I said, I didn't mean nothing by it.'

'You're right about us having been picked and profiled to come here. When I was taken by the Guards and locked in the overnight cell, I heard them talking and there's going to be some kind of test at the end of this training. It won't be good for the three Pods who come last in the Rankings.'

'Is that what the Guard meant when he said he was going to come looking for you when this was all over?'

'I don't know. But if we're going to die in here, we should at least die trying to escape. None of us in our Pod are *Denounced* and we have to hold onto that. We were nothing but in the wrong place at the wrong time. Spencer's right – we should all have had a second chance.'

'Getting that second chance is going to be hard if not impossible.'

'Impossible for some, but not us.'

I almost smile. 'Yeah, and how do you work that out?'

'Because we've got you. You just have to accept people are going to stare at you and there's nowhere to hide. I can teach you how to handle that, but I can't teach you to believe in yourself, Ned. For all our sakes, you have to do that for yourself.'

28

I'm seething.

Rasa's planned all along to dump a whole barrel load of responsibility my way, which I don't want and didn't ask for. Why do I have to carry our Pod, just because someone tagged me with a label and gave me a job I didn't want? Kuro, Chantal, Spencer, Diego and even Rasa have to step up to the challenge instead of getting more scared each day. If they want to escape or cheat the Obstacle Course, to get up the Rankings, it has to come from them, not me. Their lethargy will get us all killed and I don't know how to tell them any other way then I already have. Rasa pushing the problem back my way is just another way to avoid it.

I'm about to let her know how I feel when a noise from the dorm, like somebody getting up, takes our attention. Before I can say another word, Rasa starts pushing me out of the girls' bathroom in a flustered hurry. It would be a difficult moment to explain to anyone in our Pod, or to one of the Trainers. I open the door to our dorm and step through, all in a rush. It's like entering another world, another dimension, with the soft light and the gentle sounds of sleep humming in the air. I'm dizzy with adrenaline, like I've drunk five cans of fizzy drinks and eaten a dozen sports bars.

Relieved, I don't see anyone awake and I decide the noise must have been one of Diego's volcanic snores that erupt now and then. I quietly climb up into my bunk and wait for Rasa to re-enter, which she does several minutes later. I don't watch her, more sense where she is at any given moment, still seething, as I stare up at the wall above the door. If there is a camera hidden behind it, I can't see it or even detect that the wall is made of a different material. It crosses my mind that I'm being lied to again, but instead of Ilse or the System, maybe it's Rasa who wants to manipulate me.

My hyped-up state eventually subsides and I'm left with a creeping sense of uncertainty about my future as I drift in and out of sleep. Then the lights snap on and I'm too dazed and slow to spot the camera Rasa is convinced is watching us. I see nothing but the wall and the door and a new Trainer demanding we move.

NOW.

He's a Marcellus clone through-and-through, and they could be brothers, even twins. Our group shares a furtive look. We don't need it spelt out that this man is trouble. My gut feeling is his allocation is down to us being last rather than any overheard conversation about escape, and his introduction is Ilse's doing and not Marcellus's.

He continues to snap orders, making everyone nervous. He singles out Chantal and Kuro for not reacting fast enough. I jump from my bunk-bed and encourage them to hurry along, telling Kuro to use the bathroom first. Without taking a pause to see I'm trying to help, he threatens me with a deduction in Ranking Points for over-talking him. I surge with an unexpected anger at his bullying. I stare at him and he steps in close, so I nudge forward. It's not a visible step, more a subtle shuffle of my posture, that could be read by a discerning eye as me not backing down – which I'm not. It's a move you learn in the System and it changes everything. The walls in our dorm feel like they've contracted and nobody takes their next breath.

'Do you have a problem, son?'

Silence.

Then I smile.

It's like the greyness has disappeared and I'm staring up at a bright blue sky and hearing the waves hit the beach. But I'm not. I'm looking at someone who doesn't scare me and I don't know why. Maybe it's because I can see right through his aggressive act and I'm looking at a man who doesn't believe in who he is and what he's doing.

He's a fake.

Like Ilse.

Like this grey wilderness that is our prison.

There's a real world outside, somewhere and I just have to find it.

We all do.

'You're not my father and I'm not your son,' I say.

I turn and head for the bathroom. I move fast and he misses his chance to call me back. When you face up to an official your nerves usually give seconds after the event, but they don't this time. I'm steady. He gave me sixty seconds to get washed and ready. I'm easily longer, much longer. I saunter back into the dorm and take my time putting on my training shoes. I can see the frustration, edged with embarrassment, building in his face, but if he shouts or starts to push me around, he will lose his power.

If he calls out for help, he loses his job.

It's like I'm back in the Holding Centre and digging and frustrating at Court Officials at every opportunity I can.

I stand and we quick-march out of the dorm in Pod order to be met by the other Pods filtering outside. It adds to my victory. Our new Trainer wanted to make us feel late, another failure to add to our growing list. It hasn't worked. We did it in our time and our timings are the same as everyone else's. I glow inside and hope the others are getting the same boost. They need it. We stand to attention and complete our morning's Roll Call, filtering off to our right for the usual and painful pre-breakfast run. Interestingly, the path we normally take is more curved than usual and the incline is markedly different from the day before. There's nothing subtle about it, and it's the first time I hear murmurings that the others have noticed our ever-changing environment. It's comforting to know I've not been imagining these things and I draw another unexpected shot of confidence that I'm not going crazy.

The internal warmth from my victories soon turns cold. Each stride pounds into my lower back and I'm forced to twist my body to compensate for the painful spasms. My back isn't improving by itself and I don't know how to cure it. These morning runs, along with the Obstacle Course and other physical activities are making it impossible to get in any recovery time and I think I have the start of a chronic injury.

'Are you okay?' Rasa says, coming up on my left side.

'I'm like this every morning,' I say, through a tight grimace. 'It's nothing.'

I wipe my brow with my hand and stare ahead. The incline is long and gradual, designed to look easy on the eye. But there's nothing easy about this new run and I start to prepare my mind for the pain ahead. Chantal drops her pace and slips in front of me and I start to mirror her step. Yesterday, she gave myself and Diego a much needed running lesson. She taught us how to roll through our feet; to keep our postures more forward, so we're fluid into each transition, making our step lighter and quicker. Diego looks ten times more efficient and I'm sure I would too if it wasn't for the pain in my back limiting my stride. This was Kuro's idea. Not only to have a lesson from our best runner, Chantal, but to stay together as a pack. The idea is simple enough and I'm irritated I didn't think of it. If we stay together the slow two – me and Diego – will increase our pace, but more importantly, our

Pod should get a better overall score. On each run, we're the most dispersed Pod, with two in the fast group, two in the middle group, and myself and Diego inevitably bookending the laggers. We've missed the main message from Ilse's propaganda machine.

Work together.

Be a functioning family.

I push through my numbing pain, getting my second massive boost of the morning. Diego and I are not last. Without much effort, and even with my stiff back, we've moved up to the top of the laggers group. We've undoubtedly slowed the others, but if Kuro's assessment of the scoring system is correct then we're showing an overall improvement. All is going to plan, but I can see the gap between the slow group and the second group opening up, as it always does about ten minutes in.

'We've got to push on or we'll miss our chance,' Rasa says. 'It's now or never.'

I nod, panting hard; Diego panting harder.

'If we get into the next group, it'll be easier to stay there,' Kuro reminds me.

Diego's fighting hard to keep up. He's doing well, but I don't see he's got any more to give. Spencer reads my mind and falls back to keep stride with his buddy. Kuro then slows to go behind Diego as Rasa tracks my pace; Chantal the head of our one-two-two-one diamond shape.

'Mirror Chantal's step and pace,' Rasa reminds me, her voice full of encouragement.

Sweating hard and panting harder, I nod as I hear Spencer tell Diego to mirror my step. It takes a few moments but then I experience a connectedness I've not had before. My heart rate drops, my stitch vanishes, and the uneven beat of running turns into a synchronised two-step sound of six people in unison. There's a beauty and togetherness in the simplicity of the combined beat. I gather strength in being a single unit, instead of the draining energy of six individuals tugging in different directions.

It's like we're sharing a single heartbeat.

Pod Fifteen aligned for the first time.

Our pace begins to increase, not by much, but enough to pull us forward. I can almost feel the ease of being in Chantal's slipstream, our pacemaker timing it to perfection. If Diego's struggling, he's not complaining and the incline, instead of being our enemy, becomes our best friend. The second group has slowed to take in the challenge and with our increased pace we've merged with them. We continue to push on and our energy moves us in and up into the heart of the second group. We hit the top of the man-made hill and our pace doubles as we career down. I'm concerned for a second we'll fall back, but I've relaxed into our united speed, the adrenaline easing the pain in my back, as we keep our shape and place in the pack.

We hit the bottom and veer right into another short incline, before I spot the Canteen and Finish Line in the middle distance. The fast group usually led by Chantal has stopped and Trainers are taking notes, probably allocating Ranking scores. Sat in a buggy with a pair of binoculars surveying the runners is Marcellus. It's my turn to wish I had a camera to capture this moment. He looks directly at us, removes his binoculars from his face before returning them with a comic speed to check what he's viewed isn't a mirage.

Your eyes haven't deceived you, I want to shout. *You saw it right first time.*

This is Pod Fifteen pulling itself out of the swamp.

29

Diego has started to call Spencer – Spence – shortening his name to a single syllable by dropping the R. It's a sign of their burgeoning friendship, which I no longer treat as a threat, more a benchmark of our Pod's togetherness. Every time I hear it, like now, it makes me think of my father. His name was Michael. My mother called him Mike when they were laughing and joking and Michael when they argued. My sister being the negative person that she is, hinted they were heading for a divorce before the accident. The image of them dying together, angry over something trivial, like my mother's lateness, has always upset me. Should I ever get married, which I doubt, or certainly not until I've surfed some serious waves, I've already made the decision that I will patch-up any disagreements with the person I love as soon as possible.

I glance across at Rasa.

She nods, it's time to start.

I swallow hard, clearing my throat, the steam from the shower filling the girls' bathroom. The noise from the extractor fan is as loud as a cheap exhaust. I've still not seen the camera Rasa is convinced is monitoring our dorm, or me, but the bathrooms have become our emergency War Room as a precaution. We keep our meetings short and to the point, which translates to me doing the majority of the talking. I'm sure I sound like a Taylor or Suki type giving out orders and uninterested in the response of others. Chantal calls it a dictatorship, but she says it with a smile and a wink, so I'm only partially offended. We hold our meetings at the optimal time, which is around an hour before lights come on, according to Kuro, who is slowly becoming our resident Professor. On the pre-arranged day, I'll go to the bathroom first, usually followed by Spencer, Diego, Kuro, Chantal and finally Rasa. Kuro is convinced the camera, if it's there – because no-one else has seen it, either – will be motion-triggered and won't snap into action if it thinks I'm sleepily going to the toilet in the night. I'm not so convinced, and we will have to find another place to talk soon, because if Ilse or Marcellus get a hint at what we are doing, the bathrooms will get cameras fitted ASAP.

I yawn. I'm tired. I wish I didn't have to do this, but I do. We are here to discuss Kuro's plan on cheating the Obstacle Course – or that's what they think. There's going to be no discussion. I've made an Executive Decision they don't know about, except Rasa, who has been pushing me to do it. The others don't want to cheat, because of the deathly consequences, but they are missing the point. It's worth the risk. We're doing better on every task, but I wouldn't say we've been outstanding, and we need an outstanding moment to leapfrog the Ranking positions. We are quicker and fitter at everything we do, but so is everyone else. So really, it's still a quicker form of slow and we're running out of time to make the big leap to excellence. I can't pretend that what I have in my mind is anything else but cheating, but if we come bottom of the Ranking we die, and if we get caught cheating we die, so we might as well take the risk. Go out in a blaze of glory, Rasa said, trying to make light of the situation, although the others don't think that, especially Spencer and Diego who are more risk averse than I would ever have imagined.

Kuro hands me a wad of papers that I've reviewed already, and have started to droop at the edges as they absorb the steam from the shower. His thoroughness at these tasks never fails to impress me. He's drawn each obstacle on the course from memory, and given it a rating from one to twelve. Twelve being the hardest. There's nothing below four, except the Wall that we've nailed as a group and he's rated that at two-point-five. He's listed the main skills for each obstacle and who is the strongest within us at that particular skill. He's drawn up a list of how we should approach each and who should go first and last, and in what order. There are dozens of tiny calculations on each of the pages. I don't understand many of the symbols and I can see why he aced the tests to get out of the *Doubters' Camp*, but my maths is good enough to spot he's worked out we can be forty-three per cent better than we are now.

Forty-three per cent better, I yell in my mind, wanting to fist the air with joy, but I don't.

I turn another dampening page to check a couple of points. There are thirty-seven obstacles in total, spread over six kilometres, or that's Kuro's guess. Personally, I think it's longer, closer to eight. I've worked that part out, because if I have any skill within our group it's seeing sizes and shapes, and especially calculating distance, which is why I knew from day one our environment kept subtly shifting.

Kuro has calculated we are naturally good at eleven of the obstacles and excellent at three, one of those being the Wall. That leaves twenty-six we need to improve on in various degrees. Kuro's been watching how the other Pods approach the problem and, like us, they are naturally good at some and bad at others. This is my favourite part of his analysis. He's made a comprehensive list of what the others do well. No point reinventing the wheel. Our biggest fault is that we come to each obstacle in our family order, me, Rasa, Spencer, Diego, Chantal and Kuro. The other Pods make the same fundamental error. But just because we were given that order from day one, approaching the obstacles in the same way is a tactical mistake. Over the full course, taking in to account different skill levels, it hinders everyone's progress. This is the moment I look them all in the eye and become the dictator Chantal joked about.

I'm going to make them cheat, no excuses accepted.

There are four obstacles the trainers don't monitor because of the way they position themselves, or the fact we are required to go underwater, through a tunnel, or have to navigate one of the derelict buildings. Since Kuro pointed them out, I've been monitoring them with the eye of a hawk and the more I look, the more I know how brilliant his analysis has been.

If we pull it off, we shave ten minutes from our time, which means we'll finish first, which equates to a much higher score, or forty-three percent better.

And this is the best bit, the slam-dunk – we only have to do it once, at the end of the week, on the final run.

The only run that is scored.

I deliver my message. It's non-negotiable unless they want to join Pod Eight in a coffin.

Five anxious faces look back at me, four really, because Rasa knows what is coming and she's being a great actress.

I get the nods I need.

Nothing else to discuss.

I pull apart Kuro's incriminating evidence and flush it down the toilet. Rasa leans in and turns off the shower. We're done and I filter out first to my bunk-bed. Spencer comes in next, followed by Rasa, Chantal and then Diego and Kuro. Each one of us stagger our entrance, making sure we are as quiet as a cat tracking its prey. I sense the tension in the air and although I feel like one of the bullies in the System

I detest so much; my gut is telling me this is the correct decision to have made.

It's an Executive Order for the greater good.

Or, so I hoped.

We couldn't have timed our entrance back into the dorm better. The lights come on and I want to shout *gotcha* as I see the camera for the very first time. Rasa was right all along as she so often is. The sudden change in light is a nano-second too quick for the secret panel to react, but you still have to be looking to spot the error. It makes another decision easy for me to make. No more meetings in the girls' bathrooms. We've exhausted that window of opportunity and we have to find another location to keep up our secret discussions.

Our Trainer looks at me and says, 'Four minutes.'

There's no aggression in his voice. No urgency. Just a simple command with a touch of respect. We all know what happens if we're late and shouting at us is proving counterproductive. He steps out, leaving the door ajar and lets us get on with it. His dog-lead of trust kicks us into our own double time and sense of pride, and we're ready to go well within our allotted time.

He re-enters our dorm, gives it a quick once over, then nods us out.

Outside, it's the standard Roll Call and I'm about to start our jog when a whistle is sounded and we're ordered into buggies that are drawing toward us. Any change of routine makes me tense and I unintentionally transmit my fears to the rest of our Pod. I'm annoyed at myself that I've sucked out their energy as I climb into our designated vehicle. The one positive is my back is getting a rest. I've been struggling with the pain and it's another reason I've forced our Pod to cheat on the Obstacle Course. I can't risk making us any slower. Rasa has worked out I have a problem. If the others know they are keeping it to themselves, although I suspect Chantal has guessed. She caught me limping after the run yesterday, but said nothing, her downward glance telling me all I needed to know.

We motor along another new road. The buildings are hard to tell apart, except for our Canteen where the steps into the building have worn from the constant use. I use the steps to get a fixed bearing. The Canteen was behind us when we climbed into the buggy. I've given the steps a North point in my mind, so we're heading due South and have been for at least three kilometres.

The buggies snake to a stop and we're ordered out. The first seven Pods go through one door and the rest of us are led through a second door on the left. Inside is cold and airy, and we head down a ramp into a basement. There's an excitement and shouts of laughter from the Pods in front of us and I soon see why. We've entered a Shooting Range with rows of long concrete alleys, like bowling alleys, and human cut-out targets of court officials and lawyers attached to motorised rails in the ceiling, allowing the targets to be moved backwards and forwards. At the front of each concrete alley is a large metal table. On the table is a handgun along with a fresh case of electronic bullets. I've seen the guns on the guards at the Holding Centre and here, but they've always been holstered. I've never been this close to one before, and I'm both fascinated and scared in equal measures.

Several Trainers, wearing goggles and protective body-armour appear and call us over in pairs into the concrete alleys closest to each Pod. Myself and Rasa go first from Pod Fifteen. The Trainer hands us a pair of goggles and protective vests. He asks us if we've ever handled a gun before. In unison, we shake our heads.

'That's a good place to start', he adds. 'No bad habits.'

He picks up the black and silver handgun from the table. The handle is made of a resin and the barrel is metal, supported by more resin to keep the gun lightweight. The end of the barrel funnels out slightly and looks odd, like it's swollen. He tells us this is a design enhancement that keeps the user from getting electrocuted if the bullets malfunction. He then goes through the basics:

Trigger.

Sight.

Safety catch.

Magazine.

Grip.

The handgun carries eight electronic bullets and one in the chamber, being nine in total. He tells us that if you keep your finger on the trigger, it will dispense all nine bullets in under half-a-second. The trigger has two settings:

Single shot.

Full automatic.

On the opposite side of the safety catch is another switch with three more settings:

Stun.

Maim.

Kill.

'As you can see, kill has been disabled on this practise gun, but it won't be on the one given to you at the end,' he says with no emotion.

Rasa and I share a glimpse of panic between us.

Gladiator School ringing through my mind, hers, too, I'm sure.

'Why's that?' I say, feeling a wedge of tension in the base of my stomach.

'Because when they try and kill you, you'll need the ability to kill them first if you want to stay alive.'

30

Phase Two has fallen into its own routine, depressing me more than I thought was possible.

Our days are full of running, shooting and survival techniques that include learning to light fires, build bivouacs and skin rabbits. I don't know why I have to learn these tasks but no-one is going to ask, myself included. Some of these techniques, I know, because one of my Community Homes was close to a National Park and we spent a lot of time outside, even in the dead of Winter.

That was fun.

This isn't.

My war speech and executive decision on cheating the Obstacle Course has fallen off a cliff. We haven't been near it for days, much to the joy of Spencer and Diego, who I'm sure were going to back out at the last minute anyway. I sense they are using each other's strength to grow in confidence. They won't openly admit it, but they still believe in Graduation and that life isn't too bad in here once you look past the obvious faults of the place. As much as I like them both, they're being dumb or at least in denial and I don't know what to do to make them see the truth of what is happening to us. I'm close to telling them about our Shooting Instructor's comment about kill or be killed, but I'm waiting for the right moment. I don't want to seem desperate to convince them or it'll work against me, only adding to their stubbornness.

I shudder at the matter-of-factness in his voice, and the more I relive the moment, the more I believe he let slip a

194

secret he should have kept to himself. I push up from the breakfast table and head toward the Collection Area with my used tray. The others are ahead of me and I'm thinking about Spencer and Diego when I see what's going to unfold before me a split second before it happens. Kuro is about to place his tray on one of the collection slots when a boy from Pod One comes up on his blind side. It looks innocent enough, but I've seen this kind of behaviour hundreds of times before, and it's the speed that gives the true intent away.

The boy is close enough to Kuro to make him think it's one of us approaching.

As he instinctively turns, the boy raises his elbow and swings it out and round.

With his violent intent and Kuro's full turning force, the impact is explosive.

Kuro drops to the floor, like he's been shot, splitting his lip from what I can see. He cries out as the boy looks all innocent, indicating his arm was raised because he was about to lift his own tray into the slot in the wall. The Trainer pushes the boy from Pod One away as Chantal and Rasa rush to help Kuro to his feet. It's the second time they've targeted him, and in the Games' Room yesterday one of the girls from Suki's Pod tried to strain Chantal's ankle with a fake collision.

Luckily for us, Chantal's quick reactions saved her.

I rush over and check on Kuro. It's worse than I thought. He's standing with his head titled back, his nose broken. In some ways, it's a complement to Pod Fifteen, although I'm not going to tell Kuro that. It's clear to everyone we've improved and the other Pods have started to take us more seriously. They now mirror our running technique in the morning. It's pushed us back in the pecking order, but we're still solidly in the second group of runners, despite my chronic back pain and Diego's heavy stride. All round, we're working better as a group and we've had an unexpected bonus – we're all good shots, especially Kuro who is excellent. He learned to shoot in the *Doubters' Camp* where they hunted giant rats for extra food. It's illegal for a *Doubter* to have a gun so Kuro has consistently lied to our Trainer about being a lucky beginner – a lucky beginner who gets a bullseye, blindfolded, but I'll take our luck where I can. We still don't know how we've scored overall in the Rankings but, whatever it is, it's better than it was and I sense we're a threat to Taylor's and Suki's unofficial Alliance.

'Are you okay?' I ask Kuro.

He nods that he is, but he clearly isn't.

I give Diego a filthy look. I'd tasked him with keeping an eye on Kuro, being his unofficial bodyguard. These are the moments Diego needs to be vigilant and he was too busy sharing a joke with Spencer. Kuro's been instrumental in looking for gaps and ways to potentially gain us points in our daily tasks, but his mood seesaws between ultra highs to depressed lows. When he's in one of his dips, he goes all silent and it can last for days. This is not the time to lose our analytical expert. I'm angry at Diego and even Spencer. I need to make them see the truth of Graduation.

We leave the Canteen and are made to do another Roll Call, before whistles direct us like cattle to a building I recognise as the one we received our haircuts. I run my hand over the back of my head. The bristle-feel has grown out, but my hair is short enough to avoid another cut, I'm sure. As we approach the building, Trainers split us, sending the girls left and the boys right. Inside is a changing room with steel benches and hooks on the wall and we're made to strip down to our underwear, before being led in smaller groups into a second chamber that has been kitted out as a makeshift medical centre. The white is glaring and reminds me of the first days here when I spent most of my time squinting from the brightness. A doctor spots Kuro's bruised face and immediately calls him over. I watch the doctor pull the tissue from Kuro's nostrils before touching his nose. Kuro cries out in pain. It's a bad injury and is going to hurt for weeks. I'm called over by a second doctor. He asks me a bunch of questions about how I'm feeling. I slip into my grunt mode. I don't trust these moments and he's noting what I say into an electronic notepad. It reminds me of my last morning in the Holding Centre when the Court Official came to finish the documentation before my pending death. The doctor asks me to turn around and then prods me in my lower back, like he knows I have a problem. I do my best to hold in the pain, but my sharp intake of breath when he prods the centre of the sweet spot gives me away. He types something into his notebook, before telling me to stand on a set of scales. To my shock, I've lost five kilos. It's the lightest I've ever been, even with all the food I've been consuming since I got here. Apart from the small mirror in our bathroom, I've not seen a full-length reflection of myself since I've been here and certainly not one in my underwear. In the glass cabinet opposite, I see I have the start of stomach muscles and my stockiness has the beginnings of a muscular definition that it's never previously had.

The doctor opens the glass cabinet and asks me to turn around. I feel something cold on my back as he vigorously rubs a small section. I then flinch and tense as he unexpectedly jabs a needle into my lower left side, close to my spine.

'That should fix it,' he says, handing me a small plastic container. 'Take two of these each night before you go to bed. Next,' he calls out not looking at me, which I assume means I've been dismissed. I walk back into the Changing

Room. Taylor is across the room and it's the first time I've seen him undressed. His body is ripped and powerful and he's proud of his physique. I suspect his body was like that before he arrived and all this fitness has improved on an already solid base. He turns and we lock stares and he flexes his arm muscles, like he's telling me he's stronger and he knows it.

'If you're trying to turn me on, it's not working,' I say.

His face falls into a murderous frown as giggles fill the room. He stares about him and the sudden laughter dies away as fast as it came. I don't wait around, pushing Kuro toward the door.

'Why did you do that?' Kuro says.

'You just concentrate on getting us more points. Let me worry about him.'

Outside, there's another Roll Call and then we're marched in double time to what will end up being the Assembly Hall. It's East of the Canteen steps and the only time we go East is when we're heading to meet Ilse. I'm not wrong and fifteen minutes or so later, we take our usual positions on the grids. Pod Eight is still marked out and I'm transfixed by the six empty spots. I finally understand it's a reminder to everyone of what happens if we don't kowtow to Ilse's commands. It's then the lights start to dim and a spotlight suddenly illuminates her like a magician has made her appear.

Seeing her turns my stomach into a knot.

My palms go dry.

Her sweet smile makes me want to vomit and I catch my own earlier thought that she's the biggest fake within this fake world.

'My children, you continue to amaze me. Your dedication to the cause and unyielding commitment to what we demand is beguiling. I can't tell you enough how much I admire and love you all.' She places her hands across the centre of her chest and bows her head. 'We have some surprise movers within our in-house competition and credit should also be given where credit is due. Our black sheep has raised its game.'

Ilse turns to the screen as the room goes dark. It flashes with an array of colours that soon fade into sparkling embers to reveal the new Rankings Order.

Pod One: 590
Pod Eleven: 588
Pod Twelve : 580
Pod Thirteen: 567
Pod Six: 567
Pod Nine: 555
Pop Fifteen: 554
Pod Two: 534
Pod Five: 528
Pod Ten: 524
Pod Three: 510
Pod Fourteen: 492
Pod Seven: 465
Pod Four: 464
Pod Eight: 0

'Yeeees,' Diego says under his breath.

'A fifty per cent improvement,' Kuro says. His voice nasal through his broken nose and not sounding like him.

'Suki's Pod Nine has dropped to sixth place, only one point ahead of us,' Rasa says.

'That's why they tried to break my ankle,' Chantal adds.

'Closer to Graduation,' Spencer says. I can hear the smile in his voice, Diego nodding his agreement, like a puppy without a thought in its head.

'Join me in giving Pod Fifteen a round of applause. It's remarkable what can be done when you apply yourself.'

The rest of the *Denounced* start to salute us, led by Ilse. The heat of being at the centre of attention crashes through me once again and I realise being Head is taking an extra toll on my health that I hadn't taken into account before now.

The applause begins to die and I turn to Spencer and Diego and mouth.

'We need to talk.'

And there's nothing friendly about how I say it.

31

Rasa tells me I did the right thing.

She's probably right, but I handled it like an amateur and I've once again fractured our Pod with Diego and Spencer in one camp; the others in another, with myself stuck in the middle, feeling insecure and isolated. Yesterday, when we left the Assembly Hall, I told Spencer and Diego in no uncertain terms this was Gladiator School and Graduation was a beguiling myth. I thought Diego was going to knock me out, but he backed down, tears flooding his eyes with Spencer walking off, mumbling something about me being deluded. After lunch, we were summoned to the Obstacle Course and they protested by going slow. It was an immature and dangerous move, which has cost us some of our hard-earned gains.

I'm angry at the pair of them.

Or maybe, I'm just angry at myself for my lack of leadership skills and my blunt approach.

Either way, so much for having gravitas.

It's a curse, not a blessing.

We enter the building I was made to punish Rasa in and those painful memories flood back. As I cross the threshold into the room, I immediately recognise the acidic plastic smell of crash-mats. This has to be Combat Training Day, and it's been a long time coming. I wonder why Ilse and the Trainers have left it this long. I don't come up with a satisfying answer other than everything they do is well thought out and we're sure to understand in time, as I glance over my shoulder to check on the others. What's in store for us this morning is slowly peeling across their disappointed faces. This is going to be an especially tough day for Kuro who's spent his life running from confrontations. He's a thinker, not a fighter, and his face is the colour of the grey wilderness outside. I put a comforting arm around his shoulder. 'You're not fighting, just learning how to. There's a difference.'

'It's easy for you to say. You can protect yourself.'

'I'll let you into my secret,' I say with a smile. 'It's hard to hit someone who doesn't stand still.'

Kuro does his best to smile as we filter into the room and fan out into a large circle, surrounding Marcellus who is stood centre stage waiting for us to enter. He's removed his track-suit top and he's wearing a white tank-top that shows off his muscular physique and hairy arms and chest. His skin is the colour of dark clay and I wonder what Quadrant he's from?

'I feel sick,' Chantal whispers. 'It would be him of all people to take this session.'

'Dude, this so sucks,' Spencer mumbles under his breath.

It's the first time he's spoken to me in twenty-four hours and the defeatism in his voice catches me off guard. Diego looks equally despondent and Kuro's right leg has begun to shake involuntarily. It triggers the memory of the boy in the Holding Centre who was stood in front of me and wet himself, and I shuffle forward to block a direct view to Kuro. It's not good for him or our Pod if people see him this nervous.

Marcellus flexes his arms, interlocking his fingers, before cracking his knuckles. Coming from him, the sound is intimating and he knew the effect it would have on everyone. He asks for a show of hands for who's been to Combat School. It's a fake question. We've all been profiled before we came here and he knows the answer even before all the obvious hands go up, and there are few surprises, for me at least. All the girls from Arianne's Pod have their hands in the air, but not the boy. He definitely doesn't have a voice in that group. Rasa is the only one from our Pod, which isn't a surprise after seeing how she dealt with Suki. Taylor, of course, was the first to throw his hand in the air. Suki's a no – I'm surprised. Marcellus scans the rest of us, making a point of stopping at me and raising an eyebrow, like I'm holding back.

I'm not and he's faking this moment.

'Ned?' he asks.

'I've never been to Combat School,' I say.

Cage fighting is the number one sport in the Non-Secular World. You can make hundreds of millions of digital credits if you're good at it. The Community Homes System is one of the biggest feeding grounds for fresh blood. Legally, the promoters are allowed to come to the schools and sign up talent from the age of fourteen. They say lots of digital credits are transferred illegally so promoters can get the heads-up on who is going to be the next biggest name, and the authorities turn a blind-eye to the activity because the sport is so popular. At twelve you can request to go to one of the Community Homes that feed the sport if you've been in the System for over a year. I more than qualified. Instead of going to college you effectively enrol yourself into fight school. I was never interested in taking that route, as my dream was – still is – to become an engineer. I want to build things not destroy them. I've learned to look after myself over the years, because the System puts you in situations where you have no choice. Maybe that's what Ilse meant when she said I had *gravitas*. I learnt fast that there's a difference between being able to defend yourself from the roaming bullies who infest the System like sewer rats, and wanting to fight everyone you meet to prove a point. Most people look at me and make the same assumption. They believe, because I'm tall and big for my age it means I'm naturally aggressive. It's not true, although I was fascinated with old-school boxing for a while – The Gentleman's Sport as it was once called. I was taught by an old PE Teacher and I liked that you couldn't hit below the belt and that there was a code of conduct. I would talk old-school boxing with Jack. He would mention people I'd never heard of, people who were born in the Old World before the Terrorist Wars. He had a way of discussing them like he's shaken their hands, especially a man called Cassius Clay who was supposed to have been the greatest heavyweight boxer that ever lived. If he was alive now, he would have moved from the Non-Secular World to the Secular World so he would have been a *Denounced*. I once shadow boxed in my cell with Jack. We laughed so much, and for a man with a heart complaint and more than twice my age, I didn't even get close to him, while he tapped me on the chin a couple of times with his fists.

That's it about boxing.

It's all about the sport and respect.

Cage fighting is all about the violence.

I glance at Taylor.

'You,' Marcellus says, pointing at me. 'Are you ignoring me?'

'No, Sir,' I say, 'never.'

Cheap sniggers drift my way.

'Silence,' Marcellus shouts. 'Then come here when I call you.'

If he did, it was deliberately quiet so nobody else heard. I jog into the centre of the room. Another Trainer joins us and hands Marcellus a knife. The gasps around the room mask my own. It's about twenty centimetres long with a serrated edge on one side and it curves at the end like the hull of a boat. My heart is smacking against my ribcage like it wants to escape. My palms are sticky. Then I realise the knife is made of silicon. Marcellus holds it up for everyone to see and then bends it in half, stabbing himself in the chest to show how harmless a weapon it is. Everyone laughs except me and our Pod, questions quick-firing through my mind so I can barely catch my own thoughts.

Why do we need to learn how to protect ourselves against a knife attack?

Why do we need to learn to shoot?

Who's the enemy?

Why are we here?

Why…?

Why…?

Why…?

The Trainer jogs out of the circle and leaves me alone with Marcellus. His eyes twitch mischievously, like something bad is heading my way. It's why he's taken this class. This is payback time for being stopped at the elevator and ignoring him on day one.

He's been waiting for this.

He points at me to take a step back. I do. He shows everyone how to hold the knife and demonstrates what a downward motion attack would look like. He drops the rubber knife to the floor and then demonstrates the countermove, which would end with the attacker on the floor. He makes it look simple. It isn't. He points me back into his space. I gulp. We go slowly. He stabs down and I lift my arm to block his, pushing his hand away so I can grab his wrist to make him release his grip of the knife, before rolling him to the floor.

My enthusiasm is zero and touching Marcellus is like licking a reptile.

We go through the move a number of times, quicker on each repeat. We switch and he gives me the knife and tells me to try and attack him. Like Chantal, I'm sick at the thought. I want to be struck by lightning and die on the spot. Marcellus takes the defensive stance and tells me to approach. I put the least amount of effort I can into the request. He blocks the attack and disarms me in text book fashion, rolling me to the floor. He tells me to go harder and faster. I come in for another attack, keeping the same pace, but he reacts like I'm a crazed maniac. He blocks my attack, twists my arm and nearly breaks my wrist as he flips me onto my back. I hit the crash mats with a loud *slap*. My breath shoots out of my lungs in a single gush and pain ricochets through my lower spine. To finish off, Marcellus grabs my throat with his spare hand and pins me to the floor, choking me enough to let me know he's boss. Like I didn't know that already. The hatred in his eyes burns bright, before a smile creeps across his evil face. He lets me go and I stand, coughing. The lesson is over and we're called onto the mats and paired in our Pods.

I get Rasa.

'Are you hurt?' she asks quietly.

I shake my head, but I'm lying. The ligaments in my right shoulder feel stretched, but it's my back. The relief I'd been feeling from the injection and pills has vanished. I start to attack Rasa. She disarms me and throws me to the floor and in a flash, we're face to face, centimetres away from each other's lips. Her breath is sweet, like fresh spring water. Her eyes sparkle with a kindness I've not witnessed before and I tremble with the same uncomfortable closeness I did in the bathroom when we had our first one-on-one. Then we stand, an embarrassed silence between us and I'm saved by the whistle for the next swap. This time I'm paired with Kuro. He pushes on the front of his glasses and holds the knife as if he's going to attack me.

'I'm not very scary am I?' he says, laughing.

I like that he can smile at himself, even through his own fear. It says a lot about his character, and I wish Diego and Spencer would learn from him. We swap around and I attack him and let him disarm me and throw me to the floor. It's more me throwing myself onto the matt and hurting my back in the process, but I tell him he's done a great job.

'Really?' he says.

'Yeah…it was perfect.'

We swap again. I get Diego next, followed by Spencer. They both refuse to look me in the eye and go through the motions like they've been semi-drugged. Lastly, I pair with Chantal and a Trainer steps in to correct movements in our technique, passing on additional tips that I don't care for. Our Trainer comes over and makes a point of chastising Kuro when he drops the knife in attack mode. He makes Kuro do thirty press-ups before we can move on. A whistle brings the session to an end and I couldn't be more relieved. We re-group and I'm waiting for the Roll Call to begin when Chantal whispers.

'I think we're being set up as prey.'

I'm not sure if Rasa has put her up to it or not, but the innocence which Chantal conveys in her statement drives the message into Diego and Spencer's heart with a force I couldn't have got close to.

'You're wrong,' Spencer says, half-heartedly.

'No she's not,' I say.

32

Our days have changed yet again, and not for the better.

The Obstacle Course, The Shooting Range and our ongoing survival techniques have almost been forgotten. It's all about Fight Academy as Chantal calls it. I'm convinced, too, that we are being woken earlier and the runs are shorter. All so we can complete three fight training sessions a day, followed by supper and then bed. It's gruelling work and the worst part for me is we've not had time to communicate as a Pod. There's an uneasy truce between myself, Diego and Spencer, but my fear is that it wouldn't take much to splinter us again. We need to try and repair the rift, but there's nowhere for us to talk in private. To add to the complication, our new female Trainer sticks to us like a second skin. At least the Marcellus clone is out of our lives, for that I'm thankful.

We enter Fight Camp. I should have guessed today was going to be different when they cancelled our run. I turn to Kuro who senses it too, his face changing colour to a sheet white. Spencer starts shaking his head, mumbling to himself, which has become a permanent habit. He's bemoaned every session to the point he's even started to annoy his buddy, Diego. Spencer won't say as much, but he detests violence and can't understand why our Non-Secular Government isn't doing more to stop abuse within the Homes. I get it. We all hate the violence, but how you cope with it is part of surviving places like this. I've tried to point this out to him and he snapped at me, calling me an *Institutional Thug*.

I'm not.

The Taylors and Sukis of the System are and you don't have to be like them to survive.

Two fight rings have been constructed in the centre of the room. The crash mats have been moved to the corners for warm-up and practice areas. There's a kit area with protective gloves, fake knives, short rubber sticks and other weapons of choice. Off to my right is a First-Aid section and between the two fight rings, high on the wall, is an electronic notice board, waiting to be filled in.

Kuro and Chantal both look like they are going to pass out.

'They're going to score us today,' Rasa says, almost to herself.

I nod. It's competition day. A competition we knew nothing about. A precursor to Gladiator Day – a thought I keep to myself, as we gather around Marcellus. He dishes out the instructions in his no-nonsense rapid-fire tone.

'There'll be three, two minute rounds unless you are scored out – meaning, in a real-life scenario the blow would have maimed or killed you. There'll be no cross-gender combat today. Controlled aggression, along with demonstrating you have implemented the techniques taught, will score high. You can enter the ring with any weapon of choice, but if you are disarmed and attacked with your own weapon, your opponent will double their points. Bravery scores high; dumb aggression will be punished with a points deduction. Everyone is to wear padded gloves. This is not an excuse to beat the weaker opponent, but an opportunity to demonstrate the skills that have been painstakingly taught. Any questions?'

No-one speaks.

We're dismissed to our Pods and I'm struggling for the correct words of encouragement. Kuro, Chantal, Spencer and even Diego look equally disgusted and terrified at what's ahead. My honest advice would be to run. There's no point putting yourself in jeopardy if you don't have to. But we can't run and cowardice will mean dropping points quicker than falling through the trapdoor of the gallows. There's nothing we can do, nothing.

I say. 'In a few hours this will be over and you heard Marcellus. This is an exercise in showing what we've learnt. It's not about who's the biggest, strongest, fastest. Let's do our utmost and protect our Ranking as best we can.'

Spencer steps in close and juts his face toward mine. 'I've had enough of being pushed around. By you, by her,' he nods toward Rasa. 'By everyone in this place. If I don't want to fight for my supper, I won't. Are we clear?'

'You're making a mistake,' I say.

'Yeah…yeah…so you keep telling me. Maybe it's you who keeps making the mistakes, have you thought about that? What if we are going to Graduate? What if Graduation is after today, assuming that is, you don't get us hanged!'

Spencer says it louder than he should to make his point and the other Pods close by look over. I flush and Spencer steps away before I can answer. Rasa tells me to leave it. I look back toward the Rings then the electronic board. First up are two girls from Pod Four and Nine, and two boys from Pod Two and Six. Both boys opt for knives, the girls go unarmed. The boy from Pod Two is taller with a longer reach, but the boy from Pod Six is lightning quick. The girls are more evenly matched regarding height, weight and size, except the girl from Four looks more aggressive overall.

The bell sounds and I'm not sure if it's the buzz of being first or just the raw nerves of the moment, but both pairs attack each other with a frenetic energy I didn't expect. The Referee immediately pulls the girls apart and warns them against pulling hair to gain an advantage, while the boys slash away in a gruesome reliving of a street fight. I watch on, feeling slowly more repulsed at what I'm witnessing. The bell goes for the end of Round One. The fighters retreat to their corners. Suki starts to give advice to her girl from Nine. It's uncompromising and blunt, and it goes without saying I want the girl from Four to win. Round Two starts and the girls bounce out of their corners, setting the same tone as the previous round. They throw hard punches and it looks as if the Referee is about to stop it for another hair pulling infringement when the girl from Nine grabs the girl from Four around the back of her head, forcing her head forward as she drives up her knee into the girl's face. It's a vicious strike that knocks the girl out. Suki shouts an aggressive cheer and the rest of her Pod join in, high-fiving each other. I'm not sure which part of Marcellus's instructions the Referee upheld and I'm so wrapped up in my disappointment of the victory that I miss the boy with the longer reach snatch victory in the knife fight.

The electronic board flickers four more names and Spencer is up next against a boy from Thirteen. The boy is smaller than Spencer with short black hair, a crooked nose and a scar above his right eye. I heard he got the scar playing football, but it makes him look tough and he knows it. He's picked a knife, but Spencer's entered the ring unarmed.

The way Spencer is stood is making me nervous.

It lacks energy and focus.

It's like he's dead, already.

'You, okay, buddy? Diego says, like he's spotted it too.

'I saw him practice yesterday,' I say of the opponent. 'He likes to swing his knife from left to right, about chest height. He's predictable.'

'This whole thing is barbaric. I never asked to be here.' says Spencer. 'I don't see why I should do this if I don't want to.'

There's a venom in his tone and he's retreating further from us when we need him to be more part of our group.

The bell is sounded.

I tense.

Spencer idles into the centre of the ring, like he's out for a stroll. Rasa throws me a *what's his problem* shrug. He's gone on strike before, but I've never seen him this bad. The boy from Thirteen crabs right, waiting, eyeing up his opponent. Spencer stops in the centre of the Ring and waits, staring at the boy. The inactivity makes the boy from Thirteen's nervous. I wonder if I'm wrong and Spencer is going to spring on the boy in a move I haven't seen before. I don't care as long as it works and we score points. The boy continues to crab closer, glancing toward his corner for support. Their Head encourages him on. I want to yell at Spencer to move but it doesn't feel right, so I say nothing. I don't want to inflame his anger toward me more. The boy from Thirteen gets within range then launches forward, stabbing Spencer under the left ribs. Spencer doesn't move, doesn't attempt to fight back, just looks at the Referee in a sign of contempt. The bell is sounded. It's over. That's it. The fight is done and awarded to Thirteen. They cheer, not caring Spencer didn't even attempt to fight back. I hear the immediate whispers flooding through the room, heads turning to catch a glimpse at Pod Fifteen imploding again. Spencer walks toward the centre of the ropes, steps under the middle section, ignoring us as a team, heading for one of the chairs in the First-Aid section.

I watch him go, fuming as I check for Marcellus who has witnessed the whole episode from his perch by the electronic board. I'm about to walk over and tackle Spencer when Rasa gives me a nudge and points my attention back to the action. Kuro has been paired against a boy from Pod One. For a split second, I think it's Taylor, but I'm only marginally relieved when I see it's Pod One's Second-in-Command. He has dark brown hair, hazel eyes and is ten centimetres taller and a good six kilos heavier than Kuro. There's nothing fair about the match and I struggle to hide my disappointment. I can't recall if the boy put up his hand up or not when Marcellus first asked if any of us had attended fight training in the past. I don't think he did, but the cock-sure smile that is ruling his face is telling everyone he thinks this is going to be over in three seconds and not three rounds.

Rasa helps Kuro on with his gloves while encouraging him to be confident in his abilities. Kuro nods, as Chantal reaches out and removes his glasses from his face, like he's an absent-minded grandfather. Diego is trying to stare out the boy from One and Taylor is telling him to ignore Diego and to concentrate on the job in hand. He'll deal with Diego later if he has to.

'Remember this is about showing what we've learnt,' I say, hoping I'm not transmitting my own worry. 'Keep your distance and your hands up. Anything that hits your arms might sting, but that's all, so don't let it panic you into thinking it's worse than it is.'

Kuro nods.

'And use the whole Ring,' Rasa adds. 'Don't let him corner you.'

Kuro isn't listening. His eyes are darting from us to the boy opposite then back to us. I've never seen anyone look as scared in their life as Kuro does right this second. His nose hasn't completely healed, either, so any contact there is going to feel twice as worse. I can hear Taylor telling his boy to throw some punches at Kuro's sweet spot. He means the nose and he's making sure Kuro hears him, too. It's all part of the psychological battle. The quicker the round is over, the more points will be scored, I catch Taylor saying. He's probably right, I think, as the bell is sounded.

Kuro stands and looks all stiff and wooden as he edges forward. The boy from One shoots out of his corner, like he's sprinting the hundred metres and goes for the show-stopper punch.

I gasp.

As do Chantal and Rasa.

'DUCK!' Diego screams.

Kuro clicks into action and bends at the knees, dropping his head and bouncing off to his right. It couldn't have been closer if it was staged and I let out a sigh of relief, thankful for Kuro's natural speed.

Rasa shouts instructions at Kuro to stay off the ropes and keep moving. It's not going to score any points, but Kuro is following her lead and it's keeping him out of trouble, which is all I care about. Chantal joins in the encouragement. I'm hoping this will bring Spencer back into our fold. If Kuro can fight so can Spencer, but he stays sulking in the First-Aid section. Kuro's one advantage is he's quick, and he's worked out that if he listens to Rasa this isn't going to be the one-sided fight Pod One had betted on. I'm wishing time away and this feels like the longest two minutes of my life. Kuro takes a quick bust of hard hits and we wince in sympathy, but he absorbs them well, better than I would have given him credit for, before ducking right and then hard left to escape the bombardment. It's a good move and I'm proud of him. The boy from One slows down and looks to use his brain rather than his raw power as Kuro's movement is tiring him out. He starts to block Kuro off and force him into corners.

I want the bell to go. We need to get better advice to Kuro as the boy throws a dummy punch and then follows it with a roundhouse kick. Kuro instinctively ducks and then like an expert, steps in close, and kicks the standing leg from under the boy.

It's a great move.

Pure Pro.

The boy drops to the floor, bending his wrists the wrong way as he lands badly.

Kuro freezes, surprised at his own luck, staring across at us in disbelief.

'The killer blow. The killer blow,' Rasa and Chantal scream in unison.

'Follow it up,' I shout. 'You have to finish him off.'

Kuro is too slow and the boy springs to his feet and throws an instinctive left jab. The jab is straight and hard and well practiced, and it catches Kuro square in the face. Kuro yelps in pain as his nose is broken for a second time. He collapses to the floor, clutching at his face. The bell is sounded for the victory to Pod One. We rush in to help Kuro, Taylor's cheers loud enough to block my thoughts.

Kuro's nose is bleeding hard and he's doing his best to hold in his pain.

'I tried,' he gurgles through the snot and blood.

'You did great.'

'No I didn't. We'll get zero points. I let us down,' he says, slowly sitting up with Chantal and Diego's help.

'The only person who let us down is Spencer,' Chantal says.

'You were great,' I say.

'You forgot to keep your hands up is all,' Rasa adds. 'Next time you'll remember.'

'I hope there's never a next time,' he adds, trying to smile again.

Me, too, I think, but this is only the start, as I look up and lock eyes with Taylor. He shoots an imaginary gun at me using his thumb and first finger. I smile back, because there's nothing else I can do, but it's like he knows something I don't.

Like he knows what the pairings are going to be.

Like he knows what our final Rankings are going to be.

Like he can influence the outcomes.

And then I know my answer.

He's Marcellus's spy, which ultimately makes him Ilse's eyes on the ground.

He's traded us all out for privileges.

Taylor is a rat.

33

I thought I was being paranoid, but I'm not. The pairs are evenly matched, except ours. To me, it's obvious we're being set up to fail and I want to warn the others, but warn them against what?

Marcellus hates us.

There'll probably be a party to honour our failure.

None of it is breaking news and they worry enough as it is without me adding to the burden that the odds are stacked against us.

I've counted three fights for Chantal, totalling nine bouts, against girls twice her size. Her natural speed and agility has kept her from getting hurt, and if she's noticed she's had more fights than anyone else she hasn't complained. I wish Spencer had more of Chantal's courage instead of throwing two more fights. I've tried to speak to him about the danger his attitude is putting us in, but he walks off and I'm close to making a fool of myself by following him around while he ignores me. I'll have to deal with him later and make sure the other *Denounced* know that I did so I don't appear weak. It's another distraction I could do without. Diego and Rasa have had one fight each, which they both won with ease. Diego relied on his strength, but in the essence of Marcellus's instructions, I can't see it gaining us many points for demonstrating newly acquired techniques. Diego's not going to lose unless it's against Taylor or possibly Sean from Pod Eleven, the other Head with Gravitas. Rasa's already proved she can beat Suki, which means no other girl is going to get close, except, maybe, Arianne from Twelve.

I can't help but see this as another tactical play from Marcellus to stop us gaining points.

Which leaves me.

'You haven't fought yet,' Rasa says, as we walk over to help Kuro, who's been forced into another contest. A pairing he'll lose within the first round unless he has the most unbelievable stroke of luck, which he won't. He doesn't complain as he drags himself into the Ring and the bell is sounded. The contest is against a boy from Three who I remember had his hand in the air when Marcellus asked for the count of those who had been to Fight School. The way he swaggers toward Kuro makes me want to call for an ambulance. Rasa starts shouting advice and Kuro puts up a brave defence, lasting most of the round before he takes another powerful jab to the face which ends the contest. We rush in to help him to his feet and he apologies again for not getting us any points.

Spencer, I hope you're listening, I think.

I let my eyes wander the room, looking for Taylor.

He's sat against the far wall with the rest of his Pod. They're laughing and joking around, like today is a minor inconvenience in their timetable. I'm not sure collectively how many fights they've had, but of the ones I've seen they've eased through. Taylor had one pairing with a boy from Six who was practically wetting his pants as he stepped into the Ring.

It was the biggest non-event of the day.

Game over within ten seconds.

I know I'm being saved for the main event like some prized exhibit. Instead of wearing me down with pointless fights, Marcellus is using the psychological approach, zapping my mental and emotional strength before my pre-destined fight with Taylor. The more I think about it, the more it's all falling into place: Marcellus further inflaming my back and damaging my shoulder when he demonstrated the knife attack and counter-move. The breaking of Kuro's nose in the Canteen, and the attempted breaking of Chantal's ankle. Diego and Rasa, our two strongest contestants, have had little input to gain us points. And Marcellus has lucked-in with Spencer who's handed us all on a plate to the System.

I could vomit on the spot.

I leave Rasa and Chantal nursing Kuro, to get a drink of water. I haven't seen Diego for a while, but I hope he's having a quiet word with Spencer and drilling some sense into his buddy's thick skull. Kuro's name has been removed from the electronic board, finally ruling him out of any more action. It's been too long coming, but we're effectively a person down and I wonder how many points we'll lose for being five instead of six?

I'm sure Marcellus has some math formula that works against us – just us and no other Pod.

I gulp more water when a rushed hush cascades through the room. The speed of it catches me off guard and I go light headed and think for a second I've fainted. It's then I catch Marcellus pointing at me, calling me into the Ring. I steal a look at the electronic board to make sure I've not been paranoid.

I'm not.

Not that I ever doubted myself.

Taylor is climbing into the Ring.

Of course, he is, I think – this has been planned for days.

Taylor is gloved and beckoning me to join him, like I've been deliberately delaying this moment, instead of getting the drink I wanted to quench my thirst. I put my water bottle back on the table and head for my corner, making sure I don't rush.

'You're dead meat,' Suki hisses as I pass.

I want to have a smart reply, but one doesn't come, so I ignore her. It's all I can do. Diego appears, but I still don't see Spencer as Diego starts to help me on with my gloves. Rasa slides over and nudges him off the job, taking over. 'Taylor will play to the crowd to see if he can unnerve you. His kicks are powerful and I wouldn't put it past him to try and break one of your legs. He'll say it was an accident, but it won't be, so you need to be careful.'

'Watch out, Ned, we need you,' Chantal says all sombre.

I smile back at her.

'Be careful, bro. We can make up the points on the Obstacle Course. You know…we can cheat,' Diego says, looking all embarrassed.

'I thought you didn't want to?'

'I don't. But don't hate him, he's panicked. He can't help himself.'

I want to say it's okay, but it's not and Diego knows it.

He pulls the ropes apart, allowing me to step in. Taylor has already moved to the centre of the Ring. He's jogging on the spot and throwing dummy punches, breathing out loud. The bell is sounded for Round One. I step forward shaking out my shoulders. Ringing in my ears is:

Go Taylor.

Go Taylor.

Go Taylor.

I glance toward my own corner to see four worried faces. Then, from the edges of my vision, I spot Marcellus circle left to get a better view of the pending fight.

His spiteful smirk lights up his face, only adding to my distraction when a jab come straight toward me. It's slick and fast, and I slip the punch in the nick of time. The shock of nearly getting hit with the first strike brings my mind back into the Ring. I blow out my breath along with some of my fears. Rasa was right and Taylor starts playing to the crowd, the adulation feeding his energy. He juts out his chin, inviting me to punch it, but he's dancing left, then right, then left again, his hands held low by his waist. I ignore the taunting. This has nothing to do with demonstrating the techniques we've learnt, but more about destroying my credibility, along with Pod Fifteen's chances of survival. Taylor steps in quick and lets fly with another jab. It's much faster than the first. I pull my head back and feel the whoosh of air caress my chin. The mood in his eyes has switched from show-off to intent. He moves right and I counter. Not only do I have to watch his hands but I need to watch his feet.

I've done some kick-boxing, but I'm not good at it.

I don't have the speed or balance.

Suddenly, Taylor turns a hundred and eighty degrees and lets out a vicious flying back kick. The crowd roars with anticipation. I see it in time and skip out of its way. As he continues to swivel round he lands poised, following it up with two sharp jabs. I duck under the punches and step in close and land a right into his ribs as I stick my elbow up and into his face. The first punch catches him by surprise and he grimaces, but not before he throws a hook that smacks into the top of my shoulder. I stumble sideways as pain ricochets through my muscles and up into my neck. The crowd cheers and it encourages Taylor forward. I catch Marcellus smiling. It's the shoulder he jarred when he threw me to the ground and Taylor knows it's sore, and he probably knows my lower back is a problem, too. To confirm my fears, another kick is aimed at my waist, which is the closest he can get to my back. I block it and step in close so he can't kick me again and jab him twice with my left. The first misses, but the second connects. It's a good punch that he absorbs well and he throws another hook toward my chin. I block it with my right arm, but the pain smashes through my wrist and I stumble sideways from the sheer power. He steps in to follow up, but I bounce back onto the ropes, effectively running away.

It makes him drop his hands and play to the crowd that I'm being a coward.

Boos fill my ears.

He lifts his hands and beckons me into the fight with a single hooking motion of his first finger. It's then I spot it. Our fight gloves are more like gym training gloves with cut-off fingers and thick padding across the knuckles and the back of the hand. It's so you can still grip a weapon and use your fingers, but your own knuckles are protected, also giving protection to the person you strike. The padding on Taylor's gloves is more protruded, and from the dead-arm I now have I realise they are filled with something stronger than foam.

Metal.

Ball bearings, maybe.

But definitely not foam.

I don't buy into the beckoning routine, so he comes hunting instead. He's trying to get me into one of the corners so he can finish me off. I duck right, then a quick left. I come up and twist to miss a punch and duck again, giving me a direct punch to his solar plexus. It's a poor shot from me and my back is starting to seize. I'm not sure I can go another two seconds, never mind another two rounds when the bell is sounded to end this one.

Blowing hard, I head for my corner. Diego and Rasa jump into the Ring. Diego's holding a stool and Rasa a bottle of water.

'You did good, Ned, real good,' Diego says, as I sit down.

'His gloves are padded with metal,' I say.

'I thought so,' Rasa whispers. 'No punch on the shoulder should send someone your size spinning sideways.'

'If he connects on my chin, I'm cooked.'

'We should complain,' Diego says. 'Get this stopped.'

'Don't be stupid,' Chantal says from outside the Ring, Kuro stood next to her. 'They'll call Ned a coward and deduct all our points. Then those gloves will mysteriously disappear.'

'She's right,' Rasa says, holding the bottle so I can take a sip.

I take two long gulps of water and then say. 'Any ideas?'

Rasa purses her lips as the seconds to the next round tick down.

'You got a hard punch to his ribs. It hurt him. Keep trying to hit the same spot. It'll bruise him up and sap his energy. Then go for a dummy to the ribs, switching it to his chin. You'll get one chance. If that doesn't work, then take the metal punch. Getting knocked out is better than breaking a leg. Chantal's right, we need you.'

I can't say I like my choices, but I nod as the bell is sounded for the start of Round Two.

Chantal reaches in and gently touches my arm. I shudder as her hopes and fears surge through me.

'You can do it. I know you can.'

I stand and Diego takes the stool.

Taylor glides toward the centre of the canvas, like he was born to fight. He's rolling his shoulders and loosening his arms, taking a fighter's stance.

Go Taylor.

Go Taylor.

Go Taylor.

I brace myself, getting a flashback of myself on the first day I was left in the System with my red trunk. I was seven years old, left alone to fend for myself with my parents gone, the world against me. That same loneliness descends through me at a hundred kilometres an hour. But this time is different. I'm not alone any more. I have responsibilities. I have a new family. The one Ilse gave me and the one Marcellus wants to destroy. I'm raging at Spencer for letting us down, but I will still do everything I can to protect him as I would Rasa, Chantal, Diego and Kuro.

Taylor steps in and tries to smash his foot into my shin. I spring out of his way. I've survived six Community Homes and one hanging, so I don't see why I can't beat an *Institutional Thug* like him. He steps in for another kick, but I match his move and close off the space, bending right and going low to enable me to use all my upper body leverage. I drive a huge punch into his ribs. It connects in the same spot as before. I hear *ugh* as he grits his teeth and backs off. Again, I track his step and follow it with another punch to the same spot. It's a better shot than my first and he lets rip with a wild punch to force me back, but I've already seen it in my mind and I bob down watching his punch sail over my head. As I come up, I hit him with two more quick punches in the same spot on his ribs. That's four connects in under a second and he's winded because he tries to push me back with both hands.

As he does, I grab his wrists, splitting his hands apart, feeling the metal in his gloves.

They are ball bearings, big ones.

It froths my anger at him and the System.

I'm innocent of being a *Denounced*.

I'm Ned Hunter.

Not: Ned 5-7-9-0-1-2-3.

It's then I head-butt him with all the force I can generate.

His nose breaks and blood splatters across his lips and chin, and he drops to the floor, holding his face, his energy gone. He's squealing like a baby pig as he struggles to breathe. It takes me a couple of seconds to hear the silence in the room and to realise I've won. So much for our learnt techniques, but Pod Fifteen is victorious.

'Aren't you supposed to raise the hand of the winner?' I say to the Referee.

He looks embarrassed, glancing at Marcellus for confirmation, as he reaches for my wrist, raising my arm into the air.

I smile toward our corner.

Chantal is jumping up and down, and has the loudest cheer of anyone I've ever heard.

Or maybe it's not that loud after all, because she's the only one cheering.

34

The last few days have been some of the toughest I've endured since I've been here. It's not one thing in particular, more the overall pressure. Taylor is wearing a metal strip across his nose like a badge of honour. His eyes are the colour of a Panda's with a dash of yellow and purple to add to his freakish look. Every time I see him, I feel guilty at my own viciousness, forgetting his ball bearing-padded gloves and the victory afforded to our Pod. His new look has generated a sympathy vote in his favour, adding to his power. Taylor is now the unofficial Head of the other twelve Pods. He wanted to have thirteen under his wing, but he's no chance there.

We've been appointed another Trainer. I've lost count of how many we've had and they've merged into one in my mind. I'm convinced we've had more than any other Pod. This one is female but looks more like a man than a woman, with her short hair, flat chest and compulsory muscular frame. She's spiteful on a whole new level and finds fault in everything we do. We've been late for every Roll Call while she inspects our room making us re-do our beds or tidy our wardrobes because some imaginary speck of dust has settled at a wrong angle. She's even sat with us in the Canteen, making it impossible to discuss anything as a group. One small light has been Spencer who's apologised for his cowardice at the fight competition. On reflection, I'm not so sure it was cowardice, more a protest against being here and it came out that day. I get where he's coming from, but his actions were mistimed and jeopardised us all, and considering how long he's been in the System, he should have known better. His punishment still hasn't been dealt out and I know it's coming, so it's adding to my underlying tension. As is not knowing our final scores, but every task we do is being monitored closely and the line between being scored and learning seems to have been crossed.

I hope these days come to an end soon.

The buggies stop at the mouth of the Obstacle Course. I step from the vehicle using the moment to subtly stretch out the pain in my back. I'm terrified of anyone outside of our Pod knowing, although I'm sure Taylor has probably leaked my secret, which he learnt from Marcellus. I've taken the last of my pills and although I mentioned it to our Trainer, she hasn't organised any more or even a visit to the doctor. I can't say I'm surprised, but it's another problem, on my ever-growing list, which I'm going to have to find a solution to.

The area feels unexpectedly cold and there's a fine layer of dust that has a red tint to it, like sand. It's odd to see this unexpected wash of colour and I wonder where it's come from. Is it deliberate or a surprise reminder there's a world outside? It's hard to track time in our grey world, but I'm confident it's been two weeks since we've completed a round of the Course. The decision to cheat or not hasn't been resolved, but my victory and our lack of privacy to discuss means we probably won't, or not today. I'm still not over confident when it comes to our Ranking and it dominates my every waking thought and most of my sleeping ones. I know it's a huge risk, but I've become more and more convinced we should cheat.

Off to our right is a marquee with food and drinks. It tells me the rest of the day is going to be spent here. If we follow what we've been doing for the last few days then it'll be two rounds: a warm up-come-practise, followed by a scoring round. The usual hubbub of the Pods has died down, so I'm guessing everyone is thinking the same.

A whistle is sounded and we're lined up for yet another pointless Roll Call. We had one before we climbed into the buggies from the Shooting Range, so why we need another one now is beyond me. It's the same dull routine each time. Taylor starts by shouting out his name and number. His Number Two then does the same, followed by his Number Three. When Pod One is complete, the same order is followed for Pod Two, then Three and, so on, until it comes to us. A Trainer at the front marks off our names against a list he has in his notebook. Chantal is always last. When she's finished reciting her name and number, the Trainer taking the Roll Call gives it a beat while he taps away at his screen. When he's finished, whatever notes he's taking, a whistle is sounded to bring the whole pointless practice to an end.

Taylor reels off his number.

His voice has a nasal twang from his injury. As his Number Two calls out his name and number, I tune out and let my mind wander into the grey wilderness beyond the Obstacle Course. The vastness has always emotionally engulfed me and left me feeling helpless and alone. But over the last few days, I've viewed it differently. It's more like an optical illusion and if I had the opportunity I'm sure I could find the door that would lead us out. As always, in the silence of the Roll Call, I can hear the faint hum of the extractor fans high above my head, but in this part of our world they always sound louder, like outside is closer. The real challenge isn't the escape, but how we survive once we get out?

Girl six from Pod Fourteen recites her name and number, which is my cue. Without breaking my thoughts of what's beyond the Obstacle Course and how we might escape, I call out my details. Rasa comes in on cue followed by the others.

Chantal finishes and I look back at the Trainer taking the Call waiting for the whistle. Kuro's plan to cheat drops into my mind. It's well thought out and I'm sure it would work. I don't know why but each time I run it past myself I have the memory of taking a psychometric test at my last Community Home. I thought it was the start of my college enrolment, albeit premature, but now, I'm more and more convinced it is somehow connected to why I am here today.

I suddenly realise the whistle hasn't been sounded and I tense.

Suddenly, two Guards push through the first two rows and heads our way. My stomach churns and acid rinses the back of my throat. Before I have time to take another breath, one of the Guards shoves me out of the way and makes a grab for Spencer. They haul him to the front, pushing him to his knees in front of Marcellus. Taylor glances over his shoulder toward me, checking that I'm watching before he returns his gaze to the front. The casualness of his action makes me sick. He knows what's coming. I think I hate him more than I do Marcellus. Taylor is one of us and he should remember that. If he thinks aligning himself to the Trainers is going to help him in the long-term he's mistaken. In their eyes, he'll always be a *Denounced* even if he's been innocently accused, which I doubt.

'We take our training seriously,' Marcellus says, addressing us all. 'Much thought and hours of preparation has been put into this program. You were warned at the beginning by your mother that your full co-operation and commitment was paramount. We have been tolerant of growing personalities and those struggling to come to terms with what has been asked of you, but we will not tolerate insubordination that puts a Pod at risk of failure.'

The Guard who pushed Spencer to his knees, draws his electronic baton. A blueish arc dances from the end, mesmerising everyone's attention, sucking the air from the space. Marcellus momentarily looks toward me as the Guard steps forward and lashes Spencer.

Once.

Twice.

Three times in quick succession.

Spencer yells out with each new strike, falling to the ground with the first, arching with the second, and curling into the foetal position with the third.

I feel every stroke.

I feel Spencer's hatred, overlaying it with my own.

I yearn for fairness and acts of kindness in my life.

I hear Rasa start to cry. It's the first time her emotions have broken the surface. Tears are rolling down her face and Chantal has her head buried into her hands, her shoulders shuddering up and down. Kuro is staring at his feet and Diego has his fists clenched. After the third lash, the Guard looks across at Marcellus who gives a short single nod. The Guard takes a step back and lashes Spencer one more time, before shutting off his baton and walking away. The only sounds are Chantal and Rasa crying and the ever constant hum of the ventilation system. I knew something was coming, but I'm numb with shock at the speed and violence of what I've witnessed. Everyone has grown emotionally hard since being here, but I sense justice has been righted, and Spencer and Pod Fifteen have little sympathy from anyone else. I blame Taylor. He's forgotten he's one of us and if anyone is being selfish and risking the health of their Pod, it's him. Marcellus sounds his whistle and points us toward the starting line of the Obstacle Course. The other Pods pull away and we're left staring at Spencer.

'Wait here,' I tell the others.

I walk over to Spencer and kneel beside him. He's curled into a foetal ball, crying to himself, and he flinches as I lean in and whisper.

'We have to complete the Course. If you don't get up and join us, Pod Fifteen will be dead by the end of the day.'

I stand and offer my hand. Spencer doesn't move, but continues to lie at my feet whimpering. I don't need to look across to know most of the other Pods and Trainers are watching us.

'You need to stand. Mostly for yourself, but also for me, Diego, Rasa, Chantal and Kuro.'

He doesn't move. Just continues to cry. I have the urge to kick him, to scream at him to stand and even pull him to his feet, but I can't. He has to do this by himself. He has to care enough about something beyond his own pain and hatred and anger. I learn something watching him lying on the floor. There comes a point when you have to take responsibility for your actions and nobody can help you but yourself. I'm about to turn back to our Pod when I spot it. My heart smiles, my face doesn't. Spencer wipes his eyes with his hands and stops crying. With a painful grunt, he pushes up onto his front and takes a pause. I lean down to help, but he shoves me off. I get it. He's taking his responsibility and I respect him for it. He then pushes up onto his knees and slowly uncurls himself into a standing position. His face is creased from the pain.

'Thank you,' I whisper.

'After this, we're quits,' he says.

I step in close and stare into his eyes. 'No we're not. We're in this together. To the end.'

He stares at me, then slowly blinks his agreement.

I let Spencer lead the way. The other Pods have turned their attention back to the Obstacle Course and a Trainer is giving out the instructions for the afternoon session. It looks as if we're to go first. No surprise and more points potentially lost had Spencer not dug into his reserves and raised his game. He's limping and his body is lopsided from pain, but he's not going to be defeated. We re-group and Diego says one word.

It's like food for my soul.

A sunshine burst above my head.

'Cheat?'

I nod.

So does Rasa.

Followed by Chantal and Kuro.

We look at Spencer and he nods with his eyes.

The final instructions come in from the Trainers. This is a practice run, then lunch with an opportunity to rehearse any of the Obstacles before a final scoring run. It's the last scoring competition of *Phase Two*. It determines *Phase Three* and who goes into the final rounds towards Graduation. None of our Pod believe in Graduation any more, but we know we have to get to Phase Three to stay alive.

It's motivation enough.

'We use this as a practise run and we cheat the second round. For the next few hours, Kuro is Head. What he says goes. No debate. No discussion. Agreed?' I get five quick nods. 'Are you sure about this?' I say to Kuro.

He nods. Jaw clenched. Lips pursed. Eyes alight with determination.

'Pod Fifteen. You're up first. Make it count,' a Trainer shouts, sounding his whistle and pointing to the start line.

We jog to the start and I notice that my back doesn't hurt any more and I swear I catch Spencer chewing on a smile.

35

I wake, feeling something close to happiness. It's the first time our reputation worked in our favour. The other *Denounced* and Trainers expected us to come last, especially following Spencer's beating, so they left us to ourselves on the Obstacle Course – our failed result pre-fixed in their minds. It took the pressure off and we used it to our advantage, taking the first round deliberately slow while we worked through Kuro's plan. It was a dummy run to cheating in full, courtesy of the Trainers. Kuro had not only found the weak spots in the Course, but also where to maximise our strengths. It was a lesson in efficiency and one I'll never forget. If I do get out of here alive, it'll be something I will look to improve within myself. I have a tendency to lean toward the tougher solution. Interestingly, Kuro told me that before he was picked to take the exam to leave the *Doubters' Camp*, the leaders of his clan used his observation skills as a scout when teams ventured into the nearby towns to steal food and supplies. To finish, we were helped by a boy from Pod Ten breaking his leg and the small commotion that followed, seeing our first Ambulance buggy.

After lunch, we completed all we had rehearsed with a practised slickness Ilse would have been proud of had she only known. I'm glad that Marcellus wasn't around to witness the final round, which I see as another piece of luck, but the open mouth on our Trainer's face when we trotted past the finish line said it all. I was concerned we were too good and we would give ourselves away, but none of us showed any pride or elation at smashing our previous times. We played dog-tired and feigning injuries, making especially sure we didn't let our guard down once we entered our spied-upon dorm. I heard whisperings in the Canteen that we must have been helped, but we stayed united and kept up the appearance we'd barely scraped through.

We all know it's results day.

We are up later, almost a lie-in and our morning run and Roll Call has been cancelled.

As ever, with the break in routine, it puts me on edge – it's my biggest panic-trigger – we all sense what is coming and it's making it hard for the Pods to concentrate. We head into the Canteen for breakfast and I can feel the quiet victory still having a force of its own within our Pod, except for Spencer. There's a blankness in his eyes I've not seen before, and I'm concerned this place has finally tangled itself into his mind since his punishment. His mood is rubbing off on Diego and in turn it will seep down to Kuro and then onto Chantal. Rasa is strong enough to hold her own thoughts and feelings, but it reminds me how fragile we are as a group, and how easy it would be for everything to unfold and collapse around us. We're due some luck and I just hope Kuro made it happen yesterday and there isn't a nasty surprise waiting for us after breakfast.

I sweat at the thought.

Pod Eight, hung, flashes through my mind.

I do my best to shake away the thought.

I'm hungry and I shovel extra bacon and sausage onto my plate when Chantal whispers.

'I don't see Pod Ten. Do you?'

I stare through the Canteen and it takes me a moment to see that she's not only right, but their table has been removed, too. I wonder if that's why the Roll Call and run were cancelled this morning?

That way, everyone would have noticed immediately.

'Keep it to ourselves. We haven't spotted it, right?'

Everyone nods and we head to our table when our Trainer decides to join us. She doesn't speak or even try to engage us, not that we'd do much more than grunt our replies even if she did. I'm not sure what's she is trying to achieve by sitting with us, but we all stare at our plates; say nothing, eat too fast and wait for the end whistle to be sounded. I think that moment is never going to arrive, but it does, and we scrape our chairs back, and stand and stack our trays and head outside, the buggies waiting to collect us.

I climb in and we motor toward the Assembly Hall.

It's the one route that never changes in a place of shifting landscapes, where size and distance is almost impossible to gauge.

The Assembly Hall doors loom in the distance. I've never noticed the light electrical fog that simmers high above the doors, much like the Wall of Fog that separates this grey world from the one with the glass towers and trees and clear streams. I wonder if it's there for a reason, as the buggies slow to a stop. It's then the Trainers switch from their relaxed selves to the ones we are more accustomed to. Whistles are sounded and we're lined up and quick-marched into the Hall. Dotted around the edges are additional Guards, more than I've seen for a long time.

Rasa nudges me in the arm and nods toward Pod Ten's box.

It's empty.

'What do you think it means?' she says.

'Be thankful it's not us,' Spencer says. It's the first time he's spoken since yesterday, but his voice, like his eyes, are distant. I'm worried for him, and for our Pod.

'Right now, Pod Ten is none of our business. Don't even look that way.'

A whistle is sounded and we stand to attention. The room fades into darkness as a spotlight illuminates the end of the stage. A moment later, Ilse steps into the light and in the shadows behind her, I can see the man with the salt-and-pepper hair. We start to clap and Ilse waves to us as she heads for the lectern. The smile I'm forced to hold makes my jaw ache.

'Thank you, my children,' she says as our clapping subsides. 'You are always so generous to your mother and it never fails to fill me with gratitude. I thank you, again. We have gathered today as you have reached another landmark in our growing relationship. It brings me both happiness and some sadness. New beginnings always see the passing away of something old. Our time together is drawing to an end and you'll soon be heading into the most difficult part of your new lives. Yes, my children, *Phase Three* is upon us.' Ilse pauses and there's an uncomfortable silence before she continues. 'Some of you will complete *Phase Three* and Graduate and I'm sorry to inform you that some of you will not. But let's not dwell on those negatives and instead let us celebrate the wondrous success most of you are.'

The screen behind Ilse flashes and dances in an array of colours that seem even brighter to my eyes which have become accustomed to grey hues.

Music pumps through the room.

My heart is pounding in my chest.

I'm holding my breath and my lungs feel like they are about to burst, and I don't want to look at the screen, but at the same time, I can't pull my eyes away when our results appear.

Pod One: 1205
Pod Fifteen: 1204

Pod Nine: 1203
Pod Eleven: 1202
Pod Twelve: 1201
Pod Three: 1143
Pod Five: 1135
Pod Four: 1107
Pod Seven: 1100
Pod Thirteen: 1087
Pod Two: 1080
Pod Six: 1054
Pod Fourteen: 1036
Pod Ten: 0
Pod Eight: 0

We're second.

One point behind Pod One.

I stare over to Taylor who has glanced over his shoulder towards me. He's shaking his head in disbelief, but smiling at the same time. It's the first moment, he's let his guard down and shown any form of respect toward our Pod. I ignore his arrogance and look back at the results to make sure I'm not dreaming or seeing things, or worse, like this is another of Marcellus's cruel tricks.

It's not.

Pod One is first and we are second. Suki and Pod Nine are third. Sean, the red-haired boy and Pod Eleven, are fourth and Arianne, the girls from Pod Twelve, are fifth. Ilse said five of us had *gravitas* and if I was right in my guess then all five Pods occupy the first five spots with only a point between us. I scan the bottom of the list. Like Pod Eight, Pod Ten has been given a zero. The boy who accidentally broke his leg has cost his Pod the ultimate sanction. I know deep within myself they must be dead, murdered by Ilse for not living up to her expectations.

The lights dim and the spotlight picks out Ilse standing at her lectern.

'A round of applause is called for Pods One, Fifteen and Nine. We've never had such a close competition.'

A spotlight picks out our Pod as it does Pod One and Nine. Everyone is clapping including the Trainers. I find myself staring at the floor wanting the attention to end, but I'm thinking about what Ilse has just said.

We never had such a close competition.

That tells me they've done this before.

How many times, I wonder?

I think of my psychometric test.

I think of all the other *Denounced* who have walked within these walls.

If I look hard enough, I can see their ghosts.

How many of them were innocent like us?

We all took a test in our own ways and ended up here.

For what?

For Phase Three?

For Graduation?

Eventually the applause comes to a stop and I'm glad of the silence.

'As in any competition there are winners and there are losers, and your Rankings will determine your release into the *City of Hope*. There you will have the glorious opportunity to determine your own freedom. The winners will Graduate. For those Pods who are not in the top three, do not despair. Look at Pod Fifteen. They danced in the footlights of danger and through their determination and sheer willpower they were two points from winning. They are proof you can be victorious. Remember that on your travels, and may the

Powers-that-Be, who ultimately govern us all, shine their light upon you, and lead you to the glory you all deserve.'

Ilse turns and walks from the stage to a fanfare of lights and music.

The Trainers applaud and we join in. It's only when she disappears from view that the celebrations slowly come to an end as the lights return to reveal Marcellus stood centre stage, surveying us all. His face as stern as ever.

'Pods One, Fifteen and Nine, please follow your Trainer.'

Pod One jogs off to their right, led by Taylor. We're next, followed by Suki and the rest of Nine. I'm struggling to think coherently and all I can hear is Chantal and Kuro whispering questions to each other about the *City of Hope*. We enter a large room and our Trainer points to a second door directly in front of me. I'm hesitant, but I remind myself we were second from the top and not second from the bottom.

I step through the door and freeze.

In front of me are six plastic crates with our individual names on the front. Inside are our original *Denounced* Purple Tunics. Next to them is a utility belt similar to the one the Guards wear along with a handgun, knife, and a small black backpack.

'Get changed,' our Trainer says. Her spiteful smile, exposing yellow stained teeth. 'It's time to go to war.'

36

From day one of being in this grey jungle, I've craved to see more colour – especially after I experienced Ilse's oasis. But now that I'm back wearing the Purple Tunic of the *Denounced*, it feels like a cruel joke.

We motor on.

Nobody speaks.

We're going to war and I don't have the words to describe how I feel. Chantal is crying softly behind me and the fear from everyone else is as palpable as my own.

Ahead of us is Pod One and behind is Pod Nine.

All around me is the endless undulation of the same sterile terrain that seems impossible to navigate unless you've driven this route a hundred times and it's embedded into your memory.

We broach another small incline and it's then I spot the pulsating Wall of Fog and its shadow soon engulfs us. My skin goose-bumps as the temperature drops. Our Trainer says nothing, like it isn't there and I'm surprised Chantal or Kuro don't comment. Maybe their fears have rendered them speechless. Pod One's buggy splits to the right and I glance over my shoulder to see Pod Nine's buggy turning and heading for another spot in the Wall. I guess we've been allocated different entrance points.

First.

Second.

And Third.

As we approach, the Wall looks impenetrable, even dangerous to be near and then, like Ilse's appearances, an opening materialises from nowhere. Gasps from the others fill my ears and I forget that I've done this twice before, if you include my return journey. The sensation feels different this time, like I'm being sucked in by an invisible force rather than driven. The sharp hiss of sparking electricity sounds above our heads. It's wrapped within a grey foam and is slightly damp and smells of stale milk. I get the occasional hot spark snap at my skin, like someone's pinched me. We soon break through the other side and the change in light makes me blink hard and fast. I squint through the glare, hoping I'll see the oasis, but I know I am going to be disappointed.

And I am.

In place of the grass and the flowers and the meandering streams is a vast derelict city. It's grey and black, living under a sky that looks full of rain and pending thunder. The sheer size of it dwarfs me emotionally and I'm back being that seven-year-old with my red trunk, seeing the Community Home in front of me that I thought was a castle.

I've seen this City before in pictures at school about the end of the Terrorist Wars. Shelled and bombed; deserted of people and life; a stillness that only comes from death and destruction. Through the man-made rubble, I recognise famous fractured landmarks from the Old World. Places I've had to memorise for pointless exams: part of Big Ben from London. A section of the Golden Gate Bridge from San Francisco. The front of the White House from Washington, D.C.. The Arc de Triomphe from Paris. The Steeple of La Sagrada Familia from Barcelona.

I'm staring at a City within a City; a place without shape; thrown together; a world created by Ilse. *The City of Hope.*

But for who?

Her?

Or me?

I dare not think of the answer.

Our buggy stops and our Trainer yells at us to get out. We stand in line and she throws us our backpacks, making sure mine hits the floor. Marcellus's buggy comes through the Wall and bounces to a stop. He steps out, smiling, all spite and venom. He leans back into his buggy and reaches for six loaded magazines for our handguns.

'The top three teams get a morning's start compared to the other Pods. Pod One will be two hours in front of you and Pod Nine an hour behind. That gives you the best part of a full day on the five Hunting Packs. In case you didn't get it, there'll be no prisoners. They can kill you. You can kill them. If you're smart enough to make it to the other side, you're free. Ilse has high hopes for you. Personally, I'm not convinced you stand a chance.'

'What constitutes the other side?' Kuro asks, pushing on the front of his glasses, glancing toward the City.

Marcellus walks over and stands in front of him, nose to nose.

'Are you challenging my authority?'

'Uh…uh…no, sir. I wanted to know what makes us successful in this mission?'

'I told you. Getting to the other side.'

He shoves Kuro to the floor with a vicious push to the chest.

I step forward, my feet scraping along the floor.

The Guard reaches for his electronic baton.

'He asked you a question. Now answer it.'

Marcellus turns to me, stepping in close, grabbing my Tunic, raising his hand to strike me…

'Touch me and I won't move from this spot.'

'You'll be dead by the morning if you do.'

'Not before I come to your hanging if you mess with Ilse's plans.'

He smiles, but it's laced with worry.

'We ain't going anywhere until you answer Kuro's question.'

I push Marcellus's hand away and sit on the floor. The others look shocked, but follow what I've done. Marcellus licks his lips then puts his hands on his hips, smiling. There's another flash of uncertainty that sparkles within his eyes before he hides it with a vindictive smile. But it lacks the confidence I've so often seen within him. He nods for the Trainers and Guards to get into their buggies. He collects the magazines he put down to assault Kuro and drops them on the floor next to his buggy.

'It doesn't matter, because you're not going to make it. But for the record. There's a map in your kit. Marked are exit points. You've been dropped in Zone Three, Alpha Point One. You'll find it highlighted on the left. You make it to one of the Exit Points, you get to go home. Your *Denounced* record will be wiped clean.'

He leans forward and makes a point of picking up a magazine and placing it into his pocket – my magazine. He gives me a wink, climbs into his buggy and tells his driver to pull off. The two buggies skid as they make a fast half circle, speeding toward the Wall before disappearing into the pulsating electrical fog.

We say nothing, as we stare at the empty space vacated by Marcellus.

'You can have my magazine if you want?' Chantal finally says, breaking the silence. 'I think the leader should have a loaded gun.'

'You're a better shot than me. You keep it.'

I walk over to Kuro.

'Are you okay?'

'He broke my glasses.'

Kuro hands them to me to inspect. It could be worse. The right lens is cracked through the centre, but it's not deep and the frames are intact. I know he doesn't have a spare pair and relies on them more than he lets on.

'Can you still see out of them?'

He nods. I pat him on the shoulder, looking across at Spencer who is staring catatonic into the distance. I decide to give him a few minutes to himself, as I unzip my backpack and shake out the contents. Pre-packed food in compact sealed packs spill out first. There's a torch that I can clip to my utility belt. A short length of thin rope, about a metre long, and a lightweight sleeping bag, which folds to the size of a jumper. It's made of a material that will trap your body heat and keep you warm even in freezing temperatures. There's a piece of flint to start a fire and a small bag of kindle. They've given us a spoon and a cup that will double as a cooking pot, and a litre bottle of water with a snap-open nozzle, plus a First-Aid kit.

All items we are used to using.

In the inside pocket, I find the fold-up map. The others empty their packs onto the floor. We all have the same items. Nothing more, nothing less.

Rasa opens the map and starts to work out our bearings, but I'm watching Kuro divide his rations into meals. I know what he's doing, because it's probably the only time in my life I will ever beat him on a calculation. We have enough food and water for three days. If he thinks that's how long we'll be here for, he's mistaken. The calculation is based on how long Ilse believes we're going to stay alive.

'So much for the head start. They've dropped us at the furthest point they could from any Exit Points,' Rasa says, kicking at a small stone in frustration.

'I can't believe how many streets and turns there are. It's going to take longer than three days to navigate out of here if you factor in we have to hide and move slow,' Kuro says, examining Rasa's map.

'Five Hunting Packs doesn't sound much,' Chantal says, trying to sound upbeat.

I want to say they'll be highly trained and have advantages over us, but I keep my thoughts to myself, walking over to Spencer who's still staring at his backpack like it's a giant spider about to bite.

'Out here, we need you more than ever, but if you want to cut it alone or stay here nobody's going to stop you.'

Spencer flicks his eyes to look at me. He's wanting to look tough and mean, but he's fighting the tears. His face is the colour of a newbie who has stepped into the System, knowing he has nothing but pain ahead. He turns from me to the others and then back to the endless City.

'I hate what they've done to me. I hate what I've become. I was two years from being out. I'm sixteen and smoked one joint. I mean, come on!'

'We need you, but we need all of you, not ten or twenty per cent. You in or out?'

I watch him chew the thought. I wish him all the best, because we wouldn't have got to *Phase Three* had he not found it within himself to stand up after his beating.

'In.'

I pick up his backpack and hand it to him, turning to Rasa and Kuro.

'What's the quickest route to the first Exit Point?'

Kuro and Rasa hold a quick discussion before Rasa says. 'If we go directly ahead until we reach Fifth Street, then take a first right and second left...'

'...so that's not our route. We loop away from the nearest Exit Point. In fact, we don't go near any of them for one day. Any objections?'

Nothing comes back.

'Can you two run and map read?'

Kuro and Rasa nod.

'You take it in turns. Everyone take a short drink and we double time out of here. They've trained us to be soldiers, let's not disappoint.'

I take the lead with Rasa, making the others spread out so we're not bunched. I put Diego in the middle with his buddy Spencer and Kuro and Chantal at the back. I don't want Diego falling behind and he's good at keeping pace in a pack. He seems to forget he can't run when he's surrounded by runners. As we have an official head start, I decide it's okay to run the centre of the streets where it's the flattest to use our first start advantage. I've been around Ilse and Marcellus enough not to trust them, but I do believe we have a few hours of unhindered time.

This is Ilse's competition as much as it is ours.

We head out, keeping an even rhythm.

I'm not sure why, more a sense that we should change than anything tangible, but I swap tactics and make us stay close to the buildings, checking streets before we enter. It halves our speed. We stay like this for a while then the light starts to fade and I nod us into the empty building at the end of the street. It looks like the place has been modelled on a shop. Half the roof has been blown off and most of one support wall is missing, or that's how it's been designed. At a first glance, you would say the building is close to falling down, but it's all part of the illusion. The walls, like the roof and the structure itself, is solid and made of the same toughened plastic that is the core material used everywhere – including our dorms and training quarters.

We find a spot to sit and rest, reaching for our water bottles.

'Go easy, we don't have much for three days. We have to make it last.'

'There's one water purifying tablet in the First-Aid kit,' Chantal says.

'That's good to know, but even so, let's treat this as the only water we have. To purify water, we have to find it first, remember.'

'We can run and hide all we like, but they'll be tracking us. Like they watched us in the dormitory,' Spencer says.

I glance across at Kuro, who nods back.

It's kind of what I was thinking earlier. The Hunting Packs will have advantages we don't.

I stand.

'Everyone strip. Check the lining on your clothes. Backpacks, all the pockets, and the same with the utility belts. Everything!'

'What are we looking for?' Chantal says.

'You'll know it, when you see it.'

I search my Tunic along the arms then the neck, followed by the inside seam. I'm slow and careful and methodical. Diego sits back down to rest, but he's diligent in how he searches every seam and pocket in his backpack. Rasa takes her knife and prods at the thick webbing of her utility belt. Chantal and Kuro work through their backpacks. I remove the lid of my water bottle, careful not spill its contents, and even check under the screw top.

Nothing.

'Damn it,' I hear Spencer shout.

I glance across to see he's snapped his knife, digging at the heel of his boot, cutting his palm in the process. Chantal opens her First-Aid kit and pulls out a large plaster and moves across to help him. If Spencer's hurt you wouldn't know. He's smiling as he holds a small black transmitter between his bloodied fingers, which he's dug from the heel of his boot.

'These knifes are poor quality and there's no kill setting on our handguns. This is the worst one-sided fight I've ever been in,' he says, tossing the small transmitter toward me.

I catch it.

It's black and about the size of a couple of grains of rice stuck together. It gently pulsates in the palm of my hand.

'Check both heels,' I say.

It's a good call from me. We dig out a transmitter from each heel. Twelve in total. I'm passed being angry. I'm more pleased we found them. Spencer gets a hug from Chantal and it brings another smile to his face. It's good to have him back in the fold. I collect all twelve transmitters and am about to toss them into the street.

'No, don't', Chantal says. 'Cats!'

I turn to see her pointing at a set of designer rubble. Wedged between the false blocks of concrete are a dozen or so wild cats.

'Chantal's right,' Rasa says with a smile. 'Feed them to the cats. They'll keep moving with them inside their stomachs for a day or two. It will look like we're still moving, too, or at least moving here.'

'What's with all the cats?' Diego says. 'I can't stand them, they make me sneeze.'

'A place this size must have rats,' Spencer says.

'But the rats got here by themselves, which means there's a way in. If there's a way in, then there's a way out!' Kuro says.

I like his thinking.

I dig into my backpack and search through the food rations. On the front of one of the packs it states: *steak*. It's not steak as I know it, but it'll be some processed food that will taste as good. I hate to lose the best meal I have, but it's worth the victory. I tear open the top. The smell floods out. The cats start to meow. It's enough to give them confidence to venture out of their hiding place. I squeeze out my steak meal onto the floor in a long line and feed the transmitters into the processed food, stepping back. The cats spy us suspiciously, but the smell is driving them wild. The Tom ventures out first. He hisses, his fur pointed and angry along his spine. He sidesteps across the room, but the smell, combined with his hunger, overrides his fear. The second he starts to eat, the other cats dart out. They devour the food in seconds, squabbling amongst themselves, consuming the transmitters in the process, before scampering away.

We laugh.

It's a full-on belly laugh like I haven't had in months, maybe years.

'Let's move out,' I say. 'We still have some daylight on our side.'

I turn to check we're all ready.

Chantal starts to walk towards the door when the floor snaps open beneath her and she disappears from view.

37

'CHANTAL!'

Rasa screams, as she runs toward the gaping hole that has appeared in the middle of the floor. I'm the wrong side to stop Rasa, but Diego's spotted it and shoulder-barges her to the floor. It takes me a few moments to assess the situation, but thanks to Diego we are only one down and not two. In Rasa's panic for Chantal, she's missed what Diego was quick enough to spot. The hole is a two-part hatch. Like a hangman's drop. I'm not sure if it's faulty, or because Chantal is so light, but only one side has sprung open and Rasa was headed straight for the other half.

I circumvent the hole, making sure the edges aren't weak, almost too scared to peer over the edge, fearful of what I'm going to see. Pumping through me is the thought that our Pod is now five strong and not six. The idea that one of us has died makes me go lightheaded and nauseous. I brace myself, take a deep breath at what I might see as I catch Spencer from the corner of my eye pulling Rasa to her feet. She's calmed, realising Diego has saved her life, but she still pushes past them and takes the same route that I have and joins me as we slowly gaze into our abyss.

I sigh, long and loud.

So does Rasa.

Chantal is crying, and it's the first time I'm happy that our resident crier is in full voice.

'Don't move,' I say.

I catch the stupidity of my statement, but it's meant to be more reassuring than factual. Chantal cranes her neck to look up, nodding. I stare beyond to assess the situation. The drop is over twenty metres and the floor has been modified with wave like structures. If the fall hadn't killed her, she could have been crippled had she hit any of those structures at the wrong angle. The hatch has broken away from its hinges, wedging itself into the side walls. It's pure luck that it's jammed itself into the corners and Chantal's waif like frame has played to her advantage.

Kuro comes hurrying over to join myself and Rasa. He's taken the length of ropes from our backpacks and is tying them together. Each one is only a metre long and all five are enough to reach Chantal, but my instinct is the rope isn't strong enough, plus the cord is thin, so it's going to be like gripping a razor blade.

Diego and Spencer join us at the ledge.

Five on top.

One below.

'We can do it,' Diego says. 'She's close enough.'

Like all those torturous morning runs helped us today, I'm suddenly grateful for the Obstacle Course. We've built an understanding on how to work together in certain situations. There are no long discussions or argumentative debates.

Chantal is close enough from the top that a human chain should reach her.

Diego braces himself as the anchor about half a metre from the edge.

'I can feel I'm slipping,' Chantal calls out, desperation bouncing in her voice.

Spencer and I shoulder ourselves into Diego's waist, jamming our feet into the ground. Rasa hooks her left arm around Diego's looped arms and creates a full hook by gripping both her wrists together, like a double lock. Kuro hooks his left arm through Rasa's arm-loop to complete the chain. Still simple, but it's about to get a whole lot harder as we slide forward to lower Kuro over the edge.

A human rope.

Kuro's ankles give something for Chantal to hold onto, with Rasa the fulcrum that pivots the edge, and myself, Spencer and Diego the anchors.

Diego blows out hard as he takes the strain.

'I need more,' Kuro shouts.

I look at Spencer. He nods an *okay*.

'One, two, three,' I say.

In unison, we allow ourselves to be dragged toward the hole. Rasa is now half over the edge. The extra weight drives into my knees and it's the first time in a few days that my back twitches with pain. Sweat bubbles on Spencer's forehead. Diego's arms start to sway gently left and right as Rasa must be swaying, which is ultimately coming from Kuro. I picture him at full length, stretching out his leg, lopsided in an attempt to connect with Chantal. I dare a glance at Spencer. We both know that we have to shuffle back some more. That means, we'll be holding Rasa, Kuro and Chantal if she manages to grab his ankle. I'm scared we're all going to tipple over the edge like a pack of cards. My feet skid back. Diego grunts as he fights gravity. Spencer digs in and my feet are close to the edge with not much more room to manoeuvre. Then I hear a scream at the same time the extra weight bites into my thighs, knees and back. Chantal has made the leap to grab hold of Kuro's ankle. The sudden momentum goes against us. We slide back, my left foot skidding over the edge, Rasa dangling, nothing but a chain link between us and Kuro. The veins in Diego's neck protrude like tires on a bike. He grunts hard as myself and Spencer find our footing and dig in. I skid again, but after the third attempt, get a solid grip. I sense Rasa trying to get a foothold in the side, like a step on a ladder rung, but she's having to hold Kuro and Chantal. I can't think of anything else other than to push Diego with all my strength.

I start.

My back alive with pain.

Spencer is pushing with all his gym built force.

Diego's grunting and pulling hard.

Then it gives.

The pressure is off as quickly as it was on and we topple forward, rather than backward, and collapse into each other. I snap round to see Chantal tangled between Kuro's arms. He must have somehow reached down and grabbed her. It doesn't matter how, because she's back in the Pod. Alive. We're six, again and not five. I couldn't be happier.

I'm not sure how long it's been since Chantal's near-miss, but the light is finally fading, like we're outside and this is the real world. I'm not sure what the real world is any more, but it's not this place and there is something better waiting for us, I tell myself.

I turn to check on the others. They look exhausted, especially Diego. The running's been harder on him than any of us, plus we've been extra vigilant since Chantal's incident which has drained us further. Nobody has complained and I'm proud of our effort on what's been a long day. My desire to stay alive tempts me to push them on, but one of the positives I learnt from our training was the power of rest. I order everyone toward the building opposite. It's a four-storey house with most of one side blown away and only part of its roof remaining. The designers have modelled it on an upmarket Town House that should belong to a diplomat or politician. Cautiously, I enter first as the others spread out behind me. I'm not sure if it's the narrow shape of the inside, but it has suddenly gone dark and I catch Diego reaching for his torch.

'Dude, we don't want to signal our whereabouts.'

He acknowledges his error. It's a mistake born out of tiredness. I remind everyone to stay alert as we begin the tedious, but necessary task of checking for traps.

I don't believe every building is booby trapped, but there must be some kind of ratio the designers used. Like, one-in-a-hundred buildings, or maybe one-in-five-hundred. We were unlucky this morning, but it was a lesson, and perhaps the best lesson of the day, because at least we are alive to tell the story.

We clear the building and decide to camp on the top floor where it feels safer. It's grown darker, almost to the point you need to feel your way around, but I still don't let anyone use their torch. Once we eat, sleep is going to be easy and from tomorrow we'll be live targets, if we're not already.

During training, we were taught how to build a fire, heat water then place the packets of food into the cup-cum-pot. After a few minutes, you'd have a hot meal. Easy to do in a controlled environment, but out here we can't risk wasting valuable water, or even lighting a fire. If we did, we might as well ring a bell and turn on a neon sign to tell a Hunting Pack where to find us. So, our evening meal is cold. Spencer offers me a bite of his steak paste. The portions are small, so I only take a mouthful. Even cold, it tastes good and I can see why the cats went crazy for it. I thank him and tear open a packet of processed potatoes that taste like French Fries.

I'm hungry and I could eat more, but I need to ration my intake accordingly.

I remind the others to do the same.

Full darkness descends and I can barely see the other side of the room. Diego stands and unpacks his sleeping bag, as do the others. I want to sleep myself, but we need someone to watch over us. The War has started and we're the underdogs. Rasa volunteers to go first. I shake my head. I'll take the initial shift. It's the sign of a good leader, I decide. She doesn't protest and goes to lie next to Chantal as I feel my way to the smashed wall that is shaped like a half moon. I hear a cat hiss then scramble away as I spot a pile of fallen bricks that make a perfect sentry watch-point. I settle myself in and my eyes begin to adjust to the darker light. I'm used to being on my own and it reminds me of a time before I had my new family. A lonely time if I'm being honest, but one I'd grown used to. I'm not sure what I would do if I lost one of them now. Thinking Chantal was dead nearly tore my heart in two.

The street below slopes away into a gentle lean and affords me a panoramic view of the surrounding streets.

I smile to myself.

There it is.

The gentle hum of the extractor fans. The beautiful noise of *hope*.

A flicker of light catches my eye as I hear Rasa come up behind me.

'What's that?' she whispers.

Her voice is soft and comforting. There's a natural perfumed fragrance to her skin. Its smell sends thoughts of my real home and my mother crashing through my mind. I want to hold Rasa, kiss her. I've wanted to for some time, maybe from the very first time I saw her. I want to taste her in a way I've never done before, because that's what she is to me. This powerful female who is my equal. Someone I can be in love with, who I can trust and won't leave me with a red trunk to fend for myself.

'They're torches,' I say.

'The Hunter Packs?'

'They're the other Pods, I think. They must be in the last groups that were released and they're trying to make up time.'

I count five sets. They look like flickering stars in the night sky. I wonder how Taylor and Suki and Sean's Pods are doing, and if they've been caught by a trap? I doubt it, somehow. I'm confident they're safe, and not out there flashing their whereabouts like amateurs.

Rasa eases forward to get a better view of the street below.

We're shoulder to shoulder.

'What's all this about?' she asks.

It's the one question I've asked myself the most since I've been here.

'It's an experiment, isn't it?' she adds, turning to face me, answering her own question.

We are so close our lips can almost touch.

But I pull back, not much, but enough.

I can't risk the rejection or what it might do to the others if Rasa allows me in.

'Do you remember the pictures from the Terrorist Wars at school?'

She nods.

'Most of our Trainers and Guards look like the people in those pictures. I think we've been kidnapped into the Non-Secular World. They've watched us and learned from our behaviour. They've trained us to be soldiers and now they're hunting us down. I thought it was a sick game, but it's bigger than a game. It's an experiment, you're right. That was the word I've been searching for.'

'An experiment for what, exactly?'

'I don't know and we're not the first. It's evolved. I bet there's ninety more *Denounced* on their way to start the training over again. Another ninety who have been pre-tested. Ilse gave me permission to use the *Soul* Word, which I haven't, and I wouldn't, but when she talks about the *Powers-that-Be* I think that's what they call a God and it's connected somehow to your soul. It is something bigger than people. Something out there, somewhere.'

Rasa turns from me. I can almost hear the cogs of her mind clicking through its options as she looks into the grey wilderness of semi-derelict buildings.

'They're not going to let us live even if we do get to an Exit Point, are they?'

'No.'

She nods, but says nothing. I recognise her survivor's instinct. The System has been extra tough on her. Maybe it's harder for beautiful girls than for people like me, something I'd never thought about before. I regret those early thoughts I had towards her. I didn't see her for the person she is and the problems she's had to overcome. We are all the same really. Just trying to work it out as best we can.

'I have a crazy idea. Actually, Kuro gave it to me, so we can blame him,' I say.

'About what?' she says, attempting a laugh.

'That we go back. The only sure way out of this place is the way we came in.'

'We'd be walking into a trap.'

'This whole City is a trap.'

'That idea is nearly as bad as those Pods with their torches on.'

The harshness and snap have returned to her voice.

'Go and get some sleep. I'll wake Spencer next.'

I stand and head back to my sleeping bag, smiling to myself.

I know Rasa and I know her tone.

She's in.

She just needs time to think about it a little more, is all.

38

'Let's do it,' I hear.

Or that's what I think I heard.

I blink open my eyes to see Chantal crouched by my side, gently rocking my left shoulder to wake me up.

'Let's do it,' she says again, smiling.

I was right and it's always a good sign to see her not crying. I push myself up, my neck stiff from having slept on the hard floor. I yawn and blink through the grey morning light to suddenly see everyone is packed and ready to go.

'I thought you could do with the extra sleep,' Rasa says.

She hands me her breakfast ration. 'I never did like breakfast,' she adds.

I take the pack and start to suck on the protruding straw, as I climb out of my sleeping bag, feeling unnerved that everyone is watching me. The porridge is cold, but I'm hungry. I've become accustomed to the large portions we were allowed in the Canteen, so I'm sorry when the pack sucks dry.

'What's the plan?' Spencer asks, as I finish eating.

I stare at their expectant faces, knowing there must have been some kind of Pod Meeting I wasn't invited to. I look at Rasa, who's avoiding eye contact with me.

'We're going back, but first we have to go to where Chantal fell through the floor. I've an idea.'

I'm expecting a rush of questions, some pushback to full on objections. But nothing. Just silence and smiles. Rasa slips her backpack onto her shoulders and then hands her map to Kuro.

'Can you find a quicker way back, via the side streets?' she says. 'The main roads will be dangerous now.'

Kuro shrugs. 'It shouldn't be a problem.'

I'm not convinced it's a genuine question or answer, as I'm sure Kuro has already worked out the route. I pack my things while the others stand around and watch. There's a tension in the air, but it's weighted to the positive side. Waking to their confidence fills me with an unexpected self-doubt, but I'm sure of one thing.

Win or fail, staying in the *City of Hope* means a certain death.

It's not an *if*, but a *when*.

I finish up and we move out, we've still not discussed what I have in mind.

I'm immediately glad we didn't do three sessions of running yesterday because that would have meant three sessions of running back and a greater risk of being in the open. I ask everyone if they want to stop for a rest when we are half way back but nobody takes up my offer. I'm not sure I like this no-questions-dedication and it's me now that wants to challenge them. But I don't, and I let Rasa drive the pace while I oversee the route. The only thing I insist on is that Kuro acts as our lead scout. He's done it before when he lived in the *Doubters' Camp* and has an eye for it, and Rasa can read the map so it's a better use of our skills.

We keep a steady pace and I'm filled with relief when I spot the shop up ahead. The cats recognise us and come out expecting food. Diego *shoos* them away, not before sneezing. I tread carefully up to the hole, checking each step before I place one foot in front of the other. The trap door Chantal stood on is now at the bottom of the pit, resting on the crest of a ridge designed to break your bones. It's a stark reminder of the vindictiveness of our regime, led by Marcellus and overseen by Ilse.

I've no hesitation about what I have in mind.

I'm guilt free.

My mind at rest.

We gather debris from around the shop and re-camouflage the hole. We take our time and Chantal's creative input makes the difference. Now comes the hardest part: *the wait*. The cats still have our transmitters inside of their stomachs. Or that's my hope. I gather everyone around and go through my plan a second time. It's more an idea that's morphed into an action. Rasa and Kuro refine it further then we spread out and take up our positions. Time gets lost in my mind and begins to merge with my fears about what will happen if one of us gets hurt and how I will always blame myself.

For ever.

Then it happens.

A hundred metres of so from where I'm hiding, a man dashes from the cover of one of the buildings in the next square. Spencer was right. The City is way too big to search without some help and the Hunter Packs must have been given an indicative location of where to find us if nothing else. The man has crouched behind a wall and is peering above it to check the way. He nods to his buddy who zigzags down to the next building. It's textbook manoeuvring from one position to the next. We were taught the same technique and have used it ourselves today to get here.

I watch and wait as the Pack moves up another block. I count four men in total, exactly as Marcellus had said. A pack of four to hunt a pack of six. The men are dressed in camouflage clothes of black and grey with touches of white. It's the exact same pattern as the buggies and even this close they merge into this giant set and are hard to track. It makes me look at my own Purple Tunic. It was a good idea from Diego to cover them with dust and I hope it works. I look back at the approaching men. They don't even have backpacks to slow them further, just utility belts and machine guns. All four are wearing large blizzard like goggles and a wraparound hat that covers both their face, head and neck. They are better armed and no-doubt better trained. Panic starts to bolt through me that we don't stand a chance, as I watch the men grow in confidence for their final assault.

Two one side of the street, two the other.

The man at the front has some kind of electronic device that he keeps checking. It has to be reading the signal coming from our transmitters and my guess is right as he indicates toward the shop.

Good, I think.

I check on Kuro and Chantal, the two best shots we have. They are both in position. I count to three in my mind, as I see Kuro's arm slowly protrude from the window of the building opposite.

He fires.

To the enemy, it appears a poor shot.

It's not.

It's perfect, spot on, a bullseye.

The electric arc explodes by their feet. The men snap round and fire back. I can't see their faces, but judging by the man staring into the device they've been caught off-guard by our ambush. Chantal starts firing next. Her bullets explode near the men's heads, covering two of them in an arc of blue. Another set of perfect shots as Kuro lets off two more. The men return fire, but are slowly being backed into the shop entrance. The next bit scares me the most. Spencer fires then makes a dash right. It's designed to take their attention and draw them into the shop itself. It's my turn next. I take a deep breath then run out and fire straight at them as if I'm going to attack all four.

It looks suicidal on my part, but I U-turn and skid back on myself and sprint into the shop, Spencer a couple of beats in front of me.

We're running flat out when an electric arc explodes near my back. It's a close miss. Rasa returns fire from above. The idea is to try and stop the men from having time to take aim. By the electric arcs that are bouncing around us it must be working or they're not as well trained as I think. Spencer and I skid into the main room. I'm running hard. Spencer is in front of me and I see him hit the mark in the floor. It's our lift-off point. Spencer is flying through the air, acrobatic and graceful. Mine is going to be all fear and power. I hit the same mark and leap with all my might, scissor kicking to give myself extra momentum. More shots explode nearby, but I sense they belong to Kuro and Chantal and Rasa. Diego should be blocking the door so if nothing else we are all trapped in the shop, which was my Plan Two – a poor cousin to Plan One.

More shots rain in and it's then I hear the trap door we reset spring open, and the fall of debris hit the floor.

Silence.

A cat meows.

Followed by the groans of what sounds like two men in a lot of pain.

Are the other two dead or did they get away?

I'm more concerned that we as a Pod are safe, but I have to crawl to the edge of the pit to check. Rasa has come around through one of the windows and is doing the same as myself on the opposite side. I check everyone is okay before I edge forward the last few centimetres and snatch a look into the pit. One man is dead, I'm sure. His body is so bent out of shape it would be impossible for him to still be alive. The other two have hit the crests at bad angles. One of them has a broken leg. I can't see what's wrong with the third, but it could be a broken back or neck as spasms twitch through his shattered body. The fourth man is standing between two waves and is looking up at us. He has his hands in the air. I'm not sure why he isn't hurt. Pure luck, maybe, that he landed on top of one of his buddies and it cushioned his fall, rolling between the waves of death.

Who knows.

Who cares.

It's not one of us.

'Take your goggles off?' I shout.

He doesn't move.

'Take your goggles off?'

Again, he doesn't move.

'He doesn't understand you,' Spencer says. 'OI...' Spencer shouts, catching the man's attention. Spencer mimes taking off a pair of goggles.

The man nods then lowers his hands and removes his goggles then his scarf like hat.

'He's a BOY! Younger than us?' Chantal says. 'I don't believe it. We've been running from boys?'

I stare back at him. He's tall, but he has a baby face and looks about fourteen. I point with my gun at the others lying on the floor. The boys removes their goggles and head scarves. They are the same, or could be younger.

'What's this about?' Rasa says. 'I thought they'd be men, not kids.'

'I don't know and I don't care.' I hand my gun to Diego. 'Kuro get the ropes and tie them together like you did before.'

He hurries off. I look back into the pit. I mime taking my top off then my trouser and then I point to him. He nods that he understands and starts to strip. I point to the others lying on the floor, including the dead boy. He starts to strip them all to their underwear. The two that are hurt groan with pain as he moves their bodies. The boy with the broken back doesn't look like he has long, but I ignore my twitches of guilt and remind myself that could have been any one of our Pod.

Kuro lowers the rope and the boy ties all the clothes, guns and utility belts to the end. It's then I see it. The boy has a thin chain around his neck with a tiny silver cross dangling from it. My breath shortens. Crosses are banned in our Secular World. They are deemed an incitement to War, a crime punishable by death.

If anyone else has spotted it, they say nothing, and I don't have time to think through what it means. Instead, I pretend I didn't glimpse it and maybe I didn't. Maybe all this grey looks too close to the colour silver and it's become confused in my mind in the stresses of the moment.

We haul up the clothes and equipment and they clatter against the sides of the pit.

'We should kill them,' Diego says. 'They were going to kill us. Hunt or be hunted is what Marcellus said.'

'We're not killing anyone. We're not like them.'

'Maybe we are,' Spencer says.

'We're not. Forget it.'

I look back at the two who are injured. They are in deep pain. I know these four boys would have killed us without hesitation, but we are not going to do what they would have done to us. I have to live with myself and I'm not what Ilse has tried to make me become.

I'm Ned Hunter.

I'm innocent of being a *Denounced.*

I'm getting out of this place and I'm leaving with a clean conscience.

And when this is all over, I'm going to ask Rasa for that date. Maybe even get that kiss.

'Whoever these clothes fit, wears them. The other two are going to play at being prisoners.'

I open my backpack and throw my bottle of water down, followed by my First-Aid kit. It's the best I can do without jeopardising myself or my Pod any more than I have already. The cats still have our transmitters and I'm sure another team is going to come by, and hopefully these boys will be rescued, but not before we are long gone.

'We should kill them. It gives us the best chance of survival,' Spencer says to me. He's more forceful this time, his tone set, and there's a vengeful look in his eye that I don't like.

'You said yourself you don't like what they made you. So don't be it. You always have a choice on how you behave. Always.'

'He's right,' Rasa says. 'And if we get caught and we've shown mercy it might work in our favour. Have you thought about that?'

Chantal hands me a soldier's uniform.

'It's too big for anybody else.'

Reluctantly, Spencer walks away and I change into the uniform and slip on the goggles. There's an instant relief from the ever-present glare. I'd forgotten how strained my eyes have been at times even in the grey light. I glance up and see the roof of the dome for the very first time. It's hundreds of metres above my head; a crisscross metal frame supporting a roof with giant spotlights that act as our false sky. I see one of the many extractor fans bolted into the frame. It makes me smile.

The dome has just lost some of its fear factor.

It's a building like any other building, and all buildings have doors – even prisons.

We move out. Chantal and Kuro play prisoner while myself, Diego, Spencer and Rasa become a Hunter Pack. The goggles and head scarves work wonders. You can't tell our age or even recognise who we are, impossible to even tell who's female or male. The new formation means we can stay in the middle of the main road and keep a good pace. I'm convinced, too, that the other Pods will be further into the City, so we shouldn't be attacked by our own. I don't even know if the Hunter Packs are allowed to take prisoners, but we'll worry about that if and when it becomes a problem.

For now, we head to our own *Phase Two*.

And it starts at the spot where Marcellus dropped us off.

39

Throughout our training, we were pushed to accept the best made plans will change and we need to be adaptable at all times. A workable, flexible plan is what we were taught and I see that happening now and that we're comfortable with the unexpected. It's also good to be carrying one of the Hunter Pack's machine guns. There's a weight and substance to it, and the option to switch to kill has given me an added confidence that we can genuinely protect ourselves if a situation arises.

I hope it won't, but I have my doubts.

We run on.

I'm not tired, not even close. It's the adrenaline and I'm sure my tiredness will come later. The others are the same. Kuro waves us on that the route is clear as Rasa points to a spot on her map. We're about to enter Zone Three and shortly come to Alpha Point One, our entry to the *City of Hope*. We turn another corner and Kuro is pointing for us to stop and take cover. We do as we're told and I stay close to a building as I join him to see what's brought his caution. Ahead is a buggy with two Guards and two Workers who have set up a small camp. There's a stove and some seats, with a cover protruding from the top of the buggy, like it's the front of a shop and people are ordering cakes and coffees. All four of them are preoccupied by looking into a screen. One of the Guards peers over his shoulder and looks in our direction. I can tell by his body language he hasn't seen us, we're too far back and our camouflage is excellent.

He looks back at the screen and it's like they're monitoring the action, even waiting to pick up or assist a Hunter Pack.

Spencer was right. So much for the equal fight, I think.

'What do we do?' Rasa whispers, as she joins our vantage point.

'Keep going. We're a Hunter Pack, remember, so let's act like one. Guns to stun.'

We slow jog on. Myself and Rasa at the front. Chantal and Kuro behind us with Diego and Spencer pulling up the rear.

The Guards turn well before they could have heard us and I wonder if the Hunter Pack uniforms have some sort of tracking device, as did our boots.

It's highly possible.

'Up the pace,' I whisper, hearing my own urgency and fear. The surprise on the Guard's faces tells me they didn't expect to see prisoners and it's thrown them. They shout something in a language I don't understand and have never heard before.

'Don't stop,' I say, upping my own pace.

One of the Guards shouts a new instruction. I have no idea what it means, but he's tense and he wants us to stop running that much is obvious.

'Look out!' Rasa shouts.

The second Guard is reaching into the buggy as the Workers duck behind the front of the vehicle for cover.

'Fire,' I shout.

Myself, Rasa, Diego and Spencer spray the group with electronic bullets. Blue arcs fill the space in a blitz of fireworks. It's over in seconds and four men in front of us lay on the floor, stunned and unconscious. In our panic, we've fired all our bullets. It was stupid and against how we've been trained, but for all our training we're not professionals and that was our first battle and the first time I've used a machine gun.

I'm happy we won and none of us are hurt.

'Kuro put on the Worker's uniform. You're driving. Chantal get changed into one of the Guards' uniforms.'

'They'll be too big,' she says.

'It doesn't matter. We tie these lot up and we go through as a Hunter Park, Guard and one Worker. It's the best disguise we've got. Marcellus trained us well,' I add with a smile.

I realise, the training they've put us though is paying off. We're sorting out the mess without having to check with each other. Rasa helps Chantal get changed while Diego and Spencer tie up the Guards and Workers, dragging them to the cover of the make-shift awning. I get them to lift the two Guards into their seats so it looks like they're monitoring the screen, while I check with Kuro he can drive. He nods he can. Another advantage of having lived in a *Doubters' Camp*. He's not only stolen food to survive, but cars as well. I hand him a small set of beads on a string and tell him to hold these in his hand while he drives. He looks at me confused, but it is part of the costume, I tell him.

We climb in and head for the Wall of Fog.

It's only with the goggles on that you can see the openings. We head for the one we came through and the fog sparks at our skin and rolls over us in a white foam like haze. If we do have trackers attached to our clothes, we don't have time to check.

We break through the other side into the grey wasteland I hate so much. I count five roads, which veer off in various directions. Kuro heads for the second road on our left and soon we're cutting through the middle of the open space. This side of the Wall our map is useless, but I trust his judgement. If anyone is to remember the route back it's him.

I don't have a plan and we all know we're going to have to ad-hoc it as we go. I'm relaxed as I can be, but I start to worry that we've come the wrong way when we loop over a small brow, Kuro slowing the buggy to a stop. In the middle distance is a crop of buildings that make up our Canteen, Sleeping Quarters and vast majority of the Training Rooms that have been our life for months.

I nod for him to continue on the road. As we draw closer, Kuro veers right. I'm about to question his decision when I see we are heading for the open space between the main buildings and the Assembly Hall. When we reach that point, we will need to go straight. From there, it's unknown territory, but it's the way Spencer, Kuro and Diego would have headed had they been successful with their original escape attempt. As I survey what's ahead, made more simple with these goggles, I notice the road tapers out.

It's a road built for wide vehicles – maybe trucks?

The thought makes my heart trill.

I can see the road starts to curve back toward the Canteen. I don't want us to get dragged into going that way and I scan the area for another route, realising the maze of paths converge in the centre of our mini town before we can turn off and continue in the direction we want. I relax into the unexpected route, confident of our disguise, telling Kuro to keep a steady speed. It's then I feel it, almost hear it as two buggies come around the bend and head straight for us. A Worker is driving the first buggy with a Guard by his side. Sat behind them is Ilse and a man dressed in a dark suit and tie, whose face I can't make out. Sat behind Ilse is her Head of Security, the man with no name. He's wearing orange mirrored sunglasses, which stand out worse than our Purple Tunics did.

I can't see who's in the second buggy as Kuro hesitates and starts to slow.

'Don't,' I say. 'This is business as usual for us.'

Kuro nods and accelerates to our original speed. I see Ilse glance across to see who is coming toward them. My guess is they weren't expecting guests. Kuro pulls over to the right so we can pass each other when my world stops. My breathing ceases. I forget where I am. It's like I'm floating above myself and doing the one thing I told the others not to do. I'm staring hard, gawping at the man sat next to Ilse, not wanting to believe what my brain is telling me. I'm looking at Dr Andreas Lee. He was the Warden in my last Community Home. The man who insisted I take the psychometric test for the non-existent College examination. The man who I could never work out why he was kind to me when he could be so cruel to the other children in our Home. It was the place I've lived and detested the most.

'What are you doing?' Rasa whispers.

I hear her, but I don't hear her.

I want to stop myself, but I can't.

It's then I spot Marcellus in the buggy behind with two Trainers, a Worker driving and one Guard. Marcellus is staring at Chantal and does a double take at Kuro.

Then, people start shouting.

I can't focus, my world still in shock.

The buggy with Ilse speeds off. Then an arc of blue encases the Guard in the second vehicle.

Spencer has shot him with his side arm.

'Put your foot down!' Rasa screams at Kuro.

Her panic snaps me out of my suspended trance as Spencer fires a second shot. It hits the Worker who is driving. He slumps forward, jacking the steering wheel hard right in the process. Kuro reacts too slow and their buggy crashes into our left side, smashing us off the path. We bounce up and tip to one side, and if there wasn't six of us making the buggy heavy we would have flipped. A siren is sounded. I see Marcellus jump from his buggy, grabbing for the Guard's side arm. He switches the setting to kill, the license to suddenly annihilate us creasing his face into a snarl-cum-smile. I lift my machine gun, realising that it's empty. Marcellus aims at Rasa. I yank her towards me as a blue arc crashes into the front of our buggy and bounces over our heads. Spencer returns fire, but Marcellus dives under the arc. My own gun is trapped between myself and Rasa and everything is unfolding in double time. Marcellus aims again as I reach across and pull Rasa's handgun from her holster and fire at Marcellus. A blue arc engulfs him. He flexes with pain, like he's been stabbed in the back. I fire again and again, rage coursing through me, every ounce of my anger pouring into my shots. Marcellus slumps forward and falls to his knees and then the floor. I take aim again when I feel Diego grip my wrist with a firm hand.

'We've got to get out of here.'

Our buggy is a write-off. The Worker and the Guard are stunned. I walk over to Marcellus who is lying on the floor. He's dead. I've killed him. Rasa was wearing the Hunter Pack's utility belt and their handgun default setting was kill, not stun. I want to be sorry. I'm not a killer. But I'm not sorry. Marcellus was an evil man who tried to kill Rasa and he would have killed any one of us given a second chance.

We climb into Marcellus's buggy and Kuro reverses back. The front is all damaged where it smashed into ours, but it's working. Kuro powers off, the siren in the dome growing louder as I hear more shouting and whistles.

'They're behind us,' Chantal yells.

I turn to see four buggies in close pursuit, gaining ground. Our buggy is working but the damaged front is slowing us down, plus it's carrying six.

'In front of us,' Rasa shouts.

I turn to see three more buggies heading straight for us. Kuro swerves hard right and we bounce off the path. It's away from the Assembly Hall and heading into the heart of the buildings we know so well. He turns hard left again, but it's too sharp and we start to skid. I brace myself, as he loses control, and the back of the buggy swings round and smashes into the building. I'm flipped out, but I roll forward and come straight up on my feet. It's a trick I learned in our training. The others are either picking themselves off the floor or climbing out of the buggy. Nobody is hurt. Blue arcs start to explode around us. We sprint to the next building for cover, Chantal leading the way because she's as quick as a hare. She throws herself against the wall as she dives under an electric arc.

She vanishes in front of my eyes.

Gone.

Sucked from the dome.

I shout her name and run to the same spot, hearing her screams but I can't see her. More blue arcs explode around us; the Guards closing in. I bend down to avoid another round of bullets and see a gap has opened up between the building and the flooring which supports it.

'Go,' Rasa screams, firing another round at the chasing guards.

I'm bigger than Chantal so I unclip my utility belt and jump feet first. I'm falling through the air then I hit something metal. It's soft and bends and reverberates under my weight. I'm skidding forward. It's like I'm on a toboggan and I'm tearing down a snow packed hill. Then I hit the hard floor and career across the flat ground. My skin burns from the friction of slowing down. Disoriented, I stand. Next Rasa rolls towards me, followed by Spencer and Kuro. I don't see Diego. I swell with anxiety. The gap was narrow and Diego isn't. Then he crashes along the floor, smashing into Spencer and Rasa, sending them flying in the process. I run over to help Spencer to his feet. Chantal does the same for Rasa. Diego picks himself up as I look through another vast open space of buildings and finally get it. I wasn't losing my mind and can see why everything looked different each day. We've fallen into the floor below – a basement and giant building storeroom in one. And there are stilts and lifts and hydraulic platforms everywhere I look. Sections of paths and roads are rested one on top of the other. Parts of buildings have been stored against other buildings and half assembled rooms dot the space. Workers stare at us in disbelief. We've fallen through a fissure and have skidded down some kind of alloy conduit. I'm bruised and scratched, as are the others, but nothing is broken. Spencer fires a warning shot above the Workers' heads and they scatter like frightened chickens.

'Which way?' Rasa says.

I look around me and see more light coming directly in front of us then from anywhere else.

'That way.'

I've never run so fast in my life. My legs are working double time. Diego's in the mix and there's no way he's going to be left behind. I hear footsteps gather behind us and I glance over my shoulder to see three Guards in close pursuit. One of them fires. The bullet explodes above my head. Spencer returns fire. We run on, finding ourselves in a narrow corridor that resembles the walkway we took from the Holding Centre to the Execution Room. Ahead is a steel ladder disappearing into a vertical circular tube. We head for it as more explosions clip at our heels. Spencer and Rasa return fire as I stop at the bottom of the ladder. There's a hatch above my head. There's no way that it can take us back to the main floor of the dome because the ladder's too short. I climb up to see an old-fashioned slide bolt. I snap it back and push at the hatch. It doesn't move. I step up a rung and try and use my shoulders for extra strength. It still doesn't budge.

'Diego,' I shout.

He joins me at the top. It's a squeeze. Below Spencer and Rasa are returning fire, keeping the Guards at bay.

But for how long?

'They're nearly out of bullets,' Chantal shouts.

'One, two, three.'

Together we shoulder barge the hatch.

It flips open.

Bright sunlight floods my eyes and for a second I forget where I am and the danger we're in.

'Move,' Diego screams.

I scramble out, pulling Diego with me. Chantal is right behind him and Kuro runs the ladder like a rat, with Rasa close on his heels. Spencer's holding the Guards off on his own. He's being too brave and I'm scared for him. He has nothing to prove.

'SPENCER,' I roar. 'NOW!'

He drops his handgun and strides up the ladder as a blue arch narrowly misses him and me. Diego grabs Spencer's arms and yanks him the last metre and I slam the hatch shut. There's a bolt on the outside and I drive it home. A second later, the hatch rattles against the lock, but it's not going to open.

Not yet, anyway.

I stand, catching my breath as I take in my new surroundings. I can't see anything but sand and sand dunes. I look up and see a bright blue sky and an orange sun setting.

I smile to myself.

What I'm looking at is real and not generated by a lamp.

To be continued…

READ AN EXTRACT OF BOOK 2

SHIFTING HORIZONS

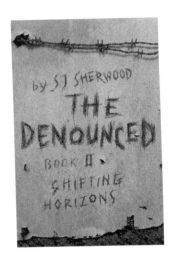

Pod Fifteen has escaped Ilse's cruel regime only to fall into the hands of a strange Nomadic Tribe. Their charismatic leader, Omar, begins to fill Ned's mind with ideas about his destiny. A possible future that puts the Pod's hard-fought friendships to the test, cuts loyalties to the bone and further exposes character flaws. Nobody is sure who they can trust and what they should do next, but Ned is convinced he must travel home if he has any chance of fulfilling his truth and changing the course of history.

1

Two things are happening to me at the same time, neither of which I like or I'm used to.

One is a sense of relief.

The other is the claustrophobic grip of chaos.

Combined they leave me rooted to the spot, giving me a detached sense that I'm more alive than I've ever been in my sixteen years on this planet. I've lived in Urban Worlds with digital credits and corrupt Systems, where embracing *hope* often costs you your life.

It's been one Community Home after another, before I ended up in the Holding Centre, kidnapped to Ilse's Dome. I wish it were different, but since my parents died, standing somewhere that is not surrounded by institutional walls has become a place of my imagination.

Somebody shouts my name.

Ned.

But I don't really hear it.

It's more a distant echo, like an aftershock that I don't have to pay attention to if I don't want to.

And I don't want to as I'm more interested in the warmth from the sun, which heats my skin in a way I had completely forgotten.

I glance left, Spencer is dragging a large smooth boulder across the top of the Hatch, which is being forced hard from underneath by the guards that chased us. He's straining with the weight of the rock as blood leaks across his forearm and runs onto the sand faster than he seems worried about. Diego is struggling to walk the soft sides of the sand dune, which encases us from all sides. His weight and short legs aren't built for this doughy, moving terrain. Kuro and Chantal have made it to the top and are looking down, pleading for me to move, so I guess it's them who are echoing my name, but really they are only adding to this strange emotional charge that is pumping through my veins.

Rasa tugs at my arm, while she shouts some kind of instruction at Spencer.

I want to tell her that I never thought we'd make it out.

So my plan is both a victory but also a defeat.

I'm flat out of ideas and I just want to stand here and enjoy the tangerine sun and warm breeze, which continues to tickle my face.

'NED,' she screams. 'WE HAVE TO MOVE. MOVE!'

Even through her pained face, she looks as beautiful as she did the day I first saw her sitting on the steel bench waiting in line to be hung. She's different from the rest of us. There's a mental strength I recognise and admire, but she's tougher than me in many ways.

And I'm tough.

I've had to be.

I know that much about myself.

'WHAT'S WRONG? COME ON!'

'There's nothing's wrong with me,' I say.

It comes out calm and contained, and it zaps the panic straight out of her.

She nods and I can see she is thinking again.

I look towards Diego and she knows immediately what to do. She ploughs up the side of the sand dune and grabs his arm and begins to drag him forward. I step across to Spencer and help him position the boulder, inspecting his arm before I guide him to the top of the dune.

At first, I think he's been shot, but it looks more that he's ripped open the skin as he careered down the alloy conduit pipe from heart of the Dome into the industrial core below.

Once at the top, I have to count that we're all present.

One.

Two.

Three.

Four.

Five.

Six, which includes myself.

It's stupid, I know, and I'm pointing at each of us as I'm doing it, taking in the new surroundings at the same time.

Rocks and sand dunes in every direction, all under the deepest tangerine glow of the like I've never seen before.

It's beautiful.

And dangerous.

Dangerous, because it's open ground and we have nowhere to hide.

Kuro hears it first, but I'm reading his mind as he cocks his head and looks straight ahead.

'Assault Buggies,' he shouts. 'Lots of them,' he adds.

'Ned,' Chantal says, pointing behind me.

I turn to see the start of a mountain range, which I'd somehow missed through the heat haze of what I think is the dying light. I'm not sure what skills I really possess for this life, especially compared to the others in our Pod, but I do have a knack for calculating distances.

We are two and a quarter kilometres from being out of the open.

Diego has already started to run towards the cover of the rocks, and it triggers us all into a sprint for freedom.

Chantal and Kuro soon overtake him, powering on.

Rasa and Spencer pass him next and although I'm at the rear, I suddenly digest Diego's fear at being last.

Left behind.

To die.

Picked off, as the weakling of the pack – another *Denounced* caught running away; to be hung at the next session.

Nothing could be further from the truth, but struggling to climb out of the sand dune has taken its toll on his strength and he was never built for running. I wasn't either, but Ilse's Military Camp has taught me some new skills and honed all our fitnesses to a different level.

'Concentrate on yourself and don't think about the others or what's behind you,' I say.

'They're close … I can hear them,' Diego pants out.

'Close is still not caught.'

I could run faster, but I match his stride, then up the pace after a couple of seconds.

It works.

Chantal and Kuro are pulling further and further away, but we're now matching Spencer and Rasa's pace.

I have another worry suddenly hit me.

Spencer's trailing blood.

His gash must be deeper than both of us realised and you wouldn't need dogs or special equipment to track us. Anyone could follow this trail, and it wouldn't matter if it were pitch black with a storm howling around them. For some reason it makes me ignore my own advice and I glance back, wishing I hadn't.

Three guards are stood at the top of the sand dune from which we've just run from.

The guard at the front takes aim, but even I know he can't hit us from there with his handgun.

He fires anyway, more out of frustration than hope.

A blue electric arc webs out and dies within seconds, far behind me. What worries me more is they don't appear concerned about making chase. Then I see why. The Assault Buggies we heard have appeared on the horizon.

Six of them in total.

They are the same as the ones that transported us around the Dome, but different, too. Instead of the grey and white camouflage, these are two-toned sand colour with splashes of black. They are bigger, too, and no doubt quicker, and they seem to merge into the background, disappearing at times into the heat haze.

These ones are built for war and that's what Pod Fifteen has just become.

Ilse's Number One enemy.

The frontline of resistance.

We've escaped the *City of Hope*. We weren't supposed to, but we did. We beat them. And the guards who came out of the Hatch aren't chasing, because they know they don't have to. They've worked it out, like I have, that although we are in this vast open space, our chances of making the next kilometres before the Buggies catch us are next to …well…

Zero.

'NED!' Rasa screams.

I realise I've stopped running.

But it's okay, because Diego doesn't know he's just given me an idea.

'GO RIGHT!' I scream at the top of my voice. 'GO RIGHT!'

I start running diagonal to the mountain range. It looks suicidal. Like I've made the Assault Team's job half as easy again. Diego trusts me enough to do the same. Kuro and Chantal have almost reached the start of the mountainous section so they keep going straight, but Rasa pulls Spencer right, and the four of us are running into what looks a certain disaster when it happens.

The drivers of the six Buggies had veered right to cut us off and are now slowed by the soft sand that I recognised from the dune by the silky glow it gives off in this dying light. Their vehicles are designed for this topography, but the soft terrain has taken the sting out of their speed and their wheels are spinning on every third turn.

Sapping energy.

I don't have to tell the others to turn left and head the way we had originally intended.

It's done in an unconscious synchronised movement.

The temporary flood of hope gives Diego another gear and we gain on Spencer and Rasa. Chantal begins to frantically wave at me. She must have spotted another danger, I think. Another Assault Crew on our tail. Maybe an Airborne Crew, as I search the sky around me.

But I'm sure I've just glimpsed a smile on her fear stricken face.

I run on, wondering.

Spencer's dripping blood marking our way.

Diego and I reach the edge of the change in terrain. It's gone from medium soft to hard sand to treacherously sharp rocks in less than four strides. I pause to catch my breath and my bearings. Rasa is pulling Spencer through a rocked path and I can now see what Chantal was pointing at. There's an entrance to a cave. Or more a man-made entrance to what looks like a Mine. Attached to the outside wall is a sign with a giant wave, like we're at a beach and the seaside is close.

It doesn't make sense and Rasa clocks it too and gives me a look to say: *what now?*

The six pursuit Buggies have one driver and four armed soldiers each.

That's five per Buggy.

Thirty highly trained and armed men against six of us.

I glance hard up.

The rocks get bigger and sharper and steeper as my eyes search for a path to the summit. The Buggies can't be driven up a mountain. It means we'd all be on foot, so maybe we'd have a chance, but beyond another half-kilometre it's like we'd need ropes and special shoes and those hooks that professional climbers use. It maybe wouldn't matter even if we had all that equipment, because none of us are trained that way, and Diego is never going to make a sheer rock face with or without special tools.

I won't either.

The Assault Buggies slow and the Teams leap from their seats and fan out in a hard-drilled formation, assault rifles held high across their chests.

We've fallen within shooting range, but they haven't raised their guns.

Yet.

We have nowhere to go and are cornered. But it's more than that, I think. Ilse wants us alive. She knows how we escaped, but she wants to know how we came to the conclusions we did, or more to the point – how I did.

If I can deny her that pleasure for a fraction longer then I'll take whatever the Mine has to offer.

I nod on that we should enter, and we scramble up.

Chantal and Kuro duck inside first.

I'm expecting pitch black beyond the first few metres, but instead a flickering grey light seeps from deep inside.

I help Diego over the last of the rocks and watch Spencer and Rasa duck into the entrance.

I'm about to step inside when I deliberately turn and snatch a glimpse at the setting sun.

I've spent far too much of my short life in grey empty worlds and I'm about to enter another.

I wonder if this one will be my final destination.

ACKNOWLEDGEMENTS

I will be forever grateful for those who gave me their time and support so I could strive to be the writer I wanted to be. This book is for you, and for the many friends I've been fortunate enough to accumulate along the way.

However, in getting *A Grey Sun* published, I would personally like to thank the following:

James Rennoldson and Clare Povey at Bloomsbury for their connections and insight into Indie Publishing. Cressida Downing and Sara Starbuck who edited the book, and not only brought a vast amount of experience to the table, but were extremely supportive and complimentary of my work from day one. Leila and Ali Dewji at *I AM Self-Publishing* who finalised the process and then joyfully helped me pull the trigger: www.iamselfpublishing.com. Binatang at 99-Designs for his artwork and book-cover design. He brought to life exactly what I had in my mind. Bryan MacErlean for his help with the technical aspects of my website. Aaron Parsons who shot my profile pictures and has probably given me the best Tinder picture I could ever wish for. And finally, Juliet Carter, for her patience, guidance and support in helping me get to this point.

THE AUTHOR

If you have got this far then thank you for spending your precious time with my work. If you would like to know more about the forthcoming books in the series, plus much more, then please visit:
www.sjsherwood.com

Otherwise, feel free to contact me via my Contacts Page and I will personally answer any questions. If you enjoyed *A Grey Sun*, I would appreciate your comments on my Amazon Review. They do make a difference!

I look forward to meeting you soon for the second thrilling instalment of The Denounced with *Shifting Horizons*, available January 2019, and the final book, *Creaking Dawn*, will be available June 2019, concluding Ned and Pod Fifteen's incredible journey.

SJ Sherwood.

24836474R00173

Printed in Great Britain
by Amazon